Praise for _The Sp_

"A perfect blend of history, mystery, family, suspense. Light the fire, grab a blanket, and curl up." —Kate Braithwaite, author of _The Girl Puzzle_

"A sprinkling of 'Grey Gardens' feels in this well written novel..." —Adele Holmes, author of _Winter's Reckoning_

"If you're into moonlight gothic fiction, with haunting and heartbreaking secrets at its very core, I highly recommend this story." —Kateri Stanley, author of _Bittersweet Injuries_

"These are characters that keep you turning the pages to find out if all will end well or, if like other Gothic tales before it, the fates will deem otherwise." —Books, Cooks, Looks, book blogger

Praise for _Campbell's Boy_

"Mary Kendall expertly paves an odyssey of Dickensian proportions, taking us deep into Colusa tunnels beneath the Chinatown of Emmet Campbell's childhood and across the tumultuous plain of an extraordinary life." —Robert Gwaltney, award winning author of _The Cicada Tree_

"With a deft hand, author Mary Kendall brings to life the heartbreaking story of Emmet Campbell and the gritty world in which he lived." —Jean M. Roberts, author of _The Angel of Goliad_

"This is a story that many people will hold close and remember for a long time." —Charles Collyer, author of _Non-Violence: Origins and Outcomes_

Other Books by Mary Kendall

Campbell's Boy
The Spinster's Fortune

Bottled Secrets of ROSEWOOD

a novel by

Mary Kendall

Artemesia
Publishing

ISBN: 978-1-951122-89-8 (paperback)
ISBN: 978-1-951122-90-4 (ebook)
LCCN: 2024933274

Artemesia Publishing, LLC
9 Mockingbird Hill Rd
Tijeras, New Mexico 87059
info@artemesiapublishing.com
www.apbooks.net

Dedication

For the gals and guys at Mary Washington College in gratitude for memories made, some woven into this tale.

With special dedication to Nora Collins Mason who loved a good story and left too many untold.

Part One
Chapter One

IT WAS THE MOST remarkable shade of blue that caught her eye. Sunlight bounced off the color, a hue that vacillated somewhere between cerulean and teal. The unusual shade had Miranda's complete attention as she picked around it with care, using the trowel. As she reached in with her gloved hand to pluck it out, a voice yelled in her right ear, "Stop!"

She looked up with an annoyed grimace at the two hundred and some pounds of brawny man with the ginger thatch of hair. "What is wrong with you?" Miranda asked.

"You don't remember the part about leaving everything intact and not moving anything?"

"Yeah, but look at this. It's blue glass or something. I didn't see the harm..."

He shook a finger at her and then peered down into the trench. He took a step back. "Whoa..."

"Whoa, what?"

"This is big. Okay...let's back up a bit and um...why don't you go take a break?"

Miranda rolled her eyes but stood up and moved aside, trowel in hand.

After all, Brian Beckett was the professional archeologist and she, the lowly volunteer. He began to call the others over, assigning specific tasks, as she walked away. "Curt, grab the plumb weights. Patty, bring the string over and Fiona, can you get my field notebook for me?" When they had started the excavation, she had been surprised by Brian's use of old-school and basic techniques in the day and age of drones and the like. But when queried, he said students had to start with the "ABCs" of archeology on his watch.

Miranda headed toward the frame colonial style house situated several yards north of the dig. As the sun beat down on its shingled gambrel roof, she felt a ripple of pleasure at the sight of her old (circa early 1800s) but new-to-her house and her annoyance began to disperse.

When Brian Beckett with his larger-than-life personality had approached her about an archeological dig within the perimeter of her property, Miranda had been all in with one caveat: that she be allowed to participate. In Tidewater, Virginia, history abounded, and she liked being surrounded by history, found it comforting. But Brian had his own caveat: that they would play by his rules.

Miranda moved over to the old well pump that served as the impromptu break station for the college kids on the dig. They greedily filled up their bottles with water deep from underground when finished for the day, hauling it back to campus. Standing by and watching as the others bustled around under Brian's directives, she began to feel superfluous and headed inside.

She closed the front door behind her and took off her work boots and moisture-wicking socks at the threshold. She breathed in the smell of the varnish on the freshly sanded hardwood floors. Running a bare toe over them, she felt how smooth they had turned out. The contractor had been able to save a lot of the original floorboards and the necessary replacement boards had blended in nicely, barely noticeable. It was finally coming together and she would soon be ready to move into it permanently.

Three months earlier, Miranda had spotted a tilted real estate sign on an overgrown drive while cycling in the area. It had been love at first sight, a phenomenon she had never believed in when it came to people. But she now believed in it when it came to houses, or at least this house called Rosewood. The logical side of her, indeed the professional side, did question it of course.

In the most impulsive move she had ever made, a quick purchase had plunged her into the adventure of homeownership. In this case, homeownership of an ancient structure that needed a lot of work. There was something bigger going on, a twist in her life plan, and she was ready to set logic aside and just go with it.

The dig cropped up in the middle of the house renovations after Brian had been clued in to her purchase through the college grapevine. When he reached out and asked if a dig could take place in the fall semester, it had been an unequivocal yes on her part. She filtered in the craziness of fixing up an old house with her college professor lifestyle while also becoming an amateur archeologist.

Cleaning up the daily mess left in the kitchen by the contractor, Miranda looked out the original bubbly glass of the kitchen window to see what progress Brian Beckett and his underlings had made. Their small group all loomed over the trench.

When she headed back outside, Brian cast an eye her way, saying, "Good timing. We're almost ready to lift it out."

She peered down into what they had all been viewing: an intact, blue glass bottle. A part of her wondered if it was really necessary to spend all that extra time to dig around so painstakingly. But Brian was the expert.

Brian's right hand teaching assistant, Fiona, was the one to actually lift it up and out. A slight young woman with white-blonde hair and vibrant blue eyes, she was quite a looker even covered up in drab dig attire. Fiona was the type of woman that made Miranda feel as though she had perpetual dirt smudges all over her face in contrast.

As Fiona almost religiously held the piece up to the light, they all stared at it. Finally, one of the students verbalized what they were all thinking. "What the heck is in there?"

Miranda leaned in closer, along with everyone else for a better view. Objects that looked like sharp pointed bits, possibly nails mixed with other things, could be seen inside the bottle. Miranda thought one of the items looked like a long fingernail, but that couldn't be right. Brian seemed to have gone into a trance, but shook himself and said, "Let's get it back to the lab."

As if carrying the Holy Grail, Fiona took it to the packing area, the rest of them trailing behind carrying miscellaneous equipment. Brian waved a hand back at Miranda when they had it all loaded up and said, "We'll keep you posted, Miranda."

"Yes, please do."

She watched the entourage as it left in several vehicles. Once alone, silence filled the space left behind by the chatter of the archeological team. It was just her and Rosewood.

After securing everything inside and making sure all was turned off, Miranda headed to her old Toyota Corolla by its lonesome in the driveway. With over 200,000 miles, it was going to have to last a bit longer now that she had taken on Rosewood. Opening her car door, she felt an eerie prickle on the nape of her neck.

Whipping her head around, Miranda cast her gaze around the yard now darkening as the sun set. Shadows from the trees swayed back and forth in the dimming light, shape-shifters in a way. The shadows, along with the thick, almost claustrophobic humidity, threw her slightly off balance. But the yard was empty. She was by herself. Giving herself a little shake, she got into the car and headed back to town.

Chapter Two

MIRANDA PASSED NO OTHER cars on the long
country drive out to the highway that crossed the York River to
Williamsburg, Route 17. It was just her and the loblolly pines
making otherworldly shapes as the car's headlights hit them
through turns and twists in the road.

Her mind wandered with the winding drive back to when
she had first been on Big Island Road. It was early summer
when she biked out from Williamsburg, mapping out a route
to take her to a glimpse of Chesapeake Bay. As the roads had
tapered off into countryside, she pedaled by the old house off
to one side that immediately commanded her attention. At the
sight of the real estate sign hanging by a thread, she made the
impromptu decision to hop off the bike and take a water break.

The property—consisting primarily of the old, white clapboard house sitting on a high fieldstone foundation—had an air
of vacancy with not a soul in sight. Miranda took the liberty of
wandering around. She looked through several windows of the
house and peered in at the various outbuildings that peppered
the property. She paused at one of them, a shed of some sort,
when she spotted a crudely etched outline of a cat on top of a
post. She traced her forefinger over the carving, charmed by its
folk-art style.

With some reluctance to leave the place, Miranda snapped
a photo of the sign. After she hopped on her bike, she cast a
final glance back, feeling a strange stirring in her belly.

Back in town, she called the listing agent immediately.
Beau Jenkins was his name and he answered in a raspy voice

after ten long rings. When Miranda asked for an appointment to see the house on Big Island Road out near a crossroads called Princeton, he sounded taken aback. "You want to see Rosewood?"

It was the first time she heard the name of her house. "Is that the name? Yes, I would very much like to see Rosewood."

"Huh." He paused and then said, "It would be my pleasure."

They arranged to meet at the property the very next day, Miranda not wanting to chance someone else coming along.

When she pulled in, tires crunching on the oyster shell laden driveway, Miranda found Beau Jenkins leaning against a late model Crown Vic, mopping his forehead with a handkerchief, the Tidewater summer humidity taking its toll.

He gave a friendly wave and Miranda took in her new Realtor. His belly hung between two suspenders and over the seersucker summer pants that he wore which aptly matched his straw hat. He leaned slightly over to one side, supported by a slightly-scuffed cane. After introductions, he looked at her dubiously and asked, "So...it's just for yourself? You'll be here alone?"

"Yep. Just me."

He nodded and then an internal click seemed to put him into salesman mode as he began his spiel. "Well, we got a real oldie but goodie here in Rosewood."

They began to walk around the exterior of the house as he continued on about the quality of construction in older houses and the value of the lot being worth the price alone.

Miranda interjected, asking, "How long has the house been empty?"

"Let's see...I think it's been five years or so since Miss Janie passed on. It was in the same family for I don't know how long. The Gwynns. Been in these parts for generations."

Miranda began to pick her way through the overgrown yard with Beau Jenkins trailing behind her, talking the entire time with a courtly Southern gentleman air about him. But she blocked him out for the most part to concentrate on the house. It sat on top of a stone foundation that seemed higher than normal in Miranda's view. She walked up closer to inspect the mortar, which looked like it had pieces of shell in it. She had noticed this around the old houses in Williamsburg too.

The frame clapboards that covered the structure seemed to almost overlap one another. Beau came up behind her and poked one with his cane tip saying, "Some of these boards are rotted out for sure but most look okay given the age on them. Pretty amazing."

"How old again did you say the house is?"

"I heard tell it was built in 1820 or thereabouts...but you gotta give or take a few on that, I think."

Miranda stared intently at the house, her mind in overdrive. The faded white clapboard looked worn, but she felt confident that a good paint job would take care of that. On either side of the front door, there were two windows. Shutters hung loosely on large hinges, one shutter hanging all the way off in fact. On the second half story, dormers cut into the gambrel roof and were inset giving off old world charm.

Beau interrupted her reveries and asked, "Ready to take a look inside?"

She nodded and they walked up the three steps to the front door. Beau struggled with the front door lock, pausing in his running commentary. When the old-paneled door swung open in a sudden burst, he gestured for Miranda to walk in front of him. A waft of lavender rose up to her nostrils. She took in a surprised breath at the scent as she made her way into the center hallway.

Looking around in amazement, she could not believe that the space was exactly what she had envisioned. It was everything she wanted, and it was where she wanted to be. She turned to Beau. "Do you smell that?"

He sniffed and said, "You mean that old house smell? So, when these older places get closed up..."

"No... no. I smell lavender."

He gave another sniff. "Huh. Nope. I just smell old house. But my sense of smell isn't what it used to be."

She turned in a circle, entranced by all she saw. Her gaze

landed on the random-width, planked floorboards that filled the main room as Beau started back in with his monologue.

"Good Southern Pine right there." Tapping it with a loafer clad toe, he added, "You don't see that much anymore."

Miranda began to move into the room to the left, feeling almost weightless.

"They call this the parlor room. I guess that's an old-fashioned term these days."

"Oh, look," Miranda said as she drifted over to the fireplace and ran a finger on the grooved mantelpiece.

"Yes, indeed. A fine example of Tidewater craftsmanship."

Continuing into the rear of the house led them to a galley style kitchen with outdated cabinets and she was reminded of her grandmother's house from long ago.

"Now, those are real wood cabinets. I've seen folks paint them and they come out real nice."

Miranda nodded. "That's exactly what I'll do." Beau did not bat an eye at Miranda claiming the house as hers already.

A side room off the kitchen was the dining space and Miranda pictured a nice oak table on pedestal legs with a colonial, tavern-style light fixture above it.

When they completed the main level circuit, Beau said, "My knee might like it better if I keep myself down here...unless you need me up there, of course."

Miranda was secretly glad his knee couldn't take on the narrow, steep stairs, leaving it all to her to discover on her own. She walked through a veil of cobwebs, pushing them aside to find two rooms on either side of the stairs with a full bathroom in between.

The slanted roofline required her to duck as she moved through the space. Each room had its own dormer that let light stream in from outside. She immediately decided one would be her office and the other her bedroom. Standing in the space, she felt the strangest sensation of being enveloped in a warm cloak. On one level, she knew what was experiencing defied reason and common sense. But she had never wanted anything more in her life than to be in this place.

Walking back down the stairs, she already felt as though the house was hers and would do whatever it took to make it so. The pull of it was so fierce that when Beau looked up expectantly at her descent, she surprised them both by asking, "How do I make an offer?"

His face broke into a smile. "You don't even want to see the outbuildings first?"

"No need. I want to buy this house."

Miranda's career as a professor of logic was an obscure one to be sure. People always asked her: wasn't logic just a stepping stone on the way to becoming a lawyer? But she had never stepped off that particular stone because...she liked it. She really liked it. It never bored her and she never tired of it. But for years, the punishing pace of an academic scholar never really allowed her to enjoy the locales of her positions even though they had been more than enchanting; Oxford, England, Cyprus, Greece, Paris, France...

A restlessness had set in, though, that had nothing to do with her interest in logic. She didn't want to write another paper for a scholarly journal. Instead, she wanted to explore her world.

A temporary stint at the College of William and Mary as a guest lecturer had freed up her time allowing her to rethink the structure of her life. Taking the lectureship had led to explorations of the multi-layered, fascinating location called the Historic Triangle. That triangle included Jamestown, Yorktown and, of course, Williamsburg. She pushed the edges even further afield to the eastern area called the Northern Neck. She even purchased a brand-new kayak and took on all the tributaries that webbed out from the Chesapeake Bay into the landscape along with biking and driving all over.

She thought back to how easy it had been after that initial meeting with Beau Jenkins to move forward with buying Rosewood and setting her life up anew. After viewing the house with Beau, she made a beeline to Dean Abernathy, the

Department Head of the Philosophy program, laying out an idea for him. She recalled asking him point blank if there were any openings for an assistant professor. Tenting his fingers, he looked at her appraisingly. "Well...Professor Fingerhut has discussed retiring. Why?"

She blurted out right on the spot that she had found a house and wanted to settle in the area.

"Where?" he asked.

"Do you know Lewiston out over the bridge?"

He raised bushy eyebrows. "Way out there? You've heard about that area, haven't you?"

Miranda had picked up some talk at a college social about the area known as Bisoux but had filed it under professors being snooty.

She decided to play dumb. "No... what?"

"It's pretty isolated out that way, isn't it?"

She shrugged. "I like the peace...the open spaces."

"Well...the people out there are different."

"Different how?"

"I mean, there's always been talk about the place. Being isolated like that for so many years, I guess it can make folks a little...you know...different."

She nodded and plowed on. "Anyway, do you think you could fit me in here?"

Again, he tented his fingers. "There could be some budget juggling. Let me approach a few folks and get back to you."

Miranda and Abernathy both knew that getting Miranda in place at William and Mary would be a feather in his cap. With her Harvard education, all her posts overseas and many years left in her career, it would be silly for him not to work it out. She knew he would come forth with something and she would take whatever he offered. She wouldn't even negotiate the terms that hard because...there was just something about Rosewood. It had bewitched her in a way she couldn't quite explain to herself.

After that, all the pieces started falling into play. Abernathy had presented her with a position and her offer on the house was accepted by the widely scattered heirs. The only errant piece was at the home inspection. A huge coiled black snake had lain beneath the bottom step of the cellar stairs. The home inspector had halted her just as her right foot was raised in the air to step on it. It sent shivers throughout her body—she hated snakes—and she had asked the man if fumigation was needed. He had said no.

Another car's high beams coming in her direction shook her back to the present and she flashed hers in return with some irritation. Her mind focused on the drive which was now filling in with more businesses positioned in multiple shopping strips. As she crossed the bridge over the York River, the outskirts of Williamsburg began to crowd the night with bright lights. Approaching the sterile apartment complex that had been her home for eight months, she felt relief that she would soon be done with it. How freeing it would feel once her evenings would be the night sky and peaceful silence. She smiled with a sense of satisfaction that she was almost there, almost living her new life at Rosewood. Only a half hour's drive but worlds away.

Chapter Three

MIRANDA SCRUBBED UP A frenzy of suds on the faux brick tiles lining the galley kitchen floor, both arms aching from the process. Removing years of grime, layer by layer, she could finally see an end in sight with the nice, reddish hue exposed. The 1970s era tiles were probably due to a resurgence of interest in all things colonial during the bicentennial, but she liked their retro-vibe and unique shade of red.

A honk out on the driveway made her jump. Other than dig days, it was rare to hear anything, especially other vehicles, during the day from inside the house. She grabbed a rag to wipe her hands and pulled herself up. Some muscles twitched and she glanced at her legs, still toned and tanned from the summer's biking and kayaking adventures. The truth was she had always been in shape thanks to inheriting her father's athletic, almost angular, build. It gave her the edge competing against others when she biked, ran and played any sports. By contrast, she had not gotten any womanly curves from her mother, Millie, who epitomized the classic hourglass shape. Instead, Miranda sported a perpetual girlish appearance even at the ripe age of thirty-three.

Pushing back a wayward curl from her tousled chestnut brown mop of hair, she stepped out the front door and was greeted by the sight of a brown-uniformed UPS driver holding a package. "Here you go, sugar," he said, handing it over with a gloved hand and immediately turning on his heel back to his truck.

Holding back irritation at the diminutive term, she said

thanks out loud to his retreating back. Looking down at the package label, someone else's name was in the address section; the last name, Maynard, and a house number one up from hers.

By the time she barked out, "Oh, wait!" the driver had already placed a foot on the gas pedal and stared straight ahead, not hearing her. Or perhaps chose not to hear her. She sighed, irritated by the interruption.

She studied the name again, trying to figure out what house it might be, not having met any of the neighbors yet. It wasn't like the in-town setting of Williamsburg with houses set on postage stamp sized lots. Out here in Bisoux, houses were not even shouting distances apart. Also, people in Bisoux were known to keep to themselves, or so she kept hearing over and over again ad nauseum. Sighing, she tossed the package aside, figuring she would need to reach out and meet this neighbor, Maynard. But her single-mindedness pushed her to finish up the floor first.

Once done for the day, Miranda headed down Big Island Road and looked for the right mailbox. On its last legs, an ancient and decrepit mailbox stood at the end of a driveway that she would need to drive down, the house not visible from the road. Tentatively driving the Toyota down the overgrown drive, she hoped the Maynards were not the types who brandished shotguns at the sight of any stranger.

The drive began to clear and opened up to a view of a one-story shack with an actual tar-paper roof. It had seen better days. Maybe there had never *been* better days. Getting out of the car, package in hand, Miranda headed towards the house taking in the place in its entirety. It could be termed a hovel.

Her eyes snagged on a bit of color in the front yard: a caramel-colored gazing ball on a concrete stand, the kind she used to see visiting her grandparents in the Midwest. A bit of whimsy among an otherwise drab and gray scene. She looked up at the sight of an elderly woman in a shapeless dress sitting in the porch's shadows.

Miranda cleared her throat and said, "Hello...I'm your new neighbor." There was no response. "Um...Miranda Chesney."

Still no response.

"Anyway...this package came for you." She looked down at the label and read aloud, "'For Bertram Maynard.'"

A gravelly voice came out of the woman in a thick almost indecipherable accent. "Maynard ain't here."

"Oh, okay. Well, I'll just give it to you then?"

"He's dead."

"Oh...I'm sorry." Miranda walked closer, wanting to just throw the package on the porch and get out of there. "So, are you...uh, related?"

With lightning speed, the woman stood up and reached over with gnarled fingers, grabbing the package out of Miranda's grip.

Miranda backed away saying, "Okay then..."

The woman had already sat back down, her gaze wandering away from Miranda. She said nothing more.

As Miranda high-stepped it back to her car, her eye caught an outline of a cat on an old outbuilding listing to one side. It was similar to, if not exactly alike, the one at Rosewood. More oddity in an already odd scene, she then made a mental note to find out its meaning. Maybe a local folk artist had made the rounds throughout the neighborhood at some point.

Driving away from the woman and the house, she took inventory of all she had heard about the locals in Bisoux: cut off, isolated, and all the rest. If that woman was an example, she fit the profile but seemed to take it a step beyond. How would someone cut off and isolated be affected in their aging years? Miranda shook off the question, not wanting to think about the answers.

But, on the half hour drive back to her apartment, her mind went back and forth between worry and minimizing. She thought about her own loner tendencies. How would it be when she was out at Rosewood by herself? Maybe now that the house was ready, she should make more of an effort to meet the neighbors and go into some of the local stores. Meet people, mingle...yes, that was what she would do. She needed to take a page from her mother's book, Millie being a natural at chit-chat. She shrugged off the funny feeling from the Maynard's as she headed back to the college.

Miranda strolled along one of the brick-lined pathways that connected most of the college buildings. She plucked at her cotton shirt to relieve the stickiness from another humid fall day. Despite the continued heat, fall was definitely coming to Williamsburg with rust-colored leaves scattered along the path. But it had not yet cut through the thick, southeastern Virginia humidity yet.

Students, young but with determined adult-like airs, filled the space as they bustled to their classes. In Miranda's mind, fall was the ultimate college season and it always took her right back to her own undergraduate years. They were becoming a faded memory, but not quite yet forgotten.

Miranda had left a message for Brian Beckett, but there had been no response on his end. It had already been a couple of days and she really wanted to see what she thought of as "her" blue bottle's contents. It was time to just show up at his office.

She thought back to that first phone call with Brian. An acquaintance in the Philosophy Department heard about her house purchase and the circuit of college doings had eventually made it to Brian's notice. His voice had been laced with excitement about conducting a dig at Rosewood for the fall semester. She said yes without any hesitation, eager to learn as much as possible about her new house.

Based on the sound of his voice and general stereotypes related to her male colleagues, she had him pegged as an effete academic with a possible bow tie involved in the mix. Upon their first in-person encounter, she had been taken aback at the contradiction of her set ideas. He was almost the complete opposite of what she had imagined, reeking of all that was masculine.

This was, however, her first visit to his office. From his open doorway, she caught sight of him lounging with jean-clad legs and work boots propped up on a desk piled high with varying sized stacks of papers. As he munched on a delicious looking pastry, crumbs fell onto his trademark flannel shirt. She still didn't understand wearing flannel in Virginia humidity but he claimed it kept ticks off when she had asked.

His eyes moved to her standing there and, rising up to his tall height, he brushed the crumbs off. "Miranda! This is unexpected."

"You didn't get my voicemail?"

He waved a hand away at the idea. "Rarely check it. Who leaves voicemails anymore?"

She grimaced a bit. "Well, I left one. What's going on with my blue bottle?"

He coughed a little and said, "*Your* blue bottle?"

"I mean...the blue bottle."

"*The* blue bottle is down in the lab...it's going to be a long process but...."

"But..."

"Well...don't let this out but..."

Miranda thought to herself wryly who would she let it out to and prodded, "But?"

"We've had to pull in some heavy-duty research on it. We found some weird things inside."

"Weird like...somebody's fingernail?"

He looked at her intently. "How did you know that? I mean, it might be a fingernail but how did you..."

"I thought I saw it when we were all looking at the glass in the light the other day."

"Good eyes." He considered her thoughtfully. "Let me show you some of what we are thinking."

He grabbed a rolled-up plat from the file cabinet behind him then spread it open on top of the covered desk, ignoring the mess of papers underneath.

"What's this?" Miranda asked.

"The plat of the property. We always start out a project with this and then add our historical layers to it. I mean, this is all loaded up in our GIS software, of course. But my preference is holding paper in hand."

Miranda stared at the layout in front of her, putting the visual in her mind of her property and matching it to the footprints of built objects in front of her. Some of the areas had cross-hatching over them.

She pointed to those areas and asked, "What's that about?"

Brian sat back in his chair and gestured for her to do the same. Miranda surreptitiously looked at the chair near her piled with books.

"Oh, here...let me move those aside."

He dumped the books on the floor without ceremony. "So, as you know, the placement of the dig is where we researched out the probable location of the kitchen midden."

"You mean the trash pile, right?"

He scrunched his face up. "We call it a midden. Anyway, I got the kids really immersing themselves in the historical record so we can figure out...."

As he continued to talk all things archeology, Miranda started to lose the thread. Instead, she appraised the man in front of her, noticing that his beard was a ginger shade lighter than the incredibly thick thatch on his head. To his credit, the beard was nicely trimmed. She really disliked an unkempt beard on a man. His eyes were a light-colored brown, almost golden in color.

She tuned back in when he was saying, "So, the potential that this is associated with other buildings that used to be there like slave dwellings—"

She stopped him, saying with a frown, "Slave houses?"

"Yes, it's an unfortunate aspect of history but has to be considered in reference to this...this bottle. It could be that we are looking at some form of tradition from Africa. But we're in early days yet on figuring this out."

"I want to see the things."

"What?"

"The stuff in the bottle. I want to see."

He scratched his beard. "Well, we aren't quite ready for that yet."

The door abruptly opened before Miranda could press the point and Fiona walked in. Miranda knew her in a vague way to be his teaching assistant and an ever-present team member at the dig.

"Hey, Brian, I...oh, I'm sorry I didn't know you had somebody with you."

She murmured hello to Miranda. Miranda's curiosity radar flared at the fact that Fiona called Brian by his first name. Interesting.

Now, out of her dig clothes and dressed up to the nines, complete with heels, Miranda did a quick tally of how different she was from this woman. Dark eyes to her light; curly brown cropped hair to her blonde hair styled to cascade down her shoulders; tan complexion to her peaches and cream; on the tall side to her petite stature. Fiona would be hard for the average male to resist. Miranda looked back at Brian and wondered if he was just an average male...or different. She had the sudden realization that she wanted him to be in the different category.

"Fiona...Miranda was wondering about the bottle's contents. I'm updating her on what we have so far."

"Yes, I was just telling Professor Beckett how much I would like to see the items," Miranda added.

Fiona looked from one to the other and said, "Uh..."

Brian let out a belly laugh. "I think Professor Chesney is baiting you. I already told her it's too soon for ogling."

Miranda knew when she had been bested and stood up to take her leave.

As she reached down for her bag, Brian said, "Let's go over to the lab and I'll show you."

"Really?" Fiona and Miranda both said at the same time.

The archeology offices were housed in a retrofitted white clapboard building that had formerly been a residence. The lab had been established in the basement of the former house and was completely modern and out of keeping with the rest of the building. Overly bright LED lighting illuminated the long tables that were strewn with various objects of all shapes and sizes. Several students were hunched over different things with tools and microscopes. It was a lot to take in. Music piped in from somewhere and it sounded like a Gorillaz song to Miranda's ears, a British tech band she had become partial to after her stint at Oxford.

"Hey, guys, you wanna turn that down?" Brian asked. One of the students scrambled off to the countertop and fiddled with a phone until there was silence.

Fiona led the way to the far end of one of the tables where a big sign had been placed saying: 'Back off! No one authorized to be here!'

Miranda raised her eyebrows at it. "Tight security?"

"You bet. We are keeping this under wraps for now." Brian then gestured widely with an arm at pieces of blotting paper on the table. "Voilà!"

Miranda got closer and could see each piece of paper held one individual object. "So...I spy with my little eyes one nail, one that looks like a twig, one fingernail and...is that a lock of hair?"

"Yeah, we think so. But we're still running tests. Also, what you can't see is that there was human urine in the bottle as well."

Scrunching her nose at that fact, Miranda said, "What is this all about?"

"We have some ideas but, like I said, we got everybody re-searching this out. We need to find out what makes the most sense."

Fiona nodded next to Brian. She had become a bobbing head to everything he said apparently.

Brian added, "Pretty crazy stuff, right?"

"Do you think there are more of them? I mean, on the prop-erty. At Rosewood?"

"Anything's possible."

A silence took over at the idea of that. When it stretched to an awkward point, Miranda broke into it. "Well, thanks for showing me. Appreciate your change of heart."

After goodbyes were exchanged, Miranda cast a final glance over the illuminated assortment of oddities from the bottle. As she made her way out of the lab, images of the strange items ran like tickertape through her mind along with the realization that her property might contain more mysteries than she could ever conjure up. With the excitement of that thought, there was also a soupçon of something else that she couldn't pin down. Was it worry? She shrugged it off once outside and headed to the parking lot.

Chapter Four

ON JAUNTS TO AND from Williamsburg and the college, Miranda had become partial to the general store at her nearest crossroads, Princeton. There were no towns like she thought of a town, streets of houses and stores in a commercial district. Instead, Bisoux, as far as Miranda could tell, was comprised of several areas where the roads crossed. While called towns, in Miranda's opinion, they were merely places given a name where a store could usually be found, pinned on the map like X marks the spot.

As she approached the store at Princeton which claimed itself a "mercantile store" on its sign, she remembered needing a pint of milk to place in the now functioning refrigerator for her morning coffee. Also, she felt a thirst for a cold soda as she swung into the dirt parking lot.

As had been the case on all of her visits to date, an elderly man in overalls with a crisp, white shirt underneath stood behind the counter nodding at her vaguely upon her entrance. He then went right back to gazing out the window at the empty crossroads. She had yet to make an entrée with him and establish more rapport than just the nodding head.

The first time Miranda had come into the "mercantile," the clutter had overwhelmed her. She had almost left without making a purchase, the chaos too much for her brain to process. But now, a few visits in, she was seeing more quirky delights than chaos. The default setting in her brain—organized—adapted by picking around the dark interior of the shop to make her selections. She now actually became absorbed by the nooks and crannies with items that might surprise. Knick-knacks, tchotchkes and old, forgotten inventory all vied for space under dust-ridden glass countertops and on rickety shelves. She plucked up a filmy container of waxed dental floss, reminded she had run out.

Lost in her explorations, she barely registered the jangly bell signaling another customer. Suddenly, she felt a hand brush her arm and was startled at seeing a woman right next to her at the refrigerator that held the sodas. Standing a foot taller, Miranda looked down on a face heavily layered with pancake makeup, slathered blue eyeshadow and several applications of mascara that almost resembled a spider's legs it had gotten so thick.

The woman looked directly at Miranda and asked, "What soda should I get?"

Miranda took a step away, unnerved by the woman's closeness before answering, "Uh...how about a root beer?"

"Okay," the other woman said. Her cut off shorts strained tightly as she reached in for the drink as the matching tank top revealed too much soft lumpy flesh.

Miranda turned and continued on through the store with the acute realization that the woman was right on her heels. Miranda tried to catch the elderly man's rheumy eyes to get his help, to no avail. He just continued to stare out into the rural emptiness in front of him.

She hastened to the counter and placed her items down; the pint of milk, a coke and the dental floss. The woman was still glued next to her. Miranda was going with the assumption that maybe the woman bore some mental challenges with a limited understanding of personal space.

The can of root beer was pushed into the pile of Miranda's items and the elderly man rang it up right along with rest on his old-fashioned cash register.

"Oh...um...okay, it's fine." Miranda mumbled to herself, holding on until she could run out to her car and peel herself away from the Princeton store.

"Your daddy know you up here, Lizzie Gooding?" It took a

minute for Miranda to translate in her head what he had spoken because of his heavy Bisoux brogue. At first, it sounded like: "Yawl daddee known yourn here, Lizzie Goodun?" But she got the gist of it.

"Yessir. He knows." The woman's reply did not have the heaviness of the brogue, just some of the intonation.

The scene was becoming slightly macabre and Miranda felt her nerves humming. Spilling some coins on the counter, she grabbed the paper bag with her items, saying, "Just keep the change." He had left the root beer out separately.

As she left the building, the woman was still right behind her. When Miranda headed down the porch stairs, she felt a grip on her arm and looked down at the woman's hand. Midnight blue nail polish, chipped off in spots, decorated each nail.

"Do you like Miss Janie's house?"

"What?" As she answered, Miranda shook her arm to remove the woman's hand.

"I saw you and all those other people at Miss Janie's. You like it?"

"How did you...do you live nearby?"

The woman nodded in response.

"Where...which house..."

"Just down the road apiece. Same road as Miss Janie's."

Miranda cleared her throat and said, "Yes, I like the house a lot." She paused and then, curious, asked, "Did you know Miss Janie well?"

The woman blinked with the heavily mascaraed big eyes. "Very well."

"Okay...my name is Miranda, by the way."

"I know that already."

Miranda nodded, not knowing how else to end the exchange. She hesitated, but the woman just looked at her. Miranda finally got into her car and started the engine.

When she put her car in reverse, she could sense without even looking that the woman, Lizzie Gooding, was still staring at her.

Miranda tried to shake off the strangeness of the scene just like she had shaken off Lizzie's grip on her arm as she drove on to Rosewood. She would try another crossroads store the next time. Pulling into the drive, she stopped short at the sight of the other vehicles. She had forgotten it was a dig day but was heartened to have some warm bodies around after the incident at the store.

Once inside the house, she looked around at her progress and thought about what she wanted to tackle next. Her zest for projects felt diminished all of a sudden and she felt deflated for the first time since purchasing Rosewood. She inwardly chastised herself for being silly. The Princeton store had nothing to do with her house. Or did it?

A rap at the door broke into her thoughts. The door opened and a voice she recognized as Brian's bellowed out hello. Not minding the interruption, she walked out to the hall to meet him.

"Hey, Miranda," he paused as he studied her. "Everything okay?"

"Oh, sure. Just tired out maybe."

"You need a break. So do I as it happens. How about I take you out to Floyd's Deck after the dig wraps up for the day?"

"What's that?"

"Just about the best seafood place on the planet. Or at least the state of Virginia, anyway."

"But why?" she asked.

"We owe you for letting us into Rosewood..." He hesitated and then added, "Consider it a gratuity for allowing us to use your property."

"You don't owe me anything at all." A part of her wondered how this would sit with Fiona, if Fiona was not just in the student category of Brian's life.

"Well, humor me. You do like seafood, don't you?"

"Of course, I like seafood. Sure, let's do it."

A couple of hours later, Miranda followed Brian's pickup

truck as they headed out further into the county to a marina that Brian said was on the bay. Once in the parking lot, Miranda took in the place from her car. Just a beat-up marina shop with not much going for it on the exterior. She hoped Brian knew good eats over bad.

As they walked in, Brian explained the set up. "Wait until we get in here to judge. They'll set us up on the porch and we'll have a million-dollar view."

The entrance was really a dark bar. Any chatter that had been going on stopped completely as they walked up to the stand for a table. "Seriously?" Miranda muttered to herself.

"What?" Brian said, overhearing her mutter.

She shook her head and said, "I'll tell you when we get seated."

As promised, the hostess took them out onto a screened-in porch area that ran the length of the building and hung partially over the water on pilings.

A soft "Wow" slipped out of Miranda's mouth as they took seats at a corner table with a round, red candle in the middle of the table on top of brown paper.

"Yeah, I told you."

The view out into the bay seemed like it went on for miles and was filled with inlets and islets. Miranda felt her nerves calm instantly just by gazing out. Once they were situated with cold draft beers with their glasses sweating on napkins and their orders had been placed, Brian beamed his golden-eyed gaze her way. She gazed right back, not minding one bit.

He broke the staring contest and said, "What's bothering you? Is it something to do with the dig?"

"No...no. Nothing to do with that. It's just...well...as much as I didn't believe in any of what I heard, I'm having some strange encounters. That kind of fit the stereotypes."

"How so?"

Miranda told Brian about her interchanges with the Maynard woman and Lizzie Gooding. Brian took a pull from his beer and seemed deep in thought. "How did she know about the dig, do you think? Has she been hiding somewhere and watching?"

"She could have been hiding in the yard, I guess?"

"That's just weird if that's going on. On the other hand, we could always use another trowel head."

"Is that really what you call yourselves? Trowel heads?"

"Nah. Just coined it this second."

Miranda grimaced at the joke and then said, "I don't think you need another one that bad. Who knows what's going on with her? I mean, I'm sure it's all quite innocent, but still."

"Well, the most important thing is that she isn't doing anything to compromise the integrity of the dig."

"Wait...you don't think she could have planted the blue bottle, do you?"

"No. No way. The strata of earth and a lot of other indicators show that has clearly been in there since the 1700s."

"The 1700s? I thought Rosewood was constructed in 1810."

Brian breathed out and then began to explain. "There was probably a dwelling there initially that they either added onto or took down. Fairly standard in historical archeological sites really."

"Hhmmm..." Miranda stopped while she was ahead. What she did not know about historical archeological digs was a lot but she didn't feel like revealing too much ignorance.

Two softshell sandwiches were placed in front of them by their server and they dug right in. After the first couple bites, Miranda said, "Whoa...I haven't had seafood this fresh...maybe ever!"

Brian nodded and said, "Yep. That's what they are known for. I told you it would be worth it."

"Indeed."

After Brian had plowed through most of his meal, he finally took a pause and looked back up. "So, tell me about Miranda Chesney."

Miranda shrugged. "Not much to tell really. And you probably know the basics by now anyway: new homeowner, philosophy professor, seafood lover...What else is there to tell?"

He gave her a dazzling grin and said, "I'm sure there's a thing or two more. That's my suspicion, anyway."

"Actually, I do have an unusual fascination with swing dancing. Haven't found many opportunities around these parts though."

He gave her a bemused look. "Huh. Swing dancing. Yeah, no swing dance clubs that I can recall."

She eyed him up and thought about his swing dancing potential. Maybe, just maybe. Out loud, she said, "Well, the rest of me is kind of 'what you see is what you get.'"

"Ha!" Moving his water glass side to side, he asked, "So when do you actually move in?

"It's this weekend."

They finished their meal in companionable silence. When the server came back and asked if they wanted more beers, Brian looked to Miranda, who shook her head.

"Probably wise. I need to get back and sort out the kids," Brian said.

"Right," she paused, feeling oddly shy. Then added, "Thank you for bringing me here. Didn't realize how much I needed the break."

He smiled and studied her a beat too long.

In the parking lot, they both began to say goodbye at the same time and then laughed. "You first," Miranda said.

"I was going to ask...do you need any help this weekend with the move?"

Miranda was taken aback at the offer. Flustered, she said, "Well...yes. That would be great. I'll text you with the details?"

After thanking him again for the meal, Miranda watched him pull out from the parking lot. She realized his offer of help didn't mean anything. Like the offer for lunch didn't mean anything. But what if it did? She could work with that...indeed, she could.

Chapter Five

WITH HANDS GRIPPING THE sides of a bulging box, Miranda pushed the apartment building door open with one foot. The moist, humid heat of Indian summer hit immediately, draping over her like a weighted blanket.

Miranda took in a breath against the cloying damp and the strain of the box. She made her way to the open back of the U-Haul truck and perched the box on the edge. Then she pushed it into the back of the empty truck. Staring at the lone box made her feel daunted by the task of moving.

Miranda glanced down at her cell phone. There were no texts back yet from the students who had volunteered to help, just crickets. Everything was boxed and ready to go but she should have remembered that Friday nights often led to Saturday hangovers. Commitments at their ages were easily broken for fancier things afoot. Unfortunately, hiring bonafide movers had been out of the question since her budget had been pushed to its outer limits.

She felt sweat start to make rivulets along the sides of her hairline and bridge of her nose. A sigh escaped at the thought of the long day ahead. Her phone interrupted, chirping out a bird whistle that she had a text. "Oh, good," she said aloud. "Calvin and Hobbes to the rescue." She had nicknamed the two students in her head but not to their faces...yet.

She looked down to see it was Brian Beckett instead. She had resisted reaching out to him with the moving details as they had left it. If she had to put a pin in it, it could be she didn't want to feel obligated to him. Maybe. But now...she needed his help. Her fingers danced rapidly over the phone keyboard with her address.

Several more runs later from the apartment building to the U-Haul, Miranda was in the parking lot when Brian pulled in. He popped out in his customary flannel, and she said, as way of greeting, "Aren't you going to get hot in that?"

"Huh?"

She pointed to his shirt, and he said, "Oh, yeah. Good idea."

He peeled off the plaid shirt down to a muscle shirt. She took a discreet peek at his physique which was not far removed from a romance novel cover. Maybe one featuring a hero from the Scottish Highlands with mussed up hair and toned muscles pressing out of his tank top. Curbing her mind from fixating on that vision, she said, "I got a head start and don't have much furniture. Just a few basics but the furniture still needs to…"

"Whoa, whoa…that needs to go in first."

"Oh."

"Didn't you say you had students helping?"

"No shows…as of yet. So, I started on the boxes."

He puffed some air out. "Okay. Keep going with those and I'll rearrange the back here."

Somewhat chastened, she headed back up for another load. On her return trip, her Calvin and Hobbes duo (really Matt and Jeff) stood by the U-Haul talking with Brian.

"Hey, guys."

They sheepishly apologized and she brushed it off saying, "Let's get to the furniture upstairs."

All of them trudged up single file and Miranda got a whiff of various deodorants mixed with various sweat odors. Once there, Brian eyed up the furniture pieces that Miranda had pushed to the center of the utilitarian and soon-to-be barren space. He began to call out what pieces would be hauled down first, second and third and so on.

Watching Brian stretch packing tape on top of the dining room table legs that she hadn't even realized came off the table made Miranda curious. "How do you know so much about moving?"

"Huh? Oh, I worked for a moving company during summers. A lot of summers, actually. It was the way I got through college and then grad school too."

"Hot job."

"It was that. But I was grateful for it. It's the way I survived."

"Were your parents..."

"Not in the picture." He didn't elaborate further as he vigorously pulled another strip of tape, that line of questioning shut down.

Miranda lifted another box, the muscles along her arms and shoulders lodging complaints all over again, and headed back down with it. As she turned away, she couldn't help but to wonder about Brian...and his secrets.

Another hour in and the move took on that never-ending quality that all moves seemed to—that point when it felt as though moving was forever. When the non-stop frenzy of back and forth from apartment to vehicle finally resulted in a loaded-up U-Haul, they all headed out separately to Rosewood for the unloading.

On the way, Miranda swung by for pizza and beer on Route 17 before heading onto Big Island Road. Even with Brian stepping in and organizing it all, she felt the wear and tear of the day and maybe even some hours shaved off her lifespan.

Later, they all sat on the bare, pine hardwood floor eating pizza and drinking the beer, conversation minimal. Once the food and beer were done, Miranda ponied up the cash she had offered and Calvin and Hobbes took their leave.

As Brian helped her pick up the empty pizza boxes and beer bottles, Miranda gazed around the space, surrounded by all the packed boxes and furniture parked haphazardly. She let out a sigh of contentment. The mess did not bother her one bit. She had time. Now at Rosewood for good, it was a canvas ready for her finishing touches.

Brian cut into her thoughts, saying, "You going to miss being in town?"

She smiled and said, "Nope."

"So...first full night at Rosewood."

"Yes, finally," Miranda said.

"Are you...are you going to be..."

"What? Say it."

"Nothing. Just keep a cell phone handy."

"Of course." Was his concern something more than friendly, she wondered. Reading the mind of the opposite sex had never been one of her talents. She added, "Thanks though. For everything."

He waved a hand around the space. "It was nothing."

Moving day exertions sent Miranda into a deep slumber. But sounds filtered into her dreams all night long, mewing sounds. By early morning, she came out of a jagged-edged sleep in her new bedroom with the slanted ceiling and became aware that the mewing was real.

She jumped out of bed, pulling on sweats and a t-shirt. Heading downstairs, it sounded like it came from the outside but inside at the same time. She stepped outdoors into the dewy morning with the first rays of dawn flaring up from the east and stopped at the doorstep to get her bearings. She determined the noise to be from the north end of the house and moved in that direction. Soon enough, she pegged it to be underneath the locked-up cellar doors. "Ugh," she groaned.

Miranda had not had cause to enter there since the home inspection when the black snake had lay coiled on the bottom step. As she deliberated, the mews became louder and more insistent. The noisy complaints propelled her to run back inside to grab the key for the hasp lock.

Back at the cellar doors, she fiddled with the key to undo the hasp. Exhaling out, she lifted up the doors. A sudden movement flitted past her. She barely made out the cat that sprung from its captivity, running away.

As she watched, it suddenly stopped and turned back to stare at her with huge golden eyes. She took in its unusual and striking markings. It appeared to be a tabby but with orange hues. She thought through her cat lexicon. A calico tabby? Or just an orange tabby?

As they eyed each other up, Miranda had the fleeting thought that the cat's eyes looked like Brian Beckett's eyes. The cat broke eye contact and began to lick a paw vigorously followed by a scrub to its face. Miranda decided right at that moment that it must be a girl cat.

"Are you hungry?" she asked. The cat paused, almost considering, and proceeded to stare at her, a soul-searching stare.

Miranda went inside and rummaged through boxes marked pantry to find a can of tuna she remembered packing. Once located, she then needed to find the can opener before finally getting back outside, open can in hand. The cat had disappeared though, and she felt a stab of disappointment.

"Kitty, kitty, kitty..." she called out. After several minutes, the cat popped out beyond the edge of the yard. The sight made Miranda inexplicably happy.

She placed the can down, wondering how far of a distance cats could smell. She slowly moved away as the cat twitched its tail, watching her.

Back inside, Miranda gazed out from the window as the cat made a tentative foray to the tuna. After delicately smelling around the can, it plunged in. As Miranda studied the cat, she puzzled over how it had become trapped in the cellar.

Later, going out to collect the empty tuna can, the cat was nowhere to be seen. She hoped it would return, liking the idea of having a cat around. She made the snap decision to stop and get cat food next time she passed by the local farm supply store on Route 17.

Bending over to pick up the can, Miranda felt that all too familiar sensation at the nape of her neck. Whipping around to see who was there, there was no one.

"Lizzie! Come out where I can see you!" she called out.

No one emerged from of the cluster of trees on the edge of the yard as Miranda stood with her hands by her sides, feeling foolish. Walking back to the house, that same creeping sensa-

Chapter Six

WHEN THE TEAM ARRIVED for the next dig day, Miranda let Brian know they might have a visitor of the feline persuasion.

"A cat, huh? I would figure you for a dog person," he said.

"Too much work. Cats do their own thing."

Miranda and the cat had adjusted to life together, each on their own terms. She generally put a bowl of cat food out in the morning and, upon her return from Williamsburg, the bowl would be empty. At times, she could spot the cat around the property with the favored hangout being the brick steps of the potting shed where a splash of sunlight warmed its tawny striped fur.

"Well, you know a dog might be a good idea though. Being out here alone, I mean..." Brian let the thought drift off as he looked at her intently.

She shrugged it off and said, "No. A dog would be alone too much."

"So, where did the cat come from?"

Miranda told him about finding the cat under the cellar stairs her first night in. He looked over at the cellar stairs and said, "Under there? But how..."

"I know. It's weird, right?"

"Um...it had to have been placed in there by someone."

Miranda bit the inside of her cheek.

Brian added, "Do you want me to check it out down there?"

"Oh yes, please. I thought you would never ask."

She stood at the top and watched Brian's ginger head duck

to go into the space.

He emerged several minutes later, wiping his hands on his jeans, and said, "It all checks out. But smells like cat piss."

"Well, I don't blame her for that since she was trapped all night in there."

"Her?"

"I think."

"Any more encounters of the human kind?"

"Thankfully, no."

He glanced over at the dig where the students were industriously moving to and fro and said, "Let's take a little walk around. You need a primer on historic outbuildings."

"Brian, I'm sure there are no bogeymen hiding in the outbuildings. Seriously. It's fine."

"Humor me, okay? Consider it a part of your education as a budding archeologist in training."

Miranda rolled her eyes but followed behind as he led the way. As he strode towards the potting shed, she studied the back of him not for the first time, noticing how fine a figure he cut.

"You know, these outbuildings aren't original to the property, right?" he asked.

"Really? But they look old."

"They were probably done when Williamsburg got big. My guess would be whatever was left of the original buildings came down and the Gwynn family put these up as sort of pseudo reproductions. Taste of the town, so to speak. Williamsburg and its success made people want to copy buildings that they saw there. Williamsburg-tique. Or Williamsburg stink depending on your point of view."

"Huh. But they left the house alone?"

"Well, the exterior, yes. But I am guessing some of the interior was jazzed up at that time."

"Fair to say the exterior already had its Williamsburg vibe?"

He nodded. Miranda cast a glance back at the house, reassured by his words that it was original.

At the potting shed, Miranda said, "This is the cat's hang out. She likes to catch some rays on the steps here."

Brian eyed up the building. "A heavily shingled roof with a steep pitch. At one time, it was that pale cream tone we can see tinges of...now, long faded."

He continued discussing the garden fads that had waxed and waned and how this had probably been built in the early twentieth century sometime. As he talked, he pushed on the door with some effort to get it unstuck. He took in the jumble of pots and bases as Miranda said, "I know. I know. I just need some time to get in there and sort it all out."

He put his hands up and said, "Hey, no judgment here. So many projects, so many days."

They continued on to the old abandoned chicken coop, long empty. It was a faded barn-red color with a run-in yard area comprised of a mesh fence now in pieces. He turned to her and said, "Are you going to get some laying hens?"

She thought about it for a second. Did she want hens to lay eggs for her? Maybe? Out loud, she said, "Hadn't really thought about it yet..."

"Well, if you do, this coop needs to get secured up. Otherwise, the predators will get right in and take care of business."

Curious, she asked, "You raised hens?"

He nodded curtly. "When I was a kid." He didn't follow up on that thought.

They ended up at the shed. "Fine example here of a drive-in shed. These were built when carriages were the mode of travel. With its generous open space in the middle and space off to one side for storage purposes. Real nice example."

He picked up the blue tarp and checked under it. He had asked at the start of the dig if they could use the side storage space for equipment and supplies. Miranda had noticed it had become another hideaway for the cat but she didn't mention that to him now.

"Oh, hey...do you know what this means?" She pointed to the cat symbol. Miranda had forgotten about it, but now was reminded it was just like the one at the Maynard's.

They both peered closer at the etching, a crude outline of a cat, kindergarten style, on the post that supported the building on its back end. Miranda ran her fingers lightly over it then realized Brian had gone quiet.

She looked up to see a strange expression on his face. "What? Do you know what it is?" she asked.

"Huh?" He cleared his throat. "Oh...no. I've never seen that."

A charged silence took over the space and, in the silence, Miranda knew he was lying. She didn't know why it would be a reason to lie or what it might mean.

"Well, thank you for the tour and looks like everything checks out. No bogeymen."

He nodded. "Yep. Better safe than sorry."

That night, it was finally a tickle in her nose that woke Miranda, followed by a sneezing fit. Once awake in the deep of the night, she tried to settle back to sleep. All was quiet except for the occasional creak and groan, Rosewood's night sounds which she was becoming accustomed to.

She turned to one side and faced the wall where the window was. Her eyes were wide open and the room seemed brighter than usual. At first, she assumed the moon was in a full cycle but then she took note of a flickering in the brightness.

One half of her didn't want to leave the warm, cozy nest of her bed; the other half, the responsible and rational half, knew something was very wrong. With a pounding heart, she leapt up and stumbled over to the sill. A fire blazed in the yard. It formed a right triangle between the dig and the house, almost too exact in its placement.

In a panic, she scrambled to pull on sweatpants and raced downstairs. She snatched a bucket and filled it at the kitchen faucet, ruing her lack of a garden hose outside. It was still on that running list of stuff to buy at the local farm supply store along with more cat food.

Once outside, the nip in the night air hit her along with

smoke from the fire. Miranda lunged over with the bucket and splashed it on. She ran to the outside spigot that they had been using for the dig and refilled the bucket. Three bucket trips later, it was finally doused out enough to her satisfaction.

She threw the bucket down on the ground and examined what was in front of her. The set up reminded her of the campfires she had learned to construct as a Girl Scout. Wood had been stacked with precision to insure an ambitious and successful blaze. She picked up a stick and kneeled to stir the remaining embers and ash left behind, remembering again the Girl Scout lessons. Standing up, she kicked some dirt over the area. This time, she didn't call out Lizzie's name.

At the edge of the tree line, she saw a slight movement in the moonlight as the cat suddenly appeared and sat on its haunches. The animal stared Miranda down, as if to say: what are you going to do about it?

Chapter Seven

THE NEXT MORNING, MIRANDA woke up groggy with the odor of campfire filling her nostrils and one overriding thought in her head: she had to go talk to Lizzie. The cat was one thing, but setting fires was taking things to another level. A dangerous level.

After a cup of black coffee, she hopped on her bike and rode the half mile to Lizzie's driveway. Given the strange situation at the mercantile, she had made sure to suss out how close the family lived to Rosewood. Stopping at the mailbox with the name, "Gooding", barely visible, she stared down at a driveway not too unlike the Maynard's. She had yet to see Lizzie's father anywhere out and about but this kind of thing had to stop. She would rather work it out directly with Lizzie and her father before taking the more drastic step of contacting law enforcement.

She turned the bike down the rutted driveway. Unlike the Maynard's, it was filled with wildflowers all fading into fall yellows, oranges, and browns on either side. It took a little away from the rundown aspect of the rest of it. After less than a city block or so, the drive ended at a house of substantial size that had lost its grandeur but must have been a showplace in its heyday. A dog took up barking, but Miranda couldn't see where it was.

"Stop that hollerin'," a male voice bellowed out. The front porch door squeaked open and a man emerged with a walker in front of him leading the way. He squinted at the sight of Miranda and said, "I know you?"

Miranda took in the man on the porch, trying not to stare

outright. His age was indeterminate. He could be any age between fifty and eighty. But she figured Lizzie must be at least thirty or thirty-five, so he had to be at least fifty-five, give or take. He had a full head of silver hair that lent a younger look than balding would have done, despite the color. Horn rimmed glasses and cigarette in hand completed the picture. His clothes were worn and dirty. She wondered briefly how he had looked in his prime. She always did this, tried to figure out how someone used to look.

"No, sir. We haven't met yet. I'm your new neighbor. Miranda Chesney."

"Now, I know who you are. You got all those people taking over Miss Janie's house."

She set the bike down and began to approach when the porch door swung open again and a Doberman lunged towards her, growling with menace.

"Cletus! I said stop the hollerin'!" The man swatted at the dog with one hand. The dog whimpered and sat down next to the walker.

Miranda stood stock still, afraid to unnerve the dog. The man looked at her with a question on his face. "Well...I, uh... wondered if I could speak to Lizzie," she said.

"She's out in the woods. You can go find her if you want," he said, gesturing off to his left towards a stand of cedars and loblolly pines.

As Miranda looked over in that direction, he added, "I'd mind the chiggers if I were you though." With that, he turned back to the door and opened it, letting Cletus go in before him.

Assured that Cletus was under wraps, Miranda decided to seek out Lizzie. Maybe approaching her in her own space would lead to an easier conversation. She found the path that broke off from the yard into the woods, well-trodden either by animals or man, it was hard to tell which. Keeping one eye out for poison oak, sumac or ivy, she picked her way through it. The path was surprisingly dense in contrast to the Tidewater's usual sparse appearance.

Eventually, there was an opening with a choice of three

different routes to take. Sighing, she half wondered if this was a fool's errand. There were no signs of Lizzie or any other human, just a slight breeze that rustled the branches and the noise of insects to keep her company.

Miranda trudged ahead on the path that was the widest of the three until it came to an abrupt stop with just the faintest trace of footfall off to one corner. Venturing further into an even denser trail, a slight opening exposed a tight cluster of three trees in a semicircle. They were wrapped together so closely it appeared as if they were tangled. The idea of them being three sisters popped out of nowhere in Miranda's mind. She didn't recognize the species of the trees with its unusual ancient and otherworldly look and thick, layered bark so different from the surrounding loblollies and cedars.

Getting closer, she caught a sway above in the branches from the corner of her eye. When her gaze moved upwards, a ragged scream automatically escaped from her mouth. The branches of the incestuously bound trees were filled with babies. She frantically looked right and left, seeing even more hidden amongst the branches of all sizes and shapes in various states of decay. Her heart raced and her breath wouldn't come as the babies seemed to move in a macabre dance. She finally registered a clicking noise when the breeze buffeted them to touch.

Slowly, it sank in that they were actually dirty, beat-up dolls. She let out a huge breath and tamped down the next scream lodged in her throat. Swiveling her gaze around the space, she did a quick count of thirty or so of the odd toy dolls. Many were in pieces or cut in half and marked with wounds painted on in red. A closed-in feeling began to overcome Miranda and she turned to flee the spot.

Pivoting, she caught a glimpse of something blue at the base of one of the trees, its roots twisted and clumped together in the same sort of tangle as above. Holding back from fleeing right away, Miranda edged in to discover that it looked like the blue bottle from the dig. But that couldn't be right, she thought. That bottle was safely at the lab at the college. Or was it?

Miranda grabbed it and took off at a fast clip out of the claustrophobic space. She moved too quickly, causing her foot to trip on a raised-up root. She fell onto her left side, landing with a thud on her ankle. She still held the bottle in a tight grip in her right hand. It was miraculously unharmed, but her ankle screamed otherwise.

Pushing herself up to a stand, she could feel a crunch in her ankle in the process. She had done some damage but made a tentative step shifting her weight to the other side. Miranda tried a few steps and knew she could continue. "Okay," she muttered to herself. "I'm outta here."

As she vacated the place, she felt the creeping sensation on her neck, the same one. She shuffled along as quick as her ankle would allow. Upon reaching the path where it entered the yard, she turned back and stared at where she had come from. All was silent and still apart from that persistent, gentle breeze.

In the yard of the house, there were no signs of Lizzie, her father or Cletus. After cramming the bottle into the bag on her bike, Miranda hopped on it with a grimace. Her ankle throbbed with each press as she pedaled hard to get away.

While concentrating on pedaling out of there, her peripheral vision snagged on a tree on one side of the drive. Another outline of a cat, that symbol again. She didn't stop to examine it. Now in three places around Bisoux, at least. What did it mean?

With the bike bouncing down the rutted driveway, Miranda decided she was done being the nice neighbor. It was time to go to the local authorities to deal with whatever was going on at Rosewood.

Miranda firmly shut the door behind her once safely back inside Rosewood, briefly closing her eyes with a huge sense of relief. The dull throb of her ankle as soon as she shifted her weight brought Miranda back to the present and she remembered a first aid kit in the pantry that Brian had left at the start of the dig in case of mishaps. She limped into the kitchen and rifled around in the pantry until finding it.

As Miranda rinsed off the combination of dirt and dried blood from her ankle, she tried to recall the date of her last tetanus shot. Digging through the kit, she pulled out hydrogen peroxide and dabbed it on the wound. It needed to be iced, too, but she had one overriding thought in mind: to drive to the lab and compare this bottle to the one found in the dig.

She called Brian on the way into Williamsburg. When he answered, she said, "Meet me at the lab in about fifteen minutes."

"What's wrong? Are you okay?"

"Not really. Can you meet me?" She heard a muffled discussion in the background after telling her to hold on. And thought she picked up Fiona's voice.

He came back on and said, "Sure. I'll be there."

Chapter Eight

MIRANDA PRESSED OPEN THE double doors into the lab and entered, out of breath from the rush to get there as soon as possible. She stopped in her tracks at the sight of Brian and Fiona seated on stools. They faced each other with Fiona leaning in towards Brian. It felt like she was intruding upon an intimate moment, and she slipped out an "Oh, excuse..."

Brian leapt up at the sight of her and immediately said, "Miranda! What is going on?"

Without preamble, she held out the blue bottle and the two others stared at it with mouths agape.

"Can I sit down somewhere?" Miranda asked, as her ankle throbbed to the beat of her heart.

Brian led her towards a table and, once they were all seated, Miranda placed the blue bottle in the center. After some silence, Brian cleared his throat. "Before you tell us about this one, I'm going to have Fiona give the rundown of what we've found out so far."

Fiona pulled a notebook out of a big, brown leather satchel and opened it up in front of her. "So, we think...we think what we found is a witch bottle," she said.

"A...what?"

"A witch bottle."

"Come on. You've got to be kidding me."

Brian held a hand up and said, "I figured a logics professor wouldn't be too enthused by this finding, but just listen."

Miranda ignored his comment. "So, 'we' believe in witches in these parts?"

Fiona began to explain. "This area was settled by people mainly from a region in England called East Anglia. It's located..."

Miranda cut her off and said, "I know where it is." Indeed, she had spent many happy hours frolicking in the beach towns of Norfolk with an erstwhile beau, erstwhile being the operative word.

"Anyway, in that area..." Fiona paused, rifling through the satchel to pull out some loose papers, then picked the thread back up, "...in that area, there has been some research about witch bottles. We think there's a possibility that immigrants settling here in Bisoux brought the tradition over."

"What is the tradition exactly? I mean, how does the bottle tie into witchcraft?"

"As best they know so far, it was meant to protect somebody—or somebodies—close by where it was placed. Protection from evil spirits and things. Here's a description..."

Pulling a paper closer, Fiona read:

"'Witch bottles are a tradition historically dating from the sixteenth century as a method to draw in and trap evil intent directed at someone in particular. Items collected to place in the bottle might include urine, hair, nail clippings, rusty nails, thorns, menstrual blood, glass chips, wood slivers, bone shards, needles and pins, rosemary and red thread from sprite traps. The bottle might then be filled with sea water, earth, sand, ashes, vinegar or red wine. Once completed, the bottle is buried beneath a hearth, in a far corner of the victim's property or another unsuspecting, hidden spot in the house or on the property. Alternatively, the bottle may be thrown in a fire to combust. If buried, the items catch the evil and harm it before it drowns or suffocates. If thrown in a fire, the evil is eliminated through the explosion. Either way, the bottle is active as long as it exists one way or the other.'"

Fiona's gaze moved up from the paper directly at Miranda. "Warding off bad intent, I guess you could say."

Brian piped up: "It's very exciting because not many witch bottles have been found in North America. Plus, this one is quite possibly the first to be recovered in the Mid-Atlantic region." His eyes took on a gleam of excitement and he added, "We can make an important tie in with cultural traditions and people settling this area."

"Okkaayy...so what about this?" Miranda pointed to the other bottle in front of them. "I know I'm a mere amateur, but this looks like the same kind of bottle to me."

They all eyed up the bottle in front of them. Brian leaned in closer and then broke the silence. "Yeah...now this. Tell us about it."

Miranda explained about the campfire and its aftermath which had led to her wild hike into Lizzie's woods where dolls had hung from the trees.

Brian let out a repressed exhale and said, "You went there alone...never mind. It does indeed look the same." He paused and then added, "Could Lizzie, or someone, have dug up a bunch on her own?"

"A bunch? Well, I don't know. Maybe the whole place is filled with them from end to end," Miranda said snappishly.

"Miranda...I don't think that is likely," Brian said.

"I wouldn't think any of this would be likely before I found Rosewood but here we are."

"Look...we need to talk to Lizzie," said Brian.

"Clearly. Which is what I tried to do already. My next step is to go to the sheriff's office."

Fiona, long silent, jumped in and said, "Oh, I wouldn't do that."

Miranda looked at her with some surprise. "Why?"

"That would alienate people right away in Bisoux."

"How do you know what people in Bisoux are like?"

Brian interjected. "Didn't we mention it? Fiona is from Bisoux. Grew up right down the road from Rosewood."

"No. You didn't mention it."

Miranda took in the vision of the perfect college co-ed in front of her. Hair perfectly coiffed. A casual but elegant appearance that probably took hours to put together. White button-down shirt underneath a form-fitting, checkered sweater. Tailored black pants. Not like anyone she had seen in Bisoux to date.

"Do you know Lizzie Gooding well?" Miranda asked, as an afterthought.

Fiona looked down to one side, a possible "tell." Miranda waited for what lie was going to come out of her mouth.

"Not really. I mean, I've seen her around here and there."

"Here and there, huh? Well, any suggestions on how to approach her with all of this since you don't think going to the sheriff is a good idea?"

"Maybe...maybe meet her at a neutral place. Like one of the stores," Fiona said. "I could...um...set it up. A meeting, I mean."

Miranda got up and started to pace but stopped when ankle pain ratcheted up on cue. "I really don't want to deal with this at all."

She sat back down. "Lizzie told me she knew Miss Janie very well. Even though Miss Janie died years ago, could Lizzie still be hanging on to that connection?"

"It's possible. We'll talk to her and figure it out," Brian said.

As they all stood up from the table to leave, Brian added, "The house of your dreams may have come with a little baggage to sort out..."

"Thanks," she said sarcastically. "Another relationship with baggage...that's just great."

"Just sit tight for now."

Miranda threw him a glare to the effect that she did not want to 'just sit tight.'

Chapter Nine

ON THE WAY BACK to Rosewood, Miranda mulled over the fact that Fiona was a Bisoux native. How had that never been mentioned and why was it so jarring?

Her eye caught sight of the Southern States farm supply store and she swung into the parking lot at the last possible moment. Walking up to the door, the closed sign slapped on made sense for a Sunday. But, next to the closed sign, there was a flyer attached. A large photo of a cat was in the center with a caption above that read, "MISS JANIE IS MISSING".

Miranda stared at it trying to understand. It was her cat, but now not-her-cat, strangely named the same as the former owner of Rosewood. A very weird coincidence. Below the description that used the words "tawny" and "she" (a "she" just like Miranda had thought), there was a number to call. Taking a photo to save the number, disappointment seeped in that the cat would need to go back to its owner.

Once back at Rosewood, all was still and quiet. She looked askance at the ash in the shallow pit at the center of the yard, the only sign it had happened, before heading indoors to make the call.

A woman's voice answered on the other end and Miranda explained why she was calling. "Oh, goodness. You have her there? Can I come over and get her right now?" The woman practically sobbed out the words.

"Well...sure. But she comes and goes. I actually haven't seen her yet today. I have been feeding her every morning and then generally see her in the afternoon."

"Aww...you've been spoiling her rotten, haven't you? Bless your heart. But don't worry. She'll come running when she hears my voice."

Miranda explained where she lived and the woman said, "Oh, of course, she would go to Rosewood."

"Why? I mean, why would she come here?"

"Well, she's the grandbaby of Miss Janie's last cat. I'll tell you all about it when I get there."

They ended their call and Miranda wandered outside to see if the cat was out and about. There proved to be no sign of her and Miranda really doubted she would just magically appear when her owner arrived.

Within a couple of minutes, an old black Ford pickup came up the drive. A heavyset woman spilled out of it and barreled toward Miranda. She had begun talking before getting out of the truck and Miranda caught up with it as she got closer. "...can't thank you enough for taking such good care of her. "

"Oh, sure," Miranda said. "But like I told you on the phone, there's no sign of her right now."

Close up, Miranda could see that the woman was on the other side of fifty, probably. Her gray hair was piled on top of her head in a slapdash fashion and locked down with a classic stainless steel French barrette. Black polyester pants were pulled tautly over a generous backside.

The woman waved a hand and started trilling out, "Here kitty, here kitty", repeatedly as she circled the yard. Within a minute, the cat came running out of the copse at a full charge and right into the woman's open arms. "There you are, Miss Janie." It was an immediate lovefest between the two of them.

As the woman crooned to the cat in her arms, Miranda asked, "So, you named her after Miss Janie?"

"I feel like I am able to keep a part of Miss Janie around. 'Cause this is a grandbaby from one in Miss Janie's last litter of cats. She was the runt, in fact. Miss Janie was quite a lady for cats. I called her that like a familiar. Do you know what that is?"

"Yeah...I've heard the term before." Miranda vaguely knew it from watching *Turner Classics* on Saturday evenings as a kid with her mom. It was the one bonding activity they both actually enjoyed. She remembered a movie about a bell and a book that involved a black cat which was really just an instrument to act out the leading lady's wants and desires. It imprinted on Miranda at a young age and, later, she encountered the term in various works of literature.

The woman began to tell Miranda about the color variations among the kittens and some other trivia. Miranda began to think about how this might be connected to the blue bottles somehow and delicately interjected with, "When you say familiar, do you mean that there's some witchcraft involved?"

The other woman went silent, a noted contrast to her previous loquaciousness. Still stroking her cat's back, she finally answered after the silence had stretched on too long. "Nah...I don't know anything about that."

Miranda knew another lie when she heard one. In fact, the third she had heard of late; first, Brian about the cat etching on the post, then Fiona about not knowing Lizzie and now this woman about witchcraft.

The woman hoisted up the cat and abruptly turned on her heel, saying over her shoulder, "Thanks ever so much for taking care of her."

Miranda, taken aback, watched the departure, feeling bereft at seeing the last of "Miss Janie" the cat. As the old Ford made a throaty gurgle sound while heading out, Miranda realized she had never gotten the woman's name.

Inside, Miranda puttered around and ultimately couldn't settle on any particular project so she just flopped down, giving up. Her eyes wandered to the refrigerator and she wondered if there was anything in there that she could whip into something delicious. After deciding that was unlikely, she focused on the business card magnet tacked onto the front of the refrigerator.

Beau Jenkin's card. The Realtor who had sold her Rosewood. Would he know anything about blue bottles planted around the property? Or why she may have inherited Lizzie as a Rosewood loiterer? Plucking the card off the fridge, she settled back in the chair.

When she dialed his number, he answered in his customary fashion. "Beau Jenkins here."

Miranda identified herself and he paused slightly before saying, "Oh, yes. Miranda! Everything working out nicely at Rosewood? Got everything gussied up like you want it?"

"Yes. It's all come together. But a couple things have surfaced that I wanted to run by you."

"How's that?" his voice became suddenly guarded, maybe less friendly. He might be concerned she would take a dig at his commission.

She went into a brief explanation of some of the goings on and finished with, "....so, do you remember hearing anything about these witch bottles?"

"I don't know a thing about any blue bottles or witches for that matter. Not something around these parts that folks chatter about. Very peculiar indeed."

"Did you know about Lizzie and her attachment to Miss Janie...I mean, Miss Gwynn?"

"Well, sure. Everybody knew about that. She was like a mother to Lizzie because her own mama died in childbirth bringing her into the world. That said...Miss Janie was a little different."

"Different how?"

"Well, she took care of her parents 'til they passed on and then she was by herself out there. I guess you could say she became a loner. A lot of years went by for her like that and then Lizzie came along."

"Funny we didn't talk about this when I was looking at Rosewood."

He audibly huffed on the line and said, "You never asked about the local gossip that I can remember, did you? In fact, you seemed a little bored when I talked about it." He added with a coy tone, "Besides, aren't you hosting a bunch of archeology folks there to fill you in on all of it?"

"How do you know about...oh, never mind."

"In my business, it pays to know it all."

When Miranda hung up with Beau, she thought his parting

words were rich given it had taken him years to sell Rosewood. Musing over the conversation, the thought occurred that she needed to find out more about Miss Gwynn. She might be the key to some of these riddles. And Miranda knew just how to do it.

Chapter Ten

AS SHE DROVE INTO Williamsburg to the Swem Library at William and Mary, Miranda plotted out a loose strategy. If she knew one thing, it was how to research with the best of them. Her research prowess dated back to undergraduate days in the Widener Library at Harvard. Brian and his minions might know the ins and outs of objects, but she could research as well—if not better—than them.

Once parked, her sandals slapped on the brick walkway as she made her way to the interior of the campus. A faint twinge reminded her of the spill that she'd taken, but Miranda decided to just power through it. She had things to do.

The Swem Library, situated on the northern edge of campus, was encircled by a perimeter boulevard. An attractive building dating from the 1960s, it had been constructed with a mid-century modern vibe despite the rest of the colonial leanings of the campus. A sundial sat in the southern entrance courtyard, ringed by an evergreen boxwood circle. A whiff of earthy boxwood stayed with Miranda as she entered.

Once inside the air conditioned cooled and dark lobby, she headed right up the staircase that swept to the second level with clean, functional lines. Taking in the pristine and quiet space, she found the far corner where generously sized carrels were reserved for faculty. She situated herself at one of the light-colored, wood Scandinavian style tables with its smooth, polished finish and accompanying Eames style chair, struck again by the odd modernity of the place. A campus such as William and Mary seemed more suited to be furnished with dark oak refectory tables and heavy Windsor style seating.

Miranda pulled up the library database on her laptop then scrolled through randomly until landing on a few avenues to pursue. If she started with local history, she could work back to the broader context of how the local families in Bisoux tied into the bigger cultural picture of immigration from England, maybe specifically East Anglia as Fiona had posited. From there, she would tap into what folk traditions might have been pervasive in that region of England. Local historical journals were located in the belly of the building's interior. The Gwynn family would most probably make a showing in at least one of them.

She moved quietly through the room to the door that stood slightly hidden in an alcove against one wall. When she opened the entrance into the stacks, a quiver of excitement shot through her. It was always like going on a secret treasure hunt, in a way. Right away, her nostrils filled with older odors, musty and aged from the copious documents, books and journals housed within its walls. Locating the right shelf number, she picked up the heaviest load manageable and took them all back to her carrel.

Within the first half hour, a number of resources were piled up including a family tree that laid out the Gwynn family's journey from England to Bisoux. Two brothers came over together on one of the earliest ships, making large land purchases in the area next to one another but divided by Polly's Creek.

Each brother spawned large families; one, with ten children, the other, with twelve. Notable to Miranda was that the majority born were male children, so lots of Gwynns had dispersed outwards. There were three daughters in each family. Three daughters. Three sisters. That stuck in her head for some reason. A connection with an old superstition about three females in a family? Something nagged at her...was it the three sisters of fate in Greek mythology or was it something else?

Miranda studied the names on the original ship roster of those who made the journey over with the Gwynn brothers. They were roughly from the same area in East Anglia it appeared. She ran a finger down the list of names: Gwynn, Maynard...her finger stopped on an unexpected last name:

Chesney. Her own.

Miranda sat back into the mold of the Eames chair. She had always assumed she was a mutt. She knew in a vague kind of way that her father's side was English. But, as a military brat, her family had moved all over the place and never seemed to be from a single distinct locale.

She plucked her pencil back and forth on the rim of her laptop and thought. By now, she (like the rest of the universe) had seen the heartfelt commercials advertising Ancestry.com, but had never dabbled. In academic circles, it was slightly frowned upon as not in keeping with the elitist tones that predominated. And, frankly, she had been too busy to be pulled into those cheesy ads. But now, she had just cause to splash into all of it, elitist or not. It couldn't be difficult to figure out since every average Joe was doing it. She typed in her keyboard, "Ancestry.com" and it began.

Several hours later, the chime on Miranda's phone indicated a text. She dragged herself out of the metaphorical Ancestry.com rabbit hole to pull her phone out. As she did so, it felt that a thousand eyes turned her way since she had forgotten to silence it. Which ended up being a good thing because the text was from Brian, "Meet me at 5 at Princeton store parking lot."

She glanced at the time to see he had only given her an hour's notice. Miranda then noted that several hours of her life had just been sacrificed to Ancestry.com as she had begun to piece together the tale of her forebearers. In a plot twist, Miranda had East Anglia roots from ancestors who apparently hailed from the exact location where she now was.

Miranda gathered her belongings to head back to Bisoux. As she drove, she thought about her brief forays to that region of England. She remembered feeling a pull for the place, at home with its wide, open coastline and barren landscape. It was a shame she hadn't known about her connection while there. Maybe she could have pinned down the exact towns and villages of her ancestors. Maybe she could have even searched out their houses.

But maybe even crazier was her possible tie-in to those Bisoux families since they all harkened back from the same towns in East Anglia. She would not have guessed that in a million years. The question was: Did it mean anything? Brian might have some ideas about it after they met with Lizzie.

Pulling into the Princeton store parking lot and turning the car off, Miranda realized she had not patronized the crossroads shop since that initial odd encounter with Lizzie. Squaring her shoulders, she took a deep inhale, not knowing what this meeting would bring about or if it would help at all.

Within moments, Brian pulled in right next to her and gave a wave. After they both got out from their cars, he leaned his back against his and said, "Turns out Lizzie has a regular time that she shows up here every day." Then he added, "Fiona found out about it."

"So...is the plan to ambush her then?"

"Basically, yeah."

Miranda looked at her watch absentmindedly and said, "How long 'til she gets here?"

"Ten minutes. Give or take."

Miranda nodded and then said, "Okay so...what do you want to talk about while we wait?"

He cocked his head. "I don't know...you?"

"I'm curious...okay, maybe nosy is a better word," she admitted with a sheepish chuckle. "What's going on with Fiona being from this area?"

"Going on?"

"I'm just trying to get the lay of the land. I was surprised she's from Bisoux and I guess...I guess I'm just trying to figure it all out." What she left unsaid was how curious he had not mentioned any of it when they lunched together. Fiona's role in Brian's personal sphere was the other hanger-on, but it wasn't her business.

"It's simple. I'm her professor. She's a gifted and talented student, on her way to becoming a good archeologist. Her being from Bisoux is just coincidence...pure coincidence."

His eyes drifted off to the right of Miranda and he said, "We got company coming."

Miranda turned, catching a glimpse of the short and stout figure. Lizzie moved in a plodding manner down the dirt shoulder, her face lifted to the autumn sunshine. "Yeah, it's her. Ready?"

"Yep. Why don't I take the lead?"

She nodded, unsettled by a flashback from that first encounter with Lizzie.

They both faced the direction that Lizzie was approaching from. As she shuffled into the dusty parking lot of the store, she looked over and, seeing them, stopped in her tracks.

"Lizzie! Could we talk to you?" Brian asked in a hearty tone. Too hearty.

Indecision crossed her face but she moved forward. Once in front of them, she screwed up her face into a question mark and held a hand over her eyes to block the sun.

"What?" she said.

"I'm working on an archeological dig at Rosewood." He gestured to Miranda and added, "And I think you've met Miranda."

Lizzie bit her lip as she cast a quick glance over in Miranda's direction.

Miranda gave what she hoped was a friendly smile.

"So, some things have been happening at the site. I mean, Rosewood. I think you may know about that."

Lizzie shook her head somewhat violently as she said, "Nope. Nope. Nope."

Miranda caught Brian's eye and he had a look of alarm on his face that she was sure matched hers. She shook her head at him indicating that they should stop.

But he didn't. Instead, he asked Lizzie pointblank, "Did you set a fire at Rosewood the other night?"

Lizzie turned and headed to the store entrance.

"Lizzie!" Brian called after her retreating back. "Are you moving blue bottles around Rosewood?"

But she kept going.

Brian and Miranda looked at each other and Miranda said, "Welp. That went well."

"Fiona said she would talk...." Brian said distractedly.

"How would Fiona know that? And, where is Fiona? If she is that connected, how come she didn't come with you?"

He looked uncomfortable as he stuck his hands in the front of his jeans and said, "She had work to finish up. Look...she just knows the people around her and how they are."

"Well, apparently not, 'cause that didn't resolve anything. We don't know any more than we did when we got here."

"Yeah, I get it."

"My vote is to go to the local sheriff now."

"I don't think it's a good idea. Maybe she'll back off now that she knows we are onto her."

"Wait and see approach, eh?"

"I think so." He hesitated then said, "If you feel unsafe, how about I camp out on the property for a few nights? Just in case."

Miranda blinked rapidly a couple of times trying to gauge whether he was coming onto her or just being nice. Now that the cat wasn't even around, she was feeling vulnerable.

"Um...okay. If you can swing it with your schedule."

"I can. Plus, it's not too cold out yet and I've got all my gear. In fact, I'll be glad for the opportunity to break it out and use it. It's been a while."

She paused, considering if she should offer for him to stay in the house with her. But would he think she was coming onto him? Instead, she said, "How about you have dinner in the house? So, I can at least make it up to you?"

"You don't have to make it up to me. I'm frankly worried about the site. That someone or multiple someones are trying to sabotage the dig. All that we recover from it will be compromised. And your safety too, of course."

"Of course," she smiled wryly. "Well, I have to eat. You have to eat. Dinner at mine."

He nodded and they made plans to meet at the house at seven with dinner ready.

Chapter Eleven

MIRANDA'S SPOTIFY HOOKUP SPILLED jazzy notes into Rosewood's space as she moved about, gathering items together. A simple dinner of a hearty stew sat ready on the stovetop with a salad and bread on the counter.

She dug through boxes and pulled out a checkered table-cloth, placemats and cloth napkins along with a pair of pewter candlesticks. The candlesticks brought back the memory of a day wandering around the historic area of Williamsburg, be-mused and entranced by all of it. Ending up in a kitschy gift shop, she had impulsively bought the overpriced set as a sou-venir of sorts to remember her time there which she assumed was just a temporary tour, a one-year stint. Now setting two tapered bayberry candles into the hollows, it occurred to her that the same type of candlesticks had probably been used years earlier at Rosewood.

Pushing all the boxes and other detritus to the side of the living room, Miranda made space for the table and two chairs. She stepped back and felt some giddiness at the sight, her first real grown-up dinner at Rosewood. Maybe she was channeling her East Anglian ancestors with this splash of hospitality. She stood back again, and eyed up the scene, wondering if it looked intimate. Maybe too intimate. She had not intended for it to be the case. Or had she?

Back at the stove stirring the stew, her thoughts again turned to the East Anglian relations, picturing communal feasts and gatherings. She hoped in time that Rosewood would give off that welcoming vibe to anyone who entered. Or maybe it already did. Her imagination began to run away from her until she was brought back to the present with a knock at the door.

Brian stood at the threshold bearing a bottle of wine in one hand and flowers in the other. Definitely intimate, she thought as he handed them to her. "Oh," she said out loud, "You didn't have to do that."

Efforts made to tame his still damp hair over to one side worked except for an errant curl that had escaped to one cheek. A cheek, she noted, that had experienced a recent close shave. His jeans looked off-the-shelf new and his shirt was a bigger surprise. A golf-style, office-casual shirt also on the newish side in an earth tone shade which matched the golden in his eyes.

As those eyes studied her now, she moved her gaze down to the top of the bouquet of zinnias at the realization he had taken more pains than his usual slapped-together appearance. An awkwardness seeped into the space between them. She looked up from the flowers and said, "Come on in."

Miranda led him through to the impromptu dining space as a shower fresh scent, maybe a pine soap, wafted her way. The soft cast of candlelight illuminated the table setting. Brian cleared his throat then said, "Well...this is nice."

"Thanks. I figured I might as well break out some of my boxes. Have a seat."

She looked through a kitchen drawer, rustling through for a corkscrew. Once located, she handed it over for him to fiddle with the wine, then went back for wine glasses.

"Eek. I can't find my wine glasses, dangit. We'll have to go with jam glasses."

"That's my preference anyway," he said with a grin.

Miranda served up the stew and placed two steaming bowls on the table where Brian had already filled the glasses with wine. After collecting the warmed baguette and the salad, she finally sat down. Letting out a breath, she said, "Okay. Ready, I think."

She raised her jam glass. "Bon appétit."

Brian smiled and clinked his glass to hers. She noticed for the first time a slight dimple on one side of his smile.

As he dipped a spoon in the stew, he said, "This is a treat. I can't even remember the last homemade anything I've had. Been a while."

"Really? I would think those eager co-eds would keep you in baked goods at least."

He made a face. "Maybe a spirulina smoothie or two. But no. No homecooked meals."

As they ate, conversation flowed easily with the awkwardness from earlier lifted and replaced by their usual, comfortable rapport. Eventually, it led back to the blue bottle and Miranda said, "Oh...I totally forgot. I did some research today at the Swem."

"Swem."

"What?"

"Just Swem. Not *the* Swem."

"Seriously?"

"I don't want you to be made fun of by those co-eds." He winked at her.

"Anyway, this is really crazy but..." she went on to explain about her explorations into Ancestry.com and the connections to Bisoux.

"Whoa...you never knew this?"

"No, never. My family was never interested in their roots or whatever you want to call it."

Brian gazed off into the room and, after a few moments of thought, said, "So...could there be some kind of connection between you and Miss Janie and Lizzie?"

"What? No, of course not. I would know that." She hesitated and then added, "Don't you think?"

"Okay. I just mean, blue bottles are placed as some sort of ancestral concern so...."

"This is getting too weird for me. How would anyone know I could be even distantly related?"

He shrugged. "No idea. Just spit-balling here. But it's a pretty unusual coincidence."

She sat back with her wine. "This whole thing...me sitting here right now in this room. This old colonial room. It happened almost without me being in charge of it. Like out of my hands. I didn't plan on staying on at the college. I've never owned a house. Never even knew I wanted to own a house."

They both fell silent. Then Miranda spoke up. "It was kind of like…" She stopped herself from saying it was like falling hard for somebody.

"What?" he prodded her.

The wine loosened her tongue and the next words that spilled out surprised not only him, but also her. "It was like being reminded I should be open to any possibility…"

"That's a good idea," he said.

"Any possibility…" Miranda repeated the line and her voice drifted off as they stared at each other. She reached over and covered his hand with hers.

"What?" he said, looking down at their hands.

"I might be looking at a possibility."

"Oh."

With that, she guided him up with her hand and said, "May I have this dance?"

"There's no music."

"Hang on…"

Miranda fiddled with her Spotify links and found a swing dance playlist. She turned to him and waited, wanting him to make the first move in the dance. Brian did not disappoint as he pulled her into his strong chest and began to lead. Despite the small space in which to navigate, he easily kept up with all the swing moves that the music called for.

"Hey, you're not too shabby," she said over the music. In response, he maneuvered her into a dip and she let out a peal of laughter.

The song ended and they wound down as the next tune came on. A slow ballad. "We can stop…" she said.

"Shhh." He collected her closer to his body and they began to sway slowly. Miranda felt the heat building in the space between them.

As the song began to end, he pulled her close, looking into her eyes. When the kiss came, it felt electric from its start to its long, drawn-out end. "That was a long time coming," he said, as they broke apart.

"It was," she agreed.

Miranda leaned forward, nestling herself between his arms angling for more. After some more prolonged close contact, he paused to ask, "Is there a better venue for this?"

She pointed to the ceiling above. Taking his hand, she led him up the stairs until they finally landed on the bed in a tangle of limbs.

Later, her head on his burly chest, hairier than she could have ever imagined, he said, "I've still got to set up my tent..."

She swatted him and said, "No. You don't."

The next morning as Miranda came out of sleep, she opened one eye and saw she had the bed to herself. She felt a pang of regret. Had he left already? But hearing a low whistling coming from the kitchen, she smiled.

She sat up and ran a hand through her tousled hair. It dawned on her that it was Monday and she needed to head into school. Miranda flung herself into a hot shower, assuming that Brian could take care of himself downstairs. Besides, she needed a little more time to herself to process whatever it was that was happening between the two of them.

Miranda took extra care after getting out of the shower, even taking her mascara wand out. She stared at her image, opening her eyes big in front of her vanity mirror. They shined back at her with the memory of the previous evening's activities. She even blushed a little at her own reflection.

Once downstairs, she caught a glimpse of Brian sitting at the table with a mug of coffee in hand and a notebook in front of him. He looked up at her approach and gave her an almost shy smile. Smiling back, they both spoke at the same time.

"How did you sleep..." he said.

"Good morning..." she said.

They both laughed and Brian said, "Let's start over. I'll go first...good morning and how did you sleep?"

"Well, thank you," and then she pointed at his coffee and asked, "Is there more of that?"

"Of course. Also, some scrambled eggs and French toast."

She was taken aback. "Wow...I didn't expect a hot cooked breakfast the morning after..."

Her sentence was interrupted by a knock at the door and she whipped her head towards it. "Who could that be?"

Brian stood up and stretched and she soaked up his image, feeling stirrings from the night before.

"It's a dig day, remember?" he said.

"Oh, yes. Monday. I knew it was Monday but ..." She became flustered.

"Do you want me to answer the door?"

"Sure."

As he walked by, he leaned in and kissed her quickly on her neck and she felt a frisson of pleasure. So, it had happened, she reminded herself.

He opened the door and she looked over to see Fiona standing there with a look of utter confusion on her face. "Oh... Brian. What are..."

"Got an early start. You didn't see my truck parked out there?"

"No, I didn't. I was just going to tell Miranda that I'm the first here. But, obviously, you're here."

"Hi, Fiona," Miranda chimed in, giving a wave. Then she said, "I'll get out of your way, guys."

"Not joining us today?" Fiona asked, eyebrows slightly lifted.

She was suspicious, Miranda thought. "No. Department meetings today. I'll be leaving shortly."

None of them said anything and a stilted air filled the room. Brian broke into it by saying, "Thanks for the coffee, Miranda. We'll check in later."

"Yep."

They both left and the door closed behind them. Miranda stood still—and alone. It unsettled her that Brian had immediately covered up spending the night. Did he think it would embarrass Miranda? Or did he not want to upset Fiona?

She plopped down in the seat at the table that he had vacated and began to eat the plate he prepped. For her. From the window, she could see that the others were trickling into the yard and setting up for the day. She could also see that Brian and Fiona had their heads close together in what appeared to be a serious discussion. She didn't know what to think about that, if anything.

Chapter Twelve

BARELY ABLE TO KEEP her mind in the department meeting, Miranda tuned in when her name cropped up. Abernathy had officially announced that Miranda accepted the slot of adjunct professor in Philosophy at the College of Arts and Humanities at William and Mary which was followed by a round of polite applause.

In her afternoon class, when students peppered her with questions, she felt distracted. Whether or not students got proper answers to their questions, she didn't know. Later, in her office, Miranda stared at the stack of midterm papers that needed grading without picking any up. She found herself looking down at her phone a lot, thinking that Brian might text her. She thought about texting him but held back. Finally, she threw her phone to the side, disgusted with herself for acting like a love-struck teenager.

Heading back to Rosewood, she stopped by a local market on the outskirts of Williamsburg to search for dinner fixings. As she thought about the next meal to fix Brian, she was also wondering if they would end up in the same place…her bed. Which she wanted to be the case, if she was entirely honest with herself. She finally decided on a roast chicken with braised root vegetables, and also grabbed another baguette for good measure.

Back at Rosewood, all was quiet. Everyone at the dig had cleared out including, it seemed, Brian. Again, she thought about texting but stopped herself.

After changing out of her skirt and pressed linen shirt, she began the meal preparation and became lost in the meditative state that cooking always held for her. She set aside all anticipatory pangs at seeing Brian and, soon, the delicious aroma of roasted chicken wafted through the house.

When done, the clock showed it was closing in on seven, the time they had set for the previous evening. But there was no sign of Brian or any word from him yet. Leaving everything to warm in the oven, Miranda poured herself a glass of red wine and sat down in the same spot by the window where she had watched Brian and Fiona that morning. Though it was dusk, something flashing in the final light of the day caught her eye on the potting shed steps.

She stood, peering out the window's aged glass more closely. It looked like...she drew back as if stung. It looked like another blue bottle. She sank back into her chair and took a huge gulp of wine, feeling icy fingers of fear crawl up her back.

Miranda bounced back up, forgetting about her ankle, still on the mend. "Ouch!" she said aloud. She started to pace the length of the room, though in more of a hobble than a pace. The thought of going out into the now darkened night to fetch it made her go numb inside. Which was ridiculous, she told herself, since it was just another childish prank of Lizzie's, in all probability. But what if Lizzie was out there, watching her?

Glancing at the clock, it was edging towards eight. Brian was now missing in action on top of everything else. Pacing more, she went around in her head about reaching out to him via text or phone. She had been burned too many times by too many guys in the past to do that. It might have been a one-night stand after all, and, if that was the case...

Suddenly, she heard the rumble of a truck engine. Headlights coming down Rosewood's driveway beamed off the old glass in the windows. Taking a deep breath, she opened the door just as he was in mid knock, standing on the top step. They looked at each other in silence for a moment. Then he cleared his throat and said, "Can I come in?"

She stepped aside to let him in, waiting to hear what he had to say.

"I got caught up in an issue after the dig...I would have called but..."

She stopped him. "There's another blue bottle on the potting shed steps."

"What?"

"There's a blue bottle..."

"I heard you...I'm just...oh man. I really thought all this would stop after we confronted her."

Miranda tried not to sound incredulous when she spoke. "Are we assuming that Lizzie, or *someone*, thinks that I need protection? Is that the idea?"

Brian shook his head, his face inscrutable. "Did you bring it in?"

"No. It's still out there. I was waiting for you. I didn't know if you were going to show."

"Going to show? You think that of me?"

"Well...I mean...you don't owe me anything. You could have changed your mind about coming out here. I don't know...."

He walked closer to her but didn't reach out. Just stood with his arms by his side. "Last night wasn't just any night to me. You know?"

"Really?"

"Really."

"Okay then...well, I have dinner..." He grabbed her quickly and his kiss was fierce, cutting off whatever she was going to say next. When they broke apart, she felt weak at the knees.

"Okay?" he said.

"Yeah. Okay."

"Did you mention something about dinner? Because I'm starving. And something smells good," he said, looking into her eyes as though he meant something else altogether.

"Yeah...um...dinner. It's warming in the oven still."

Dinner ended up in the same place: first, a tangling of limbs on the barren floor and then, back to her bedroom. Afterwards, he reached over and intertwined his fingers through hers.

"So...the blue bottle."

"Let's just leave it for now..." She reached over to him.

In the morning, Miranda rolled over, taking in the sight of Brian next to her. He had a peaceful expression on his face in repose. His thick ginger hair was standing on end and his bare chest was out of the blankets fully exposed. As though he sensed being watched, his eyes blinked open blearily once or twice and then opened for good, moving over her way. With a lazy smile, he grabbed her close to him. They didn't speak as they acted on the desires that the morning brought.

Afterwards, Miranda shifted onto her back and sighed contentedly.

"I hope that's a sigh of satisfaction and not something else," Brian said.

"Definitely satisfaction..."

"But..."

"There's a blue bottle out there."

"Oh...yeah."

"I think I should call the sheriff's office to come over and examine things here."

He was silent for a bit and then said, "Yeah...it's probably time."

After taking a shower together with more delay tactics on Brian's part, they eventually found themselves downstairs, black coffees in hand.

"Here goes," Miranda said, dialing the number for the local sheriff's office on her cell. After she detailed to the person on the line what was happening, she listened on her end to the response and finished the call with a "thanks".

"What did they say?" Brian asked.

"They will send someone within the hour."

He nodded. "So, we'll enjoy our coffee until then." He reached over and put one hand on her knee.

She felt reassurance from his touch.

When Miranda heard the squad car pull in, she was glad to

have Brian with her. They both stood up at the same time and headed out to the yard. The officer who stepped out of the car immediately hiked up his pants to cover the protruding belly that hung at the beltline. It was not any use though and the pants sagged back down. He gave a huge sniff and made a show of staring around the property.

When he finally turned to face them, Miranda was struck immediately by his likeness to the character Otis on the Andy Griffith Show, a childhood favorite of hers. She had prided herself her whole life long to never get hung up on stereotypes but sometimes they smacked her in the face.

"'Morning, folks. What seems to be the problem out here?'"

After Miranda greeted him and took in his nametag—Sheriff Sanford—she proceeded to give him a condensed version of events and finished with "....so, we think Lizzie Gooding may be involved with this."

"Aww, Lizzie. She wouldn't hurt a fly. I doubt she's your prankster."

Brian weighed in and said, "Well, I don't think we can rule out the possibility...."

"Who are you, again? You two married or what's the connection here?"

Brian spoke up first to answer him. "No, no...this is Miranda's place. I'm here conducting the dig." Miranda could feel an almost imperceptible air of tension between the two men, finding it curious.

The officer cleared his throat and said, only looking at Miranda, "Well, I'll walk the perimeter of the property. But honestly, I think this thing is just some kids having fun out here. Wouldn't worry yourself over it. They'll get bored of it soon enough."

Brian and Miranda glanced at each other and then Miranda said, "Um...well, Lizzie..."

"Look...just drop this nonsense about Lizzie Gooding, you hear? Just leave her out of it." His voice had shifted from the easy-going Bisoux accent Miranda had come to know to almost a snappish tone.

Brian said firmly, "All right, but we're on record here...in case anything else happens."

"Consider yourself on record then. Like I said, I'll walk around some and then get out of your hair."

"Let us at least show you what the bottles look like," Miranda headed over to the potting shed and the two men followed behind her. The blue bottle sat untouched just as she had seen it the previous night.

The sheriff pulled on a plastic glove and then lifted it up to the light. Gazing at it, he said, "Looks like it's got something in it."

"Yes, they all have...stuff...in them," Miranda said.

"Huh...how about that?"

"Do you want to take it? Like, as evidence?"

"Nah... you can just toss it away." He plucked his gloves off with a snap. "Alrighty now, folks...you have a good day, you hear?"

As they watched him get into his vehicle and drive away, Miranda stood, bristling with anger, with hands on hips. "Can you believe that guy?"

Brian placed his hands on her shoulders and said, "I know, I know...but calm down. We'll have to figure this out without their help," he promised. "And don't worry. We will."

Wrapping her in a tight hug, he continued. "First things first. I'm taking this bottle to the lab today and verifying its age. Just in case. Then we can sort out if there is a copycat thing going on or if someone is digging up artifacts." He turned her towards him by the shoulders and looked down at her. "Okay?"

She nodded, trusting what she saw in his golden eyes.

Chapter Thirteen

AS MIRANDA PLOWED THROUGH the business of the day that included classes, Google sessions and face-to-face student meetings, she eagerly awaited getting back to the Swem (or just Swem, she inwardly corrected herself) to research more deeply into the local Bisoux families, including possibly her own.

At the end of the day, she set up "shop," once again finding an available spot with an accompanying Eames chair. Like before, she let herself fall into the process, hopping between her family on Ancestry.com and Bisoux families in the online local history collection. A few times, she got up from the comfort of the Eames chair to wander the stacks for a hardcover book.

While not making any new connections with her family, she stumbled upon a document from the 1800s that showed land parcels with ownership—a family surname attached to each. Using Polly's Creek as her reference point, Miss Janie's family name, Gwynn, was situated right where she would guess it to be. Neighboring parcels included Lizzie's family, the Goodings, the Maynards and then, strangely, Fiona's family name, Lansbury.

She sat back and stared off into space. Did Fiona grow up practically next door to Rosewood? Why would she not have mentioned this? In passing, at least? But then, she didn't know any particulars about Fiona's life really. They had never had so much as a single personal conversation. If Brian knew, why didn't he mention it? If he knew...

Tapping her pencil back and forth, she was snapped out

of her reverie by a ding on her phone. Suddenly aware she had forgotten to mute it again, she scrambled to pull it out of her overstuffed bag. She kept her eyes averted from the dirty looks and peered down to see a text from Brian, "Can't make it tonight. Something's come up. Will you be okay?"

She felt a stab of disappointment and pondered how to answer back. Was she okay to stay at Rosewood by herself anymore? She suddenly realized if the answer was 'no', she had an enormous problem on her hands: buying a house that she could no longer live in by herself.

She texted back, "Bummer. I'll be fine", closing it with a kiss emoji. After sending, she cringed, the kiss emoji maybe being too much. She waited for the dots to pop up if he was going to reply, but nothing happened. Setting the phone aside, she resolved that she would definitely be fine. There was no other option, after all.

Back into her research, she pieced together where Fiona's possible ancestral house would be and vaguely recalled seeing yet another overgrown driveway about a half mile away from hers in the direction of the bay. She knew what she was going to do when she headed back to Rosewood. It was about time to meet the neighbors—in a normal, civilized fashion. Given Fiona's poise and polish, if any of her people still lived there, it stood to reason they would somewhat be the same.

While difficult to tear herself away, Miranda stopped her research endeavors and hastily collected her belongings. There was still enough daylight to pay a visit to a neighbor if she headed out immediately.

Once back in Bisoux, she drove past Rosewood's driveway and slowed down to locate the other driveway she'd seen. Miranda shook off second thoughts as the car made its way down a drive that looked almost identical to Lizzie's and the Maynard's—overgrown with a stand of loblolly pines on one side.

Her tires crunched along the scattering of oyster shells that lined the way until it finally opened up to a view of a house. She gasped aloud at the sight, an almost mirror image of Rosewood.

But this "twin" had a general air of neglect hanging about, showing a lack of maintenance with missing shutters and slate roof shingles. That familiar looking old Ford truck sat off to one side of the house. A wisp of smoke emerged from one chimney. Before she reached the steps to the front door, it opened and she immediately recognized the woman who stood there. It was the cat lady. Same black polyester pants and same slapdash hairdo piled on top of her head. She wished she had asked the woman her name back at that first meeting.

The woman gave her a curious stare and walked down to where Miranda stood. "Can I help you with sumthing?"

"We met a while back about your cat. You know, we never exchanged names that first time and I apologize for that. I'm Miranda."

The woman slapped her forehead and said, "Oh my goodness! 'Course I remember. No apologies needed. I'm Caroline. But anyone in these parts calls me Caro. Did you come by to check on my kitty?"

"No, but, um...how is she though?"

"Living the life of Riley, don't you worry. She's spoiled rotten."

There was a pause and Miranda plunged in. "I'm actually here about some research I'm doing on my house." Her gaze swept over the house in front of her, again marveling at the likeness, and she added, "Which I didn't realize had a look-alike."

"Yes, indeed. They were sister houses, I've always heard."

"Sister houses? Huh...anyway, I saw on an older map that this used to be owned by the Lansbury family. Did you know them?"

"Know them? Well, of course, I know them. I am a Lansbury."

"Oh...so, it stayed in the family all these years?"

"Sure did. We wouldn't have it any other way."

"That's really interesting. We have a student at the dig going on at my house with that last name. Fiona. Fiona Lansbury. Do you know her?"

The other woman now looked at Miranda with almost a pitying expression at Miranda's ignorance. "Fiona is my niece.

This is her house. I raised her here."

"I had no idea. She never mentioned," said Miranda sheepishly.

Caro cast her eyes away from Miranda and said, "Well... she's trying to shake off her roots. Has some high falutin' notions that I think that professor of hers, the one she's in love with, set her on to."

"Professor?"

"Yes. Archeology guy. Well, you probably know him, don't you?"

Looking down at the ground to collect herself, Miranda said, "Yeah...I do."

"Listen to me going on about all this personal business."

"No, not at all. I'm just amazed that there is a house that looks exactly like mine a stone's throw away." Miranda looked back up and again studied the exterior of the house.

"That's on account of the fact that the Gwynns and the Lansburys were related. The story goes that two brothers married two sisters. Both sisters wanted the same house. That's always how I heard it told."

"So...is your brother Fiona's dad?"

"Was. He got stone drunk one night and wrapped his Pontiac Trans Am around a tree over near Gloucester. Fiona's momma was in the front seat. Impact killed them both."

The bluntness of Caro's delivery of this family tragedy threw Miranda for a second and then she said, "Oh. I had no idea, I'm so sorry."

Caro nodded. "Like I said, Fiona don't like to talk much about her past. I moved in here right after. She was just little. About four and some change. Now I'm here on my own."

"Wait...does this mean you and Fiona are related to Miss Janie?" Miranda asked.

"'Course it does. We miss her terribly. Fiona and me. And Lizzie too, of course."

"Is Lizzie a relation too?"

"No. But Lizzie was like a daughter to Miss Janie, so...we all look out for each other round here, I guess you could say."

Miranda tried to wrap her head around all the connections as Caro continued to wax on about the good times. Her gaze drifted over to an old hitching post that stood off to one side. Shadows from the lowering sun obscured her view but she could just about make out something carved into it. The light was dimming but it sure did look like yet another example of the strange cat motif. She started to discreetly edge over for a closer view with Caro still talking a mile a minute. Once nearer, she could see it was indeed the same as the others.

When close enough, Miranda placed a hand over the grooved design. Caro paused to catch her breath and Miranda took the opportunity to cut in. "Can I ask you what this symbol means? I keep seeing it around the neighborhood."

Caro inhaled sharply and her demeanor changed in a swift instant with her expression becoming furtive. "Oh, it's just a thing people round here have always done."

"But why a cat?"

"Well, cats have some tremendous qualities." And then she was on a thread about their attributes until Miranda's eyes started to glaze over. She remembered the woman referencing her cat as a familiar when they had first meant. Strangely, Caro did not bring that up and, instead, seemed to hedge around the topic of the symbol's meaning.

When Miranda could interject politely into the flow of Caro's discourse, she said, "I've got to get going, but so nice to officially meet you."

The other woman frowned at being cut off but said, "Yes, indeed. Don't be a stranger now."

Miranda was aware of Caro watching her the entire time as she walked to the car and drove away. The woman was odd, but that was surely just a function of her living on her own. Shaking off a sense of unease, her car bumped down the rutted drive and away from Rosewood's "twin."

Later, after finishing a dinner for one, she gazed over at the chair that Brian had sat in and felt a gulf open up. Did he know that Fiona was in love with him? Had he told her the truth about him and Fiona? The knife edge of doubt began to widen.

To distract herself, she opened her laptop and began to search out the mystery of the cat symbol and what it really meant. She remembered a photo she snapped on her cell and uploaded it to do an image search. Within a key stroke moment like presto-magic, the exact image popped up and left her marveling over modern day technologies. She honed in deeper, eventually clicking open a site about Depression era homeless people or, as they were derogatorily referred to back then, "hobos."

A chart depicting all the signs that hobos had used showed the cat symbol as one of them. The meaning was clear. The symbol indicated a "kind-hearted woman" so that a person knew they would be able to ask for a handout, maybe a place in the barn or a shed.

Miranda thought about it. Why didn't Caro just tell her this? It was a credit to her and the other women, wasn't it? Something just didn't add up.

Chapter Fourteen

THE NEXT MORNING AT Rosewood had Miranda feeling antsy, uncomfortable even, with no classes at the college to distract her until late afternoon. At loose ends and without thinking of any particular destination, she threw her stuff in the car and headed out by eight.

Finding herself in the commercial area of Lewiston on the main route into Williamsburg, she drove back and forth a couple of times, eventually spying a local breakfast spot she had yet to try. Excitement stirred at the prospect of a full plate, laden with all the fat and cholesterol she could manage with strong black coffee as accompaniment. She would treat herself after the goings-on at Rosewood.

Called "Joe's," the restaurant sat squarely in the middle of a 1950s, one story tall, brick commercial strip, its width and depth limited to that space. Opening the door, Miranda braced herself for the stares she knew were coming. It was a part of the deal with living in a rural area and she was trying to become accustomed, if not immune, to it.

Predictably, all heads swiveled for a moment or two at the sight of her before going back to their conversations and food. A bar counter on the left side with some stools was filled and the small number of tables on the right side were half taken. A waitress holding a coffee pot passed by her saying, "Pick any table you like, hon."

Miranda found a spot by the window, situating herself. The man seated directly across held a newspaper close up to his face. There was something familiar about his posture and, as he folded his paper up, she knew why. It was Beau Jenkins.

As recognition came over his face, he said out loud, "Well, look who it is!" He gestured towards his table and added, "Come on over here and join me."

Miranda began to demur but then thought better of it. Why not sit with Beau while she was having breakfast? Maybe she could pick his brain some more about all the strange events occurring at Rosewood.

She walked over and pulled out a chair. Glancing over at his half-eaten plate of food with yellow streaks of egg yolk left behind, she said, "You sure I'm not interrupting you?"

"Not at'll, not at'll. Sit on down." He waved to the waitress and said, "Sissy, can you bring Miranda here some of your best hot coffee.... you do want coffee?'

"Absolutely."

After Sissy served up some piping hot coffee and jotted down her order, Miranda studied the man in front of her. Dapper as ever with his face cleanly shaved and his hair Brillo-creamed over to one side, his bright, light-colored eyes looked back at her.

"You know, Beau...I have to apologize. I wasn't paying attention when you were telling me local tales. But I would like to hear more now."

His face wrinkled into a beaming smile. "Ask me anything."

"Seems funny I never asked before, but are you from here, Beau? Bisoux, I mean?"

"Nah. I'm still thought of as a 'come-here.' But that's alright. I wouldn't want to be anywhere else. Love it here. So much history."

As he continued to romanticize Bisoux's attributes, Miranda took the opportunity to take in all of random bits of Beau. His voice shook a little when he spoke but, otherwise, he bore his age well. She assumed he was on the downslide towards eighty, but she could be off. Maybe he was already there.

He wrapped up his side of the conversation by saying again, "There's just so much history here."

Miranda, curious, asked, "Where are you from?"

"The mean streets of Baltimore. A stone's throw from that fancified harbor they did up. Wasn't like that when I was coming up, though. Not at all." His eyes got a faraway look as though taking him back to another time and place.

Miranda thought about Beau being a transplant from Baltimore. Like herself, he was drawn to this place from someplace completely different.

Her thoughts were curtailed as Sissy deftly slapped a plate in front of her. Miranda felt ravenous all of a sudden as she gazed down at the Lewiston Blue Plate special; two eggs over easy on top of a Belgian waffle with crisped up bacon and hash browns on the side.

As she began to tuck in, Beau picked up the flow of conversation saying, "I'm sure you know by now how Bisoux got started up, right?"

Miranda felt chagrin as she admitted that she did not and added, "I've only been exploring the family histories so far.... Like we talked about on the phone that day, actually."

"Well, I can give you my favorite nickel version. Although you'll hear about as many variations as there are people in Bisoux no doubt."

Beau went on to explain that the original settlers of the area had a mix of currency that included French sous. They paid for goods and services largely with foreign currency from the earliest days in the late 1700s, long into the 1800s, and almost to the end of the Civil War. Supposedly. Beau finished the story by saying, "Bisoux was a twisting around use of "sou," or so the story goes."

"Huh. Interesting. It seems strange if so many of them were from East Anglia they would end up with a French sounding place name. Also, doesn't 'bisou' mean 'kiss' in French?"

Beau shrugged. "Like I said, there are other versions. But, on another note, if you haven't seen it yet, the place is known for its daffodils come springtime. You're in for a real treat."

Miranda smiled and said, "Daffodils. The trumpeters of spring."

"That's right."

Sissy parked herself by their table leaning against it with one hip, coffeepot in hand. "Top off, folks?"

They both nodded and waited while she filled them up. There was a pause as they took satisfying pulls from their refreshed hot mugs. Miranda realized she was enjoying herself, bouncing ideas off Beau. Why had she been so impatient when he had been her Realtor? She shook her head. Sometimes she confounded herself.

"What else we got?" Beau asked.

"Let's see...what else. Oh yes. The cat symbol."

Beau looked at her blankly. "Hang on." Miranda pulled out her cell and sorted through until she found the symbol of the photo. "Here it is."

Beau pulled up the glasses around his neck and then studied it. "How 'bout that? I guess I never noticed it before. 'Course I haven't been to every single property yet. Working on it, though."

"Well, I did pull off a possible explanation from the internet."

After telling him her theory on hobo signals and kind-hearted women, she finished with, "It's strange to me that Caro wouldn't fill me in on that. I mean, it's benign enough but it seemed I really offended her when I brought it up."

Beau took a big breath in. "You know, Miranda, folks around these parts get prickly about the oddest things, I've figured out along the way. But it sounds like a nice sentiment and mystery solved, eh?"

All of a sudden, he snapped a finger. "Oh, I almost forgot. After our last talk, something occurred to me. I showed that archeology fellow Rosewood when it first came up for sale. I guess that's how he got the whole idea to dig there. I should've given you a heads up about him." As an afterthought, he said, "He had his girlfriend with him, a local gal. Think her name was Felicia."

Miranda's jaw dropped. "What?"

His expression was perturbed as he said, "Yep. If you ask me, she's way too young for him but not my place to judge.

Anyways, this has been a treat, but I need to get going. 'Sure you got places to be too." Beau beckoned for Sissy.

Miranda gave a half nod, lost in thought about what Beau revealed.

After they paid up and walked out to the parking lot, she watched his car pull away. She heard the text indicator on her phone. She didn't pull it out. She didn't want to see it. Whether it was Brian bailing on her again or saying he wanted to meet, Miranda wasn't quite ready to face what either might mean. She decided to think about it later.

Chapter Fifteen

AS MIRANDA STOOD AT her lectern, the faces of the twenty or so students blurred in front of her. She tried to finish her train of thought and said, "So if you think about what Kant said about the formal logic of ....um..."

Her mind went totally blank and she scrambled around in her brain for the words. A front row student cleared his throat and spoke up. "That it was short but certain?"

"Thank you." Pointing at the student, she added, "Yes, what he said."

The class chuckled a bit here and there, but Miranda was inwardly mortified by her gaffe. She wrapped up the rest of the lecture, forcing herself to stay on point. This could not go on. She had to pull herself out of whatever was going on with Rosewood, Brian, Fiona...all of it.

As she jammed her papers and folders into her attaché case, the student from the front row came over to stand in front of her.

"Oh, Scott. Hi. What's up?"

He pushed vintage horn rim glasses up from his nose and said, "I just...I just wanted to ask if you're okay."

Miranda was struck dumb and felt tears suddenly spring to her eyes. A simple kindness bringing her to tears. It was too much.

She looked down at her papers and brief. "Oh...thanks for asking. I've been doing a lot of work on my new place. I guess the lack of sleep is catching up with me."

He nodded and hesitated. Then he said, "If you ever need

any help, I'm pretty handy with tools. I grew up on a farm."

She looked straight at him considering his words. "You know, that might not be a bad idea. I'll let you know when I figure out my master list, how about that?"

He broke out with a shy smile. "Okay."

She watched him exit out of the class before reaching down for her phone. Taking an inhale, she looked at a recent text which, as she dreaded, was Brian canceling out again. It had become pretty obvious now where she stood on his dance card. And maybe how he had used her to get into Rosewood.

Out in the hall, her mind began to swirl again with too many thoughts. Her feet began to walk in a northerly direction of their own accord behind the John Lathrop building as she formulated the choice words she wanted to say to Brian. She halfway didn't realize what she was doing until she stood right in front of the white frame building on Richmond Road. The archeology lab. Squaring her shoulders, she decided to ask Brian what the hell was going on.

She opened the door and walked into a silent building. Most, if not all, had left for the day. Her low heels made a clipping sound on the polyurethane-treated hardwood floor that reverberated off the walls. An old boyfriend had called them her "school marm" heels but her lower back would not tolerate anything higher than an inch or two.

Once at the double doors of the lab, she paused. Her intuition nudged her to peer in through the block of glass on the upper tier, instead of busting through right away. She gulped in a breath at the sight of Brian and Fiona standing in a close embrace in the corner of the room. She didn't need to see much more than that so she turned around and fled from the place.

On the way back to Rosewood, a pit-stop at the local Dairy Queen offered some comfort in the form of a big ice cream sundae. In the parking lot, she polished it off quickly. Feeling slightly nauseous, she stared off into the distance at the fading sun. When it had fully set, she swung the car in gear and headed down the road towards Bisoux, her heart heavy.

Sometimes, the drive at night into her new neighborhood

felt more dramatic than other times. On this night, the tree branches, now barren of leaves, made a stark contrast of shadows against the car's front high beams. One of her colleagues had referred to the area as a "sundown town." Not really understanding the meaning, he had to explain to her that the place had a reputation. Outsiders had no business driving around after sundown. She had psshawed it away with all those similar types of sentiments in the early days of her love affair with Rosewood.

Now, as she drove through the pitch-dark, she realized too late she should have been a better listener and not discounted all who had offered advice. She thought they had been quick to judge something they didn't know about...but maybe it had been her not judging enough.

In the quiet of the car, her mind chatter started up again about Brian. At her ripened age of thirty-plus, she should have been smarter about him. It was humiliating how naïve she had been...but she had to just let it go.

Almost too late, Miranda braked as the headlights beamed on the back of a figure walking dead center in the middle of the road. After the Toyota came to a screeching halt, she gasped for breath, heart pounding. As if in slow motion, the figure turned to look back. Lizzie Gooding.

Without thinking about it, Miranda flew out of her car and began yelling, "What do you think you are doing? Are you trying to get yourself killed?"

The woman just stared at Miranda, mouth hanging ajar.

Miranda went silent and the two women eyed each other.

"Get in. I'm driving you home," Miranda said through gritted teeth.

When Lizzie got in the car, a sickly, sweet odor quickly permeated the space. It reminded Miranda of a cheap perfume called Jean Nate, that dated back to her childhood years.

As she began to drive, Miranda said, "Lizzie...why are you walking in the dark?"

The other woman was silent. Miranda sighed and a discomforting silence took over. Then Miranda heard a slight humming. It sounded like a bird trilling at first but changed over to a chirping noise.

"What's that song you are humming?"

Lizzie stopped the strange noises. After some moments, she spoke up. "Fiona's got her claws in your man."

"What? No... I mean, he's not my man."

The trilling and chirping had started up again. Miranda spoke up a bit to be heard over it. "Do you see Fiona much?"

"Only on gathering nights."

Miranda had no idea what that could be but played along, asking, "Oh. When are those nights?"

"Full moons, mostly."

Stunned by the turn of the conversation, Miranda kept her tone neutral. "Huh. Where do you meet?"

"Places."

"Where's the next one?"

"Don't know. Caro hasn't told me yet."

"What do you do at the gatherings?" Instead of answering, Lizzie took up with more unusual humming just as Miranda spotted the Gooding mailbox.

As she turned into the drive to go down, Lizzie spoke. "Stop here," she said.

"I can drive you down..."

"No...stop here."

"Okay...okay."

Lizzie got out of the car without saying anything or looking back. Miranda shook her head and backed out.

In a few minutes, she pulled into her own drive and, too late, recalled she had not left a light on. Of course, she had thought Brian might be with her when she returned. She let out a mirthless laugh at that thought.

Out of the car, Miranda felt the need to hurry inside and get away from the night. Shapes in the yard, innocent in daylight, turned into something else altogether at nightfall, shadowed and menacing. Almost at the door, she paused at the sight of her house, eclipsed in total darkness. But better to be indoors than to stay outside in the unsettling evening. The sound of the lock when she turned the key seemed comically magnified in the stillness.

Inside, she turned on the lights, going from room to room. As she began to put away her things, her eye caught something on the dining table. She let out a piercing shriek at the sight, her pulse immediately racing. Sitting dead center on the table was another blue bottle, almost as if spotlighted by the switch Miranda had just carelessly flicked on.

Someone had been inside the house. She moved away from the bottle as far as she could get and cowered on the other side of the room, frozen in place and trying to get her mind to work out what to do next. Leave? Hide? Call the joke of the sheriff again? She wasn't safe at Rosewood anymore—if she ever had been.

There was no knight in shining armor to come in for the rescue now. It was on her.

Steeling herself, Miranda moved back to the table and picked it up. She held it up to the closest lamp. Just like the others, there were items inside. She could make out nails, fingernail clippings, and a strange netting type of fabric. A cold chill made its way throughout her entire being as she wondered who had made it...along with why and when.

Not wanting it inside the house for another second, she marched to the back door. She pulled on the handle to discover the door unlocked. With her hand on knob, she remembered distinctly checking it before leaving that morning. Somebody had a key. That must be the answer. Was it Lizzie?

It then occurred to her that *anybody* could have a key. She had never changed the locks. They were at least one hundred years old and she'd found them charming. But now she realized there must be dozens of keys to Miss Janie's doors around.

Miranda ripped the door open and hurled the bottle up in the air and out into the yard as far as she could manage. She didn't care if it was a million years old. She was done with all of it.

Chapter Sixteen

THE NEXT MORNING, MIRANDA stood by the open front door, letting a huge draft into her already drafty house. With a cup of hot coffee in hand, she watched as the locksmith wrangled with the aged, wrought iron box lock.

"Real shame to take these off, ma'am." He paused and looked over at her. "You still sure you want to?"

"Yeah. I have to. Back door, too." He shook his head and grimaced but got back to work.

After a fitful night of tossing and turning with a chair propped under the bedroom door handle, Miranda had waited for the closest locksmith business to open up and called for emergency service. Now, with a pain in her heart, she observed the man in the grease-stained coveralls tearing out part of the historic fabric of Rosewood. But it had to be done.

He gave her a choice of styles to replace it with but they all paled in comparison to the original box locks with their fine craftsmanship and crisp lines despite the age. She pointed to the least offensive.

After Miranda paid him an exorbitant fee without blinking, he handed over the originals saying, "You can probably make some nice change on these if you sell them to an antiques dealer." She nodded, taking them from him.

After he left, Miranda walked into each room and eyed it up. She checked to make sure each window lock was secure. Then she thought about other places to enter the house. There were no other places...there couldn't be.

Sun from the nice late fall day outside beamed on the floorboards, belying the state of her internal affairs and her conflict-ing thoughts and feelings. She needed to be outside, needed to shake the mood up. After pulling on hiking boots and throwing on a warm fleece jacket, she fussed for a few minutes over the new latch, not liking the feel of it, before locking up tight.

Miranda knew exactly where to go and headed to the cor-ner of her property where a deer path hooked in. It had been too overgrown to explore before, but the change in season had now cleared it up. As she picked her way through the path, it wound its way in a curvy fashion until opening up. The expanse of Polly's Creek could be seen from the flat edge of the shoreline.

Her house deed had revealed that the original land parcel of Rosewood included many feet along this shoreline. At some point, it had been cut off in a jigsaw fashion and deeded over to Lizzie's family. Now it was Gooding land.

It stood untouched and Miranda imagined that it had looked much the same when those early settlers from East Anglia eventually made their tired way up the creek. She kept walking along the waterline until the path stopped, becoming all wetlands. Oyster and clam shells stuck up randomly in the muck that was visible. The scene of untamed beauty began to rub away at her troubles. Inhaling deeply, she felt the slight tang of salt water in her nostrils.

The path headed off away from the shoreline and in the direction of the Maynard's property. Miranda followed it until hitting an impasse where branches stacked on top of one an-other barred further entry. It looked human, not nature, made. Who would have taken that kind of trouble all the way out here where there was nothingness? And why?

She got closer to see through the brambly thicket, too dense on either side, preventing further passage. The view of the woods beyond was obscure and shrouded. Shivering, she turned to head back.

Spotting a course that veered in the direction of the main road, Miranda took the path that led into thicker tree growth and soon heard a faint sound in the distance. Closer, she could discern a high-pitched mewing sound. Not like the sound Caro's cat had made in the cellar, but softer and squeakier. Stopping, she stood still and listened.

It started up again. She pinpointed the noise to a tree ahead on the path. Once there, she examined closer, finding a squirrel hole a couple of feet above the ground. Pulling out her cell phone, she flashed it down into the hole.

Blinking blue eyes looked up at her. A tiny orange kitten. With no mother in sight. Miranda made a snap decision and reached down into the hole, pulling out the little creature. Once in her arms, it trembled and mewed some more. It was the cutest thing she could ever recall seeing in her entire life. She situated the delicate passenger in the front pocket of her fleece, toting it carefully back home.

Back at Rosewood, Miranda placed the kitten in an empty box left over from the move, cushioning it with a towel. After calling the closest veterinarian's office, the receptionist squeezed her in with the last appointment of the day, making the point clear by saying, "You are darn lucky that there was a cancellation and that Doc didn't want to close shop and take off early." Unsaid was that the receptionist got ripped off of her chance to go home early by Miranda's call. Miranda thanked her profusely.

She headed out to Lewiston, the kitten mewed plaintively in the box, making it known he wasn't happy to be out of Miranda's arms. The vet's office was not too far away from Joe's, the restaurant where she and Beau had met up. It sat in a stand-alone, generic looking brick building with only two cars in its lot. After parking her Toyota, she hustled in quickly to keep everyone appeased; vet, receptionist and, especially, kitten.

Once inside, the gum-snapping receptionist handed over paperwork. After Miranda filled it out, she directed her to a back examination room. On the way there, she peeked into the box and softened some saying, "Aww, what a cute little thing."

In short order, the vet stepped into the room and reached into the box with one hand without missing a beat. "Let's see what you got here," he said in a booming voice.

He held the kitten by the scruff of its neck up to the light, examining it from top to bottom. "Where'd you find the little fella?"

Miranda explained about the tree and not seeing a mother around.

"No telling if something had happened to Mama Cat, so you made the right call."

Miranda stood to the side as the vet examined the cat even more thoroughly.

"Huh...how about that."

"What?"

"It's a little gal, not a little fella."

"Is that...unexpected?"

"Yes, it is. Most orange cats are male. Known for a specific personality. Using human terms, the personality is easygoing, life of the party jock type." He mused further. "In fact, I wonder if the same could be same for orange humans."

"But what about a girl orange cat?" Miranda asked.

"That I don't know. I'll leave you to be the judge...I assume you're keeping her?" He looked over the rim of his glasses at her.

"Yes. Yes, I am." She realized at that very moment that Rosewood had turned her into a cat person.

After the worming, flea treatments, and a couple of shots, the kitten looked pretty worked over, making Miranda feel guilty. The vet finished it all up by saying, "Now, she'll have to come back in about four weeks to be spayed."

Miranda paid the bill at the front desk with a slight wince. Between the locks and the kitten, it was getting to be an expensive couple of days.

The receptionist again peered into the box. Seemingly over her irritation, she said, "She's a sweetie. What's her name?"

"That's a good question. Haven't gotten that far yet."

On the drive back, the kitten slept the entire time, worn out by the proceedings. In the silent break from the mewing, Miranda mused over the vet's orange cat analogy about personality to orange (really ginger) humans. He had basically described Brian's personality.

That night at Rosewood, with her spirits lifted, Miranda set up camp for the kitten in the pantry where there was a door to close. Litter box. Check. Food. Check. Water. Check. It was comforting to have another living thing in the house...along with her new locks.

As she settled into bed, Miranda mulled over a name for the kitten. It came to her finally: Polly, of course. After Polly's Creek, close to where Miranda found her. As slumber began to take over, her last thought before succumbing to nod land was about the cat symbols on her property and around the area. Maybe she should get a tattoo of one...

Chapter Seventeen

UP EARLY, MIRANDA SAT with a coffee and watched the kitten's antics, chasing sunbeams on the floor. As she half-anticipated, half-dreaded the start of the day, a dig day, she absentmindedly made a mental note to pick up some kitten toys on the next trip to the store. Based on the strangeness of Brian's behavior, she was wondering if the dig would go on.

She heard the rough grumbles from his truck engine before seeing it out the window. When the knock came, she was right there to open it. Brian stood with his eyes shifted down in the direction of the door handle. "What happened to your box lock?"

She lifted her eyebrows. "That's all you have to say to me?"

His eyes stayed glued to the new, ugly, generic lock. "Well, the lock is an antique...it's almost a crime to take them off. A house dating from this era...it was probably specially ordered from England."

"When someone is breaking in using the old lock, that's what has to be done."

"What?" He looked at her with alarm.

She pointed out to the yard where the blue bottle still sat after she had thrown it. "I found that inside the house on the table the other night."

His gaze flicked over at where she pointed and he said, "Another one? Jesus Christ."

"So, I figured out about you and Fiona..." Miranda began.

He spoke right over her saying, "There's a lot you don't know. Just trust me on this."

"Well, why don't you try to explain it to me?"

He was silent, running a hand through his already rumpled hair. "I...can't. Not yet."

Miranda felt like she was in a cartoon with a thought bubble above her head showing a big question mark. And a bubble with "blah, blah, blah" over Brian's head.

"I don't have any idea what you are saying right now."

"I know...I know..." He reached a hand towards her. She flinched and backed up a step even though she felt a physical pull towards him at the same time.

What a muddle she had gotten herself into. She thought he was a friend, at the very least, and now he was a foe. "Just... just do your dig, I guess. I'll stay out of your way until you wrap it up."

He gave her a tortured look but said nothing more. She closed the door on him, leaning back against it and feeling disgust at herself. For liking him...trusting him...sleeping with him. She couldn't believe she had read him so wrong. As she told him, she would put up with him around the place until the dig was done. She had signed a contract with his archeology center and she wouldn't go back on her word.

Her mind scrambled for how to handle this and settled on the idea of leaving Rosewood every dig day, starting with the current day. Where to go was the question. Miranda floundered around for options finally remembering a neighboring town touted for its antique dealers, according to her recent googling. The county seat, in fact.

Grabbing a gallon size Ziplock baggie, she packaged the antique locks and headed out to the car. She kept her gaze averted from the dig activity while feeling others' eyes on her. She tried not to care whose eyes they were.

On the drive down country roads to Gloucester, she attempted to concentrate on the rural beauty around her rather than the most recent interaction with Brian. But she couldn't. Her thoughts kept straying back to him no matter how hard she tried to corral them until the Toyota pulled into the town of Gloucester.

Miranda circled around the county courthouse and gazed over at the handsome brick affair that took up the center of the town square. It was adorned with impressive arched windows and a columned portico that matched the height of the building. Using her newfound knowledge of colonial architecture, she judged it to be the same era of Williamsburg construction but knew that might be off by a number of years. Way off, even.

A row of one story, one room deep, brick buildings, almost as if stacked in a row, trickled down the street away from the courthouse. She edged over to a historic marker and read it from her car. Apparently, they were a collection of law offices dating from the time of the courthouse and unique in their architecture and survival until present day. The word "cute" popped into Miranda's head, but she wondered if buildings could officially be described that way. Maybe quaint was a more apt term.

After parking on the street, she strolled away from the law offices a block or so until reaching the commercial district proper. Miranda's googling efforts had pinpointed three antique dealers as possibilities, especially one that claimed to specialize in "architectural artifacts." She deemed the box locks to fall into this category.

Hitting the other two first, she struck out in terms of any interest in box locks but did find herself taken in by various pieces that would look fabulous at Rosewood when finances allowed. If she still found herself at Rosewood...she felt a twinge at that thought.

Miranda pulled the door open of the third shop: "J. Wood and Sons, Purveyors of Fine Antiquities and Objects." The musty odor that she was getting accustomed to from old buildings and things hit her nose as the door chimes jangled.

A gentleman with some age on him sat behind a desk and looked over at her above pince-nez glasses. "Hello there, young lady."

After saying hello in return, the man went back to his scribbling leaving her to her own devices. She wandered through the store, empty of other customers, to size up his inventory before approaching him. It was a mixed bag of small pieces of furniture along with many curiosities that could be labeled "architectural artifacts;" signage, mantelpieces, and interesting hooks among other things.

Miranda patted her bag filled with door locks for reassurance and headed back to his desk. She cleared her throat and then spoke. "Got a question for you."

"What's that? You see something that strikes your fancy?"

"No...I mean, yes, there are many things in here I would love to take home. But I actually have some box locks to sell that I thought you might be interested in."

He gave a sniff and placed his pencil down. "You got 'em on you?"

"Yep." She rifled through her tote and lifted the baggie out. As she handed it over, he asked, "Okay to take them out?"

"Of course."

He pulled out a magnifying glass from his drawer and eyed each one carefully, silent as he did so.

"Well...you do have some fine specimens here." He gazed at her with some suspicion in his eyes. "Can I ask where they came from?"

"My house, actually."

"Where's your house at?"

"Down in Bisoux. It's called Rosewood."

"Why'd you take them off?"

"I was having some...some security issues so I had to upgrade."

"That's a shame. Well, let me do up some figures on what I can offer. Give me a minute or two."

Miranda went back to wandering around the shop and examining the nooks and crannies. In the far back, she saw a reflection of the light off some glass and leaned in to get a closer look. Then reared back. It was a blue bottle.

Visceral reaction kicked her in the stomach like a horse, a clenching of her digestive tract. She was stuck in place for a couple of beats. How could something so ordinary get to her like this? She gave herself a shake, chastising herself for behavior that was so not her. Finally, she lifted the bottle out of its cushioned nesting box and examined it. Indeed, it was the exact same as the others.

As Miranda set it down, she saw it was on top of a dusty case filled with others cushioned like it. A dusty case of blue bottles. Her logical mind took over, racing with the probabilities. The most likely one was that somebody purchased them here to stage the pranks. And who could that be?

She went back to the desk. The proprietor looked up and said, "Okay, little lady. I'm all set..."

"What? Oh yes. But first I have to ask. What can you tell me about that case of blue bottles in the back right corner of the shop?"

He gave a chuckle. "Those have sat back there for years taking up space and now you're the second person within the past month or so to ask about them. Isn't that just the way it is in this business? He bought two cases of 'em right up." He looked at her hopefully and said, "Leaving me with just the last case...maybe you want it?"

Miranda skipped his question and asked one of her own. "Who was the first person?"

"Huh?"

"Who asked first before me?"

"Couldn't tell you his name. Never saw him before or since."

"What did he look like?"

"I can barely remember what I had for breakfast these days."

"Anything you can remember at all?"

He scrunched up his face. "Let's see. Just ordinary, I'd say. Tall, I think. A little scruffy around the edges maybe?"

Miranda held back venting impatience on the man. "Okay, can you say when it was exactly?"

"That I can do. 'Cause I got my ledger right here where I write down all purchases. It was still hot as cotton out, I do remember that...so I would say it was about a month ago, give or take."

He flipped through some pages and then pointed a finger.

"Here it is. It was on October 2nd."

Miranda worked that date in her head quickly and re-alized that was after the first find at the dig. The bottle that was actually old and original. So, somebody had found these right afterwards and started up with planting them. Or was the first bottle actually old? Had that been planted too? Could she believe anything from Brian and his group? But who was this scruffy mystery man? And why was he doing it?

"Why are you asking so many questions about this?"

She let out a big rush of breath and then said, "It's a long story. I don't want to bore you with it."

"Try me."

Looking at the kind eyes gazing at her over his pince-nez, she said, "Maybe next time."

Miranda walked out of J. Woods and Sons without the box locks but with a case of blue bottles. A deal had been struck. Mr. Woods had given what she estimated to be a fair price on the locks and kept some of that money back for her purchase of the case of bottles. She quickly decided it was a little insurance policy. If she bought them, no one could buy any more from J. Woods—meaning less chance of more to find stashed around at Rosewood. It also made her feel less helpless. It wasn't much, but at least it was being more proactive than anything else she had been able to do.

Driving home, she worked out the figures in her head re-alizing she might actually be in the black again after selling the locks. The amount covered the vet bill, the locksmith and the purchase of bottles. She would hide the case safely away, some-where discreet and out of plain view at Rosewood.

Chapter Eighteen

UPON HER RETURN, MIRANDA found the dig crew thankfully gone and she let out a breath of relief. She had timed her return for that but partly expected to find Brian still there. He wasn't, though. She chided herself for thinking he would want to talk again but, even more so, for the part of her that wanted him too.

She hoisted the case of blue bottles out of the trunk, looking around furtively just in case anyone was watching and moving as quickly as possible with its weight and her still stiff ankle. She opened the new front door lock one-handed, starting to get the hang of it.

Inside, she thought about where she could put the bottles, deciding on the closet underneath the staircase. She pushed aside paint cans and other leftovers from the renovation and plopped it down. After shutting the door, she flipped the chunk of wood across that served as its closing device.

The kitten was meowing her loud "pay attention to me" meow and Miranda smiled. She was just as eager to see her little companion. When she opened the pantry door, the kitten blinked wide from the light and struggled to get on four paws, teeter-tottering. Quickly finding its footing, Polly skirted around Miranda to get out.

Miranda picked her up handily. As if she'd pushed a button, Polly began to purr back in response with her ragged, engine-like noise. Miranda sat down, nestling and petting the kitten, the purring bringing its calm.

She stared out the window at the fading sunlight but started abruptly and the kitten jumped off her lap. A figure stood at the edge of the woods where the yard met up. A squat figure that she recognized as Lizzie Gooding. Miranda sprang up and headed out the door.

As she marched over to Lizzie, the other woman continued to stare at the house. Miranda paused, not wanting to scare her off. She yelled out with what she hoped was a friendly tone, "Hallo there, Lizzie."

Lizzie's gaze slowly moved from the house to Miranda. Then she nodded. Miranda stepped closer and Lizzie stayed put. There was just enough light left to the day for Miranda to make out Lizzie's features, especially her blue eyes. She had never made the connection before, but Lizzie's eyes were strangely the same unique color of the bottles. A weird light hue that was almost luminescent, an eerie blue.

"How are you?" Miranda asked her.

"The gathering is soon."

"Oh? When?"

"Next full moon."

"Huh...where?"

"Don't know yet."

"Did you come to tell me this?"

Lizzie nodded.

"Okay...well, thanks. Can I walk with you a ways back?"

Lizzie shrugged and turned to head off into the woods towards Gooding land. Miranda's mind spun around what she wanted to ask the woman. So many questions.

"So, Lizzie...have you ever seen any old blue bottles around Rosewood?"

Lizzie shrugged again, which Miranda was beginning to realize was a trademark mannerism.

"Did Miss Janie ever show you any, maybe?"

Instead of answering, Lizzie stopped short and stared beyond towards the waterway. They had reached a clearing that gave a broader view of Polly's Creek. Miranda waited her out, feeling a chill creep up her bare arms and regretting she had not grabbed a jacket before leaving the house. But, with Lizzie, it seemed she had to take whatever was on offer.

Lizzie began the strange bird trilling that she had done before and then broke it off mid-trill to say, "Witches use 'em."

Miranda, unnerved, said, "Blue bottles?"

Lizzie went back to staring beyond.

"Where...why..."

Lizzie began to walk off without saying anymore. Miranda said to Lizzie's departing back, "Thanks for stopping by, Lizzie. Thanks for letting me...." Her voice trailed off as she wasn't getting any acknowledgement. She watched Lizzie's figure fade away on the path before she herself headed back inside.

That night, Miranda's dreams were fraught with frantic, last minute paper grading and kittens meowing, spliced together with haunting visuals of doll babies in those twisted, gnarled trees. Fitful at best, she woke up with a slight headache, almost a hangover effect.

Hearing the kitten's angry meows, she dragged herself down the stairs with a heavy footfall. "I'm coming...I'm coming." She wondered if baby humans could be that demanding.

Sunlight already filtered into the main room and some of it reflected off glass catching Miranda's attention. She came to a sudden halt at the sight. Yet another one sitting plain as day in the middle of the table.

The cheeriness of the bright daylight belied the macabre tableau of another blue bottle filled with miscellaneous items. The knowledge that it hadn't been there the night before made her shake with anxiety and fear.

Someone had been in the house again. In spite of the locks.

Miranda sped all the way to Lewiston, halfway wanting to be pulled over for some kind of attention. Once in the police department's parking lot, she got out, slamming the door hard.

She marched up to the entrance of the generic 1960s block style building that gave off an air of shoestring budget economics. The uniformed sergeant at the desk looked up at the sight of Miranda and stifled a yawn. "Help you, ma'am?"

"I need to talk to the sheriff."

He lifted up a phone receiver and said, "Lady here to see you, Sheriff. Huh? Oh yeah," he looked to Miranda and asked, "Your name, ma'am?"

Miranda gave her name and he finished up his side of the conversation saying, "Alrighty. I'll send her back."

In the furthest back reach of the building, Miranda found him right behind an overly large name plate that declared him to be "Sheriff Billy Sanford." He lounged behind his equally overly large desk, mud encrusted boots propped up on the edge.

"What can I help you with, miss?"

"I'm Miranda Chesney. You were out at my place."

"Yeah, yeah. What seems to be the problem now?"

Miranda gave him the details on the latest: changing the locks and yet someone still managing to break in and leave another bottle. She finished by placing the latest blue bottle on his desk.

He gave a big harrumph when she was through and said, "Well, any broken glass windows? Any broken locks? Busted doors?"

"No...but..."

He threw up his hands and said, "So, no sign of a break in in other words."

"No..."

"Look...next time you get some destruction, give us a call... otherwise..."

"How am I supposed to sleep at night?"

"I'd suggest you get some kind of alarms. Maybe cameras, too. If you want to feel safer. We can give you some names of guys to call about it."

Miranda began to sputter her anger out. "I can't believe this...is this because I'm not from here? I really hope so... because this...this is not protecting your public, let me tell you!"

Sanford moved his weight up to standing. "Now look here. This all started with you throwing some wild accusations around about Lizzie Gooding. You could be making all this up about blue bottles for all I know."

She turned away from the man, boiling with rage, as she stormed out of the building, leaving the bottle behind. Once in her car, she swung it into gear and hit the gas hard. There was no one else in the parking lot to see her hissy fit but it didn't matter.

She whipped out of there and headed down the main drag. Fuming the whole time, she glanced over to the strip of shopping center that housed Joe's Restaurant and saw Beau's gold toned Crown Vic. Making a split-second decision, she screeched on her brakes and turned in, cutting it close and causing the car headed the other direction to lay on the horn. She didn't care. Maybe Beau Jenkins might know something. Remember something.

Miranda stomped into the restaurant and looked down one end and then the other until spotting Beau at the same table where they met previously. She made her way down to the table and stood in front of him, her upset clear on her face.

"Miranda! What in heaven's name is the matter?" He sat with his thumbs propped under his suspenders and his brow wrinkled in confusion.

"Where do I start?"

"Have a seat and we'll sort it out. Let's get you some coffee first though."

After she got settled and gulped down a few mouthfuls of black coffee, Miranda poured out all of the events to date, ending with her infuriating visit to the sheriff. Beau never interrupted and listened with careful attention. By the time she wound down, she shockingly felt a tinge better.

"I'll tell you what," Beau looked around the restaurant and then continued, "the Sheriff's not one to put himself out much."

Miranda put her face in her hands and said, "I don't know what to do, Beau. How is someone getting in? I mean, the cellar would seem the obvious way but those doors are padlocked tight so I just don't get it..."

Her mind conjured up the Wizard of Oz-like visual of Rosewood's exterior cellar doors secured by the shiny, silver padlock. It was the only cellar entry evident, just from the outside.

As an afterthought, she asked, "Do you remember anything funny about the cellar at Rosewood?"

Beau sat back, his knobby fingers toying with a fork back and forth with a distracted air. "The cellar? Let's see…"

Miranda could see the cogs of his mind trying to place the specificity of Rosewood's cellar among all the ones he had shown around the Tidewater region.

He gazed somewhere above Miranda's head and finally said, "I only went down there once or twice that I can recall… but nothing in particular stands out in my memory. That doesn't mean there's not another way in down there."

Miranda let out a huge sigh. She had ignored the cellar for too long because of snakes, spiders, and who knew what else. But it was going to need investigating.

Slowly, and with a measured confidence, Beau continued. "It's gotta be the cellar though. How about I come back with you right now and we go over it with a fine-toothed comb? Try to get to the bottom of this."

A wave of gratitude passed through Miranda. "Oh, would you? I just don't know who to call next. My head is spinning."

Beau reached over and patted her hand with his gnarled, liver spotted one and said, "Now, every problem has a solution. We'll figure it out."

Chapter Nineteen

THE COFFEE TABLE SAT between them. "It was right there," Miranda said, pointing to the middle of the table.

Seated on Miranda's living room couch, Beau stared at the space as if the bottle was in place. "Right there, huh?"

Miranda nodded. "You know, I was gone all day but the dig was going on. There are a fair number of students that come here." Miranda knew most of them by sight but there was a rotating roster of participants that switched out on any given dig day. She added, "It's *got* to be one of them tied to doing this."

She went back to petting Polly, who had crawled up onto her lap after she had finished tearing into the chair's upholstered legs with her jagged little claws.

"It seems more prankster-like than malicious, don't you think?" Beau asked.

"But still...how do they get in? One or more...who knows?"

Beau's gaze moved over to the staircase. "These original settlers were dang good builders. They knew what they were doing. None of this tract house crap you see all over the place that breaks down in a matter of months. I can't tell the number of the clients that call me back complaining."

Miranda stood up and walked over to the stairs, willing the answer to be revealed to her. Maybe the center of the house was the most logical place somehow.

"Would that archeology fella know about stuff like this?" Beau asked from behind her.

She glanced over her shoulder and said, "Maybe. But I'm not talking to him anymore."

"Oh."

"I'm going to have to go into the cellar to look underneath this, aren't I?'

"Yeah. We'll do it together. You got a good flashlight? I got one in the car if you don't."

Miranda moved over to the kitchen drawer and pulled out her Maglite.

"Alrighty," Beau said, pulling himself up off the couch with some creaks and groans, leaning on his cane. Miranda looked over at his knees, sizing them up for the task at hand.

After they made their way outside to the cellar door, Miranda pulled out the key for the padlock that kept the two matching doors hasped. She heaved them up and apart. Complete darkness yawned at her from below.

Beau cleared his throat and said, "I'll get down there first."

"Beau, are you sure? Can you...?"

He waved her off with his cane in the air and began to make his way down saying, "Mind you, I'll be taking my time."

"Yes. Please do." Miranda followed behind his dungaree clad legs with her Maglite shining so it reflected each step ahead of him.

As they made their descent, the smell of old earth, mold and just general age swung up. It wasn't entirely offensive, but it also wasn't something she wanted to steep in her nostrils for too long either.

When they reached bottom, Miranda ran her light over the ground surface, hard packed earth. As it had always been. Beau scuffed his shoe over it. "You don't see this too much anymore. Usually, folks pour concrete over it by this point. Now...I know there's a pull string for a bulb down here somewhere. Shine that light around, will you?"

Miranda caught the skinny string for the bulb in her flashlight beam, hanging a couple of feet in front of where they stood, and Beau gave it a yank. The space became more illuminated with the trademark halogen yellow, but it was dim at best.

Both of them began looking around to get their bearings. Miranda already knew that the space was only under half the house. Brian had told her it was common that a house of this age had started as a one room affair and then was expanded when fortunes allowed.

Miranda turned to look at the back wall. Old, stacked shelving held some vintage Mason jars of unknown origin, canned goods now distorted with what they originally contained. She shivered at the idea of hauling them out.

The wall that connected to the back would be the one that lined up to the staircase by Miranda's estimation. Walking closer to its edge with minced steps just in case anything creepy or crawly popped out, she shined the light on the floor joists above. "I don't see anything special here. You?"

Beau was poking around the front wall where old garden fencing was piled up. He worked his way over to Miranda and looked around, then said, "No, I can't make out anything different. How about on the walls themselves where a door might be?"

They both gazed around at the open space not covered by shelving, fencing or any other bric-a-brac. The areas that could be seen were made of stone and seemed to be completely solid all around.

"I don't know, Miranda. I just don't know. It looks tight as a tick down here to me."

Miranda nodded, thoughtful. "Me too. I don't get it."

"Maybe we got it wrong and there's no way in from down here. Or...."

"Or what?"

"Maybe you got a ghost."

"Beau, don't tell me you believe in that stuff too?"

"Show enough old houses to folks and you'd become a believer too, missy. The stories I could tell you..."

"No thanks to the stories, and not a chance this is a ghost. Not with those cases of blue bottles floating around that a live human purchased just recently. Not a chance."

Beau nodded and said, "True. But how are they getting in?"

"That is the question that remains."

After they emerged from the cellar, each of them took a

door and closed the cellar followed by Miranda securing the padlock.

As she dusted her hands off, Beau looked at her with a pained expression. "You got somebody to stay with you for a couple of nights? Just until this joker is done fooling around?"

Miranda thought about who she could possibly ask to spend the night and then realized it was ridiculous. If she couldn't stay alone the next couple of nights, then she couldn't stay at Rosewood at all anymore. That was something she wasn't ready to entertain.

"Nah. I'll be fine. As you said, it's just some mischief at its worst. They'll get bored soon enough."

It was the kitten's loud meows that woke her up that night. Her first thought was that if Polly made that a nightly habit, they would have problems getting along, sleep being non-negotiable. After blinking a few times, she registered a glow coming in through the window. A nice color, comforting even; it lit up the room warmly. But, as the kitten meowed louder and louder, Miranda sat bolt upright. Something was terribly wrong.

Stumbling over to the window, she could barely believe the sight outside. She ran to the other upstairs room and looked out that window too, confirming the worst. A circle of fire ringed around the entirety of the house. A string of profanities spilled from her mouth as she grabbed her cell phone and punched in 911.

The dispatcher asked what her address was, and she stuttered it out along with the problem at hand. "Hurry! I don't know if it's going to move closer to the house. And my house is old."

"The fire trucks will be out as soon as possible, ma'am. Given your location, it will take about fifteen minutes. Hang on."

The dispatcher told her to stay inside for the moment unless the house did start to catch on fire. She paced from window to window, ignoring the cat's cries. While she tried to figure out if anybody was out there, a closer look revealed more about the fire itself. She could make out what looked like poles or torches stuck into the ground. The spaces in between held blue bottles lined up like unlikely soldiers. This had gone too far. Way too far.

It felt like an entire lifetime elapsed waiting it out for help to arrive. Finally, the sirens got closer and closer. Four trucks blazing with lights and sirens filled the driveway and the yard of Rosewood. A loud banging on the door made her shake all over and she pulled it open.

The fireman stood fully engulfed in protective gear and held an axe in one hand. "Everybody okay in here?"

Miranda, wondering if he had used the axe to pound on the door with a fleeting concern for possible damage, answered him. "It's just me…and my cat."

"All right. Come on out with me, ma'am, while we put this out."

"Hang on, I gotta grab the cat."

"Sure."

Grabbing her coat and Polly, Miranda went out the front door without a backwards glance at Rosewood. The fireman led her through a doused area made in the perimeter of the ring of poles and into the safety of an open EMT vehicle.

"Now, just sit here with Stacey while we get this sorted out."

A beefy female medic said in an authoritarian tone, "Hop on up here. You okay to get up on your own?"

"Yeah. I'm not hurt. Just freaked out."

"I can imagine. This is a weird scene. And I say that as someone who has seen a lot of weird scenes."

Miranda nodded. "I'm sure you have."

"Any idea who did it?"

The thought of explaining it all to this young woman was too exhausting so Miranda just shook her head. The two of them fell silent and watched from the back of the vehicle as the group of firemen extinguished all of it out. Once done, they walked to the other buildings and around the house. Miranda assumed it was to make sure there were no little fires anywhere else on the property.

Eventually, the man in charge headed over and introduced himself as the fire chief. "Welp, you got yourself quite the trickster out here." He looked back over the scene they had just taken care of. When he turned back, he said, "Very clever setup."

"How did they do it?" Miranda asked, her tone resigned.

"They set up those wood stubs, kind of like a torch idea, and then lit them with a kerosene mixture. You must have interrupted them before they finished."

"How so?"

"We found an empty bottle tossed out in the yard away from the circle they made. They missed lighting the last couple so maybe you scared them off turning on your light or something."

"Well, that's good, I guess."

"It's funny what they used. Has citronella and cedar oil in it. Too bad there aren't any mosquitoes out right now." He gave a jolly chuckle. "You can still smell it out here, mixed with the kerosene odor."

"Yeah, funny." But Miranda didn't share in his chuckle. She did, however, finally recognize the familiar scent in the air that nuanced the smoke odors.

"Anyway, did you have any friends over that maybe left this as a parting gift or something like that?"

Miranda took a deep breath and then began to tell the man her whole saga ending with the fact that she had tried to get some help from Sheriff Sanford.

The fire chief took off his helmet and scratched at some matted hair. "Huh."

"What do I do now?" she asked.

"Well, there needs to be an investigation. Figure out if there was malicious intent even though no damage occurred. Given the empty bottle, maybe they were careless enough to leave other clues, identifying ones. And I'd suggest you go someplace else to stay for a bit. Just until we figure out what's going on here." He paused and said, "Is there a neighbor close by that you can go stay with?"

Miranda let out a humorless chuckle and said, "No. I'm

new here." Then she asked, "Do you think you can figure it out?"

"We'll try our darnedest. You can count on that."

"I'm happy to hear that. Trying to get help before this point wasn't working out."

He nodded. "Yeah, I gathered that."

They were silent for a moment and then he said, "We'll get some of the ashes tamped down some more. Why don't you go get what you need, and we'll stay here until you're ready to go."

"Okay," Miranda hoisted herself up off the gurney, disturbing the now sleeping kitten.

She looked down at her cell phone to check the time. Three in the morning and she had no idea where to go.

Chapter Twenty

MIRANDA WOKE UP TO daylight streaming through the too thin curtains that hung on her Motel 6 room windows. Bleary eyed, she looked around taking in the dismal space with its threadbare blanket, cheap looking plaid chair in the corner, and mud brown rug. It was all so vastly different from her home's space with its gleaming hardwood floors and charm at every turn.

She felt a surge of anger at being driven out of Rosewood. And she had no idea why. Why, why, why did someone—or even multiple people—feel the need to do this to her? Was it about her? Or the house? She really couldn't wrap her head around it anymore.

Her cell phone gave off its ring for an incoming call and she stretched over to the side table to grab it, feeling a twinge in her rib cage. She glanced at the time and realized she had slept in way too late.

"Hello?" she answered.

"Miranda Chesney?"

"This is she."

"Chief Johnson wants to meet with you and Billy—I mean, Sheriff Sanford—over at the police station at 11. Can you make that?"

"Uh…yeah. Okay."

She sat up fully and rubbed the sleep out of her eyes. Then she let out a huge sigh knowing she had to get ahead of this. Somehow, some way.

After a quick shower, feeding Polly, and grabbing a complimentary muffin and coffee from the Motel 6 office, Miranda pulled into the police station parking lot right at the eleven o'clock hour.

After giving her name at the front, she was waved into the back conference room. She entered the utilitarian space to see Sanford and the fire chief sitting around companionably, trading war stories. Her entrance interrupted the sheriff, and a look of annoyance crawled over his face.

Chief Johnson stood up and the sheriff followed suit. Miranda's suspicion was that Sanford would not have done so if it had not been for the chief's lead.

"Mizz Chesney. Have a seat," the chief said, pointing out an available chair. "Thank you for meeting us. Sure hope you got some sleep after last night."

Nodding, she asked, "Have you figured anything out yet?"

"So, the thing about it is this...because there was no damage...we don't have a case. So, no arson, in other words. We don't even know if there was any intent to do damage."

"Well, what other intent would there be?" Miranda asked.

Johnson stroked his chin and said, "I gotta say the torches were firmly planted in place and they would have burnt down safely. Kind of an old-style way of doing it. Interesting, really."

"I don't get it."

"In order for this to be a crime, there has to be evidence that damage was clearly intended. Now, on the other hand, if damage had happened it could have ended up being something called 'reckless arson.'"

"What's that?"

"It would be like maybe a campfire that wasn't tended to properly, gets out of hand and then causes damage. See the difference?"

"Not really. What if the torches had gotten out of hand?"

"But they didn't."

Sanford cleared his throat and interjected. "Like I told you before...I think cameras are your option now. I gotta a cousin who will fix you up at a good price."

Seeing the frown come over Miranda's face, he added, "And we'll get patrol cars out there a couple of times a night...until this thing simmers down."

"Isn't there any way to figure out who is doing this? I mean, what about the blue bottles? That's got to be a good clue."

Sanford leaned back in his chair, allowing his wide belly to expand a bit. "You told me Mr. Woods didn't have any recall of who it was."

"Yeah, but I'm not a detective and that was me asking him. Shouldn't..."

He put a hand up and said, "All right, all right. I'll go out to Gloucester later and ask him about it."

"So, given all that...you can head on back whenever you like," Johnson said.

Sanford chimed in and said, "Just say the word and my cousin will get right out there with the cameras."

"How much?" Miranda said with a sinking feeling about spending more money that she didn't have.

"Give him a call and he'll sort it out with you." He pushed a business card towards her.

She picked it up and tapped the edge on the tabletop, wondering if she could actually trust either of the men at the table. Would she just be better off coming up with her own plan of action?

Driving back to the Motel 6 room, she called Beau's number. When he answered, she said, "Famous last words, Beau. More went down last night."

"Miranda? That you?"

After she filled him in on the latest, he gave a low whistle.

"Yeah, so now they said cameras and patrol cars. The sheriff has a cousin who sets up cameras. Unless you have a better recommendation."

"I sure do. I'll get my man Bucky out there right away for you. You'll get the friends and family rate. How does that sound?"

"Great. I hate to ask, but could you meet him out there? It's near exam time with the holidays coming soon and I've been missing too many meetings."

"Sure thing. But how do we get inside there?"

"Oh, yeah. I didn't think of that." After some more discussion, they arranged to meet at Joe's for the key hand off.

After a quick change at the Motel 6, better set-up for the cat and collecting her books and notes, Miranda was soon headed back to Joe's to give Beau the key. She had kept the room for another night, not ready yet to go back to Rosewood. She would figure that out later.

Miranda finished up her lecture and meetings and headed out through the first floor of John Lathrop Hall. She noticed several students who looked familiar from the dig heading into a classroom. She paused to read the placard on the door, a materials culture class taught by a teaching assistant. The TA listed was none other than Fiona Lansbury.

Making a snap decision to go into the very back corner of the lecture hall, she squirreled herself away into a seat hoping to be inconspicuous. Fiona stood behind the lectern below, poised and ready. Dressed to a "t" as usual, she wore a casual but elegant white cardigan unbuttoned at the collar line to reveal a strand of pearls. It was paired with a tartan plaid skirt. Her blonde tresses were coiffed to perfection, not a hair strand out of place, and her makeup was smooth and just right, not too subtle and not too overstated.

Fiona greeted the class and got underway with her lecture. She was articulate, well-organized and presented all the information on clay pots and pipes in an ordered manner. The students all appeared engaged and attentive, especially one fellow who had his hand up at every turn. And seemed to be hanging on Fiona's every word and move. As Miranda peered closer, she got a visual of who it was: Scott. The student in her logics seminar who had offered his help. She sat back struck, wondering what he was playing at—if anything. Maybe he was this way with all his female professors? Or male, too? Who knew.

Fiona's perfectly modulated tone made Miranda grudgingly acknowledge that her lecture game was on point. If Miranda was the grading professor, she would have no reason not to give her the highest mark. Feeling pinpricks of jealousy, she questioned if Fiona was better than her at lecturing despite the younger woman's limited experience.

Over the course of the lecture, Miranda was reminded of a movie, decades old, called "Election", a dark comedy with Reese Witherspoon in the lead role of a character obsessed with winning. A Fiona-esque character, in fact.

After the lecture wrapped up, Miranda walked up to the lectern, waiting until the students finished with their questions. The overzealous Scott from the front row with his hand up the whole time finally shuffled off. Miranda made sure she stayed out of his view. Finally, when it was just Fiona left, Miranda stepped forward from the side. "Hello, Fiona."

Fiona's eyes narrowed as she took Miranda in, nodding curtly.

"I think we need to talk."

"I don't think so, Miranda."

As Fiona gathered her papers and files, a sweep of her blonde hair sloped gracefully across the side of her face. As she lifted her hand to push it behind her ear, Miranda noticed what appeared to be a burn mark, a recent burn mark, on the top of her hand.

"What happened to your hand?"

"What?"

Miranda pointed to her hand and said, "It looks like a burn."

"It's...nothing. I have to go." With that, Fiona headed out of the lecture hall without any further word. Miranda followed right next to her, keeping pace.

Fiona looked over at her and said, "What are you doing?"

"Following you. Until we get this sorted out."

Fiona picked up speed despite the heel height of her black pumps and exited the building, heading in the direction of the archeology lab building. Miranda half trotted to keep up, peppering her with questions.

"Why didn't you tell me you grew up right near Rosewood?" and "Why didn't you tell me you knew Lizzie, quite well in fact?" and "What is with all the hiding your connection to Rosewood about?" and, finally, she finished with "What do you really know about the blue bottles?"

When they reached the front lawn of the lab center, Fiona reeled around saying, "I am not talking to you. In fact, you need to leave here."

"As a gainfully employed professor of this college, do you really think you are in a position to order me off school grounds?" Miranda asked. She could almost see the smooth veneer of the young woman's face crack in front of her very eyes and give way to a very ugly other face, anger boiling right on the surface.

"But, now that you mention it, I am in the position to tell you that you need to stay away from Rosewood. You are not welcome there anymore."

Fiona began to almost sputter and the thought passed through Miranda's head that here was someone not used to being told "no."

"In the meantime, we can have a civilized discussion right now and you can answer a few of my questions instead."

"I am not answering any of your questions," Fiona spit out, turning and bolting towards the lab entrance.

Miranda gazed at the door closing behind Fiona thoughtfully. That had gotten her nowhere. Fiona was a closed book. With a burn mark on her hand. The unspoken thing between them had been Brian. Miranda needed to find him next and lay it all on the line. The dig could not continue with Fiona's involvement.

Marching back over to John Lathrop Hall to face it head on, she headed to the office she had been avoiding the past week. The halls were emptying out as the students made their ways to their next classes and she soon found herself alone. Stopping a couple feet from his office to collect herself, she took several deep slow breaths and then approached his open doorway.

Miranda poked her head in to see Brian seated behind his desk, pouring over a document with furrowed brow. She felt her heart give a twinge and inwardly berated herself. She spoke up. "Brian."

He looked up suddenly, a conflicted expression crossing over his face. As he stood, Miranda took in his wrinkly plaid shirt, creased khakis, and rumpled hair. "Miranda...hi. Come in."

The space became too close and tight right away and she backed up a couple of steps. "Fiona and I just had an...altercation, I guess you could call it."

His face became stone. "What happened?"

Miranda told him about the circle of fire and how she was done with all Fiona's secrets. She finished by saying, "But she didn't admit to anything, of course. I made it clear that she is no longer welcome at Rosewood. You'll have to finish the dig without her. I don't trust her there at all."

Brian closed his eyes briefly. Opening them, he said, "I wish you hadn't done that."

"Why, Brian? Why? Please...just level with me."

"I can't. If you can just hang on for a little longer..."

"How can you ask me to do that? I have someone burning rings of fire around my house and planting blue bottles inside while I'm asleep."

They stared at each other, tension almost crackling in the air.

Miranda finally asked softly, "Are you in on this?"

"In on what?"

"This...this campaign, for lack of a better word. This campaign to drive me away from Rosewood for some reason. Some reason I can't figure out for the life of me."

Another pained expression came over Brian's face and he said, "I'm not...I'm on your side. You have to believe me."

"How can I believe you? You're telling me nothing, Brian."

He held out placating hands and stepped closer. Again, she felt the closeness of the room and stepped back almost into the hallway.

"I just need a little more time to sort it out. Just a little more time," he said.

"Brian, I don't know if I have a little more time. This is escalating, not downgrading. Can't you see that?"

"I know, I know...but I think I can get it to stop."

"You are talking in circles. Look...how many more dig days are there?"

He stepped back to his desk and moved some papers off his calendar. "Two more and then exams. I also planned for a site visit as part of the exam process."

"Okay, three more and that's it. Maybe then all this will go away."

Miranda didn't know what else to say to the man in front of her that she had been intimate with. He was little more than a stranger now, on so many levels. He stared back at her intensely, as if trying to communicate something with his eyes. But she had no idea what.

"Goodbye Brian," she said, and left.

Chapter Twenty-one

MIRANDA PACKED UP EVERYTHING at the Motel 6 room the next morning. She swung out of the parking lot and headed back to Rosewood. It was time for a fresh start.

As she headed into Bisoux, she decided to hit up the Princeton store for some provisions and pulled into the parking lot. The elderly man who she now knew was named Mr. Blackwell (according to Beau) nodded at her per usual upon her entry. After she made her selections, he rang them up on his old-fashioned register and said, "$10.50."

Rustling through her change purse, she had forgotten his was a cash only operation. Counting out her dollar bills and laying them down on the counter, she said, "Shoot. I'm short a dollar."

He waved a hand and said, "You'll make it up the next time."

"Well, thank you, Mr. Blackwell. By the way, I'm Miranda Chesney. I never properly introduced myself."

He nodded and said, "I know who you are, miss. Folks around here are in each other's business. You bought Miss Janie's place awhile back."

"Yes, I did....in fact, there was a fire there a couple nights ago...did you hear about that too?"

"Yep."

"Huh. Any word on who might have started it?" She smiled to soften the bluntness of the direct question.

"Not that I've heard."

"Anything else you might have heard about it?"

He gazed back outside and, for a second, Miranda thought

that was the end of the conversation. But he looked back at her and said, "Word is that you are a witch."

"A witch?"

He nodded again.

"Maybe you could spread that word back the other way that it's not true. I am not, nor have I ever been, a witch." As an afterthought, she added, "No one ever stopped by to introduce themselves or anything....do you think that could be the reason?"

He shrugged. "Couldn't say. We kinda keep to ourselves around these parts, anyhows."

"Could it have been Lizzie Gooding spreading this rumor?"

"Nah...not Lizzie. She likes you."

"Likes me? Really?"

"I can tell."

Miranda shook her head and said aloud, "A witch. How about that? I've been called lots of things in my life, but that's a new one."

He gave a faint smile.

Walking back out to her car, she wondered if it was possible that Lizzie was the only one around here that liked her and didn't think she was a witch. If that was the case, who started the rumor and to what end? To what purpose? What was their coven meeting on the full moon and all that about if they were not witches themselves?

Miranda got into her car and just sat with her head spinning. Did she need to just move? Was that what she needed to do? It dawned on her that Lizzie might hold the answers to all of it.

She arranged to meet Beau at Rosewood at ten and took comfort at the sight of his Crown Vic already in the drive. She still was unsettled about whether the decision to move back into Rosewood was a wise one.

Beau worked his way out of his car upon seeing hers pull up. As she pulled next to him, he reached back in to get something off the front seat. He handed over an aluminum pie tin covered with foil and said, "This is for you. From the missus."

"Oh, wow. That's so nice." Miranda could feel the bottom of the tin was still warm and peeked under the foil.

"Yep. It's one of her house specialties, corn bread. She studs that sucker with cranberries. Kind of a twist. But it works."

Beau had only mentioned "the missus" here and there in passing and Miranda had a vague idea of her but had never met or seen her. She said now, "Well, it was really nice of her to think of me. I hope I can meet her in person to thank her."

"Yeah, we'll have to set that up. Anyways, Bucky got everything like we need it here with the cameras. I took the liberty of giving him your email address. He said once you get that there will be a code and then you walk through a set up that gives you a screen to watch the activity when you need to. Or want to."

"All right."

They were both quiet then Beau said, "How about I come inside with you and we rig up your computer and take a look?"

Miranda breathed an inward sigh of relief. She had not realized until that moment how much she was dreading going inside by herself. The thought occurred that maybe she was getting PTSD from seeing the blue bottles.

"Yes. Good," she said, as she collected Polly in her carrier and her belongings out of the back of the Toyota.

After opening the front door lock, she stood on the threshold for a moment with Beau behind her and scanned the main room. Not seeing anything out of turn, she moved into the room, inviting Beau to take a seat.

Once they were all settled, Miranda opened up the laptop and found the email. "Okay, here goes."

It was fairly basic with easy instructions and included about six different screen shots. "Oh, look at this. He set them up all over the place."

"Yeah. Full coverage is the idea," Beau said, peering in to get a view of the laptop. He added, "Now he said something about quadrants and how you set up a tone for each one so that when someone or something comes into a quadrant, you get a ringer."

"Huh. Well, I don't want an alarm going off in the middle of the night. That might do me in."

"How about one of those ringtone doohickeys like on the cell phones?"

"Good idea. Maybe a chime. I could probably handle that."

She finagled her way into the different audio sounds and then found another feature. "Oh, look. It has the option of giving the codes out so someone else can view if need be."

"Yeah, that could come in handy."

After seeming to have it all set up, Miranda logged off and said, "Well, Beau, I can't thank you enough."

"No thanks needed. Just sorry you are going through this, Miranda. I really am. But I think you're okay now between this and the patrol cars at night."

She nodded and said, "As my mother says, 'time to pull my big girl panties up.'" Her mother would have handled this with her usual aplomb, Miranda was sure of that. A bit of her mother's moxie would be quite welcome at this point.

Beau gave a chuckle. "Maybe so, maybe so."

"So, I had an interesting conversation with Mr. Blackwell."

"How's that?"

"He told me people around here think I am a witch. But he didn't know who might have started that rumor."

Beau shook his head. "That's terrible. You know the thing about this area being so isolated and all is that folks can get some strange ideas...." He went off on a tangent about the history of the occult in Bisoux and then a long-winded, twisted tale of a historic hanging of a supposed witch.

When he wound down, Miranda asked him point blank, "Do you know any self-proclaimed witches?"

"Well, no, can't say I have met one, specifically."

"So maybe it's just talk, don't you think?"

"Maybe so, maybe so..."

After Beau took his leave, Miranda dug out her ancestry research. It had occurred to her that the answers had to be right in front of her somehow, some way. Maybe especially the answer to why people thought she was a witch.

She shuffled through her notes, almost willing something to pop out at her, some sort of explanation. When she hopped back onto Ancestry.com, she worked on connecting the dots between her ancestors from East Anglia to the Bisoux area. There was a tree branch that was not a direct descendant but rather an eight times back great aunt. The woman had apparently never married and was the last Chesney to remain in Bisoux, the name dying out in the area upon her death. Pinpointing her exact name and dates was eluding Miranda, try as she might.

Something about her circumstance tickled at Miranda's brain. A supposed spinster who was the last of her family. It was reminiscent of Miss Janie, she realized. But what did that have to do with anything?

Several hours later, her hair was standing on end from raking her hands through it, and she was no closer to any kind of answer. As she cracked her neck from one side to the other to relieve the ache that had set in, she caught sight of the framed photograph of her parents placed on one of the bookshelves.

A tinge of guilt crossed through her as she tried to remember when she and her mother had talked last. The thought occurred that there could be the off chance that Millie might remember something pertaining to her father's side. He had not been one for telling old family stories as far as Miranda could recall but maybe, just maybe, Millie might recall some random kernel said in passing.

She punched in her mother's number, waiting while the cell connection made its blips and bleeps to reach over the hundreds of miles to Ottawa, Illinois. She imagined where it would find her mother at that moment. It was late in the afternoon, so Millie might be taking a break with a cup of coffee and a cigarette. A pause in her usual constant-in-motion playbook.

Millie's voice came on the line. "Halloo...is this my long-lost daughter?"

"Hey, Mom. How are you?"

"Better now, getting a call like this out of the blue! What a pleasant surprise!"

"Yeah, yeah...I know." Chagrin filled Miranda's voice. "I need to be better about keeping in touch."

"Well, go ahead and fill me in with all the news."

Miranda began to explain about her recent jaunt through Ancestry.com because of the possible connections between Rosewood and her father's roots while Millie murmured understanding noises on the other end. She wrapped it all up by saying, "So, here's the question. Do you remember anything? Anything at all about Dad's family history?"

Miranda could hear her mother suck in air through her teeth on the other end, which was her habit while in deep thought over something. "Hhhmmm. Let me think."

After some silence, she said, "Nothing pops out straight away, Miranda. Sorry to say."

Miranda felt immediately deflated but then Millie added, "But there is that old photo album of his family still around somewhere. I wouldn't have thrown that away."

"Photo album?"

"Yes. I think I got it up in the attic. After his momma passed, somebody sent it on to us. I guess because Rob was the oldest of the kids."

Miranda frowned. "I don't remember ever seeing anything like that."

"Yeah, well, I think we boxed it up pretty quick and never really looked at it again. I'll try to hunt it down though. So, would it be like real old-timey photographs that might help you out?"

Miranda thought about it for a second realizing the photo album might be another blind alley. On the other hand, she felt a stronger pull towards any connection to her father's past. "Probably. I should take a look at all of them."

Both women fell silent and then started speaking at the same time:

"Anyway..."

"So..."

"You first, Mom."

"You know what I'm going to ask you..."

"What?"

"Same thing I ask every year around this time...can you come out for a visit over the holidays? Especially now that I can lure you back with this photo album." Millie chuckled on saying the last bit.

Miranda's mind flashed to Burt Jones, her mother's second husband. The man her mother had scrambled to find and marry within a year of Miranda's father's death. He was the primary reason Miranda had not been home for the holidays in years. There was history between them that was possibly typical of any stepdaughter and stepfather. A tug of war for Millie's attention had put the both of them in direct opposition of one another, with her mother in the middle. It had eventually led to Miranda's preference of avoiding his company as an adult, even if at the unfortunate expense of missing out on her mother's company.

"Um...well, I've got the house now and..."

"Okay, okay. I'll never stop trying to get you out here at Christmas, though."

"I know, Mom. I'll get back to you about it."

Hanging up, the initial tinge became more of a dousing of guilt. It had been way too long since she had spent time with her mother. It felt like going to another planet to enter Millie's world, a leap and effort too huge. But now, as Millie shrewdly pointed out, there was that photo album in the mix.

Chapter Twenty-two

THE AGE-OLD TRADITION of "reading days" gave students time off to study for exams, making for a peaceful and empty campus with only the occasional student scurrying into study sessions or private cubes in Swem Library. Miranda only had to make the foray into the almost ghost-townish halls of John Lathrop a couple of times over the remainder of the semester. Rosewood was also peaceful and empty. The exception was the last scheduled dig days when Miranda would make herself scarce and head into town. So far, her avoidance strategy was working well.

Between the quiet campus and the quiet Rosewood, Miranda had become lulled into complacency, her lurking anxiety pressed down firmly underneath it all. When the disruption to the peace came in the form of the gentle, chiming ringtone she had set up for the cameras, it took her by the unawares. It was so gentle, in fact, that it took some time to seep into her semi-consciousness. Once fully awake, the slow, icy hand of terror caressed her spine. She grabbed for her cell phone and looked at the time. 4:30 am.

Miranda scrambled to roll over and look at the laptop's open screen that sat by her bedside every evening. Her eyes zoomed into the quadrant that had activity. The chime was blinking on the very bottom right one. That would be the camera on the carriage shed outbuilding, the one with the cat symbol.

The figure in the frame stood still and stared at the direction of the house, boring a hole right into Miranda's face.

Although blurry, it appeared to be Lizzie. Moments ticked by as she waited to see what Lizzie was going to do. Was she going to pull out a blue bottle? Was she going to start a fire?

Enough time went by for Miranda to realize Lizzie wasn't going to do either of those things. In fact, she was just standing still, watching the house. A silent watcher of Rosewood, much like she'd been from the start.

Miranda took action, propelling herself out of her warm bed. After pulling on sweats and a flannel shirt, she headed out the door to greet Lizzie. The cold air rose upon walking outside, a damp, almost bone-chilling cold, from the heavy moisture. As Miranda headed to the rear of Rosewood with flashlight in hand, Lizzie continued to stand statue-like within view. Miranda got close enough to yell out, "Lizzie. It's cold out. Why don't you come inside for a hot drink?"

Closing the gap between them, the light cast by an almost full moon along with Miranda's Maglite revealed the other woman's appearance. Lizzie, visibly shaking, wore a thin hoodie with jeans and Ked sneakers. Rivulets of moisture hung off the tips of her hair.

"You must be frozen. Come on. Let's go inside."

As Lizzie stepped one foot forward, Miranda turned halfway, to make sure Lizzie was following her back to the house the whole way. Once at the door, she stepped back to let Lizzie in first. Lizzie stopped a couple of feet in and seemed stupefied, looking around. Then, she spoke. "It's so different."

"Yeah, I had a lot of work done before I moved in. Do you like it?"

Lizzie puffed some air out and said, "It's not like how Miss Janie had it."

"Well, come on in and have a seat. I'll make some coffee."

Lizzie trailed behind Miranda into the kitchen, standing too close.

"Uh...why don't you have a seat at the table over there? This will only take a moment."

As Miranda set up the coffee filter, her mind frantically pulled at what she needed to ask Lizzie. But where to start without scaring her away? She began with asking her how she liked her coffee.

"Three sugars, lots of milk," Lizzie answered.

Settled at the table with coffees, Miranda tentatively asked her next question. "Lizzie, do you know who told everybody I'm a witch?"

Lizzie stared into her coffee, mute. Miranda was just about to ask another question when Lizzie answered. "You are one, aren't you?"

Miranda shook her head and said in what she hoped was a calm tone, "No. What makes you think I am?"

"It's the love triangle."

"What?"

"Don't you know what a love triangle is?"

"Well, yeah, but what does a love triangle have to do with..."

Lizzie's voice became sing-songy as she looked off to the side saying, "I don't know...I don't know..."

Miranda changed tact. "You've known Fiona your whole life, haven't you?"

The trilling started up in between slurps of coffee.

Miranda prodded again. "Fiona?"

The trilling came to a halt and Lizzie said, without looking at Miranda, "We played doll babies together. All the time."

"Oh, that must have been fun."

A frown came over Lizzie's face. "Fun...until Fiona got mean with them. Real mean."

An image of the dolls hanging off the trees in the copse of woods near Lizzie's house came into Miranda's mind. "How was she mean?"

Lizzie looked at her directly with a confused expression. "Who?"

Miranda stomped out impatience and answered calmly, "Fiona."

"She's not mean...she's fine." With that, Lizzie stood up from the table, clearly finished with the questions. Something was at play underlying the conversation that Miranda couldn't get a handle on. Was Lizzie just being loyal to an old friend? Or was she feeling threatened? By Miranda or by Fiona?

Lizzie began to walk towards the door but turned back. She said offhandedly, "It's tonight. The gathering."

"Really? Where?"

She reached into her jeans pocket and pulled out a folded piece of paper.

"Here." She handed it over to Miranda. "I drew you a map."

Miranda opened it up—it had been folded over many times with dirt marks at the creases.

"Oh, okay. Let me just see if I can..." She unfolded it and took a look down.

It was actually well done, albeit not to scale, with all of the houses on Big Island Road delineated. A big star sat between the Maynard's house and Lizzie's house connecting the two with a trail. The cat symbol lay underneath the star.

"Okay, so this trail leads to a place in the woods and I'll know it by the cat symbol. Like a landmark?"

Lizzie nodded and then said, "But you need to stay hidden. They can't know I told you, okay?" She had a gleam of excitement in her eyes that gave Miranda pause, along with the passing thought that this could be a set up.

"So, what time do you think?"

"When the moon is highest in the sky. You can figure it out."

With that, Lizzie walked out the front door leaving Miranda to gaze after her, map in hand. It seemed Lizzie had made the early morning trip to Rosewood to tell her about the gathering and to give her the map. But why?

Chapter Twenty-three

AS THE DAY UNFURLED, Miranda's thoughts went back and forth about whether she would go traipsing through the woods in the middle of the night to find out more about witch covens in Bisoux. Science had never been her strong suit, but she deduced that "highest in the sky" meant the midnight hour, with confirmation provided by the internet.

In the end, the overarching reason to do it won out in her decision-making process. Miranda knew that she needed to get out in front of all of this and take ownership for a change. It was her house, her dream and her life. Sitting around with a target on her back and waiting for the next attack was no longer an option.

But she needed to ensure all her bases were covered. Someone had to be informed. Beau was the logical choice. He was the only one who might understand. If she told any of her colleagues or friends, they would think she had gone cuckoo crazy. It would have to be Beau. But she didn't want Beau and the missus to miss out on their beauty sleep. That wasn't fair.

She thought hard about what to do and decided to set up an email to be sent the next morning. It laid out a plan that Beau was to call her right away upon receipt. If she did not respond by ten a.m., he should call the sheriff and report her missing. It seemed the fairer option. She didn't want to alarm him with the drama but she would tell him all about it the next day. Whatever it ending up being.

Leaving Rosewood at half past ten o'clock allowed enough time to hike down Big Island Road, find the spot and then lay in wait for the event. She would also avoid the patrol car's ride-by, which she noticed happened typically at half-past eleven. The "gathering" was an event already tinged with a cliché-ish start time that some might even call the witching hour.

Once outside and buttoned up with three layers and heat warmers for hands and feet, Miranda looked back at Rosewood's warm, cozy glow from a few lights she had left on. The house almost seemed alive, its own entity. Her house. But was it really her house or had she usurped it? Was it something that wasn't really hers and couldn't ever really be hers? She really didn't know anymore.

On the road, the light that guided her way was indeed from a full moon, also considered a cold moon based on her earlier internet surfing. As her footfall on the asphalt made a dull, thudding noise, she caught glimpses of it shining with brilliance and a reddish hue. The low temperature, however, quickly began to seep into her layers.

As she wandered down the road at a questionable hour with only a hoot owl and a barking dog in the distance for company, part of her feared that this was a set-up but the bigger part of her needed answers. If it weren't for her destination, she might have allowed herself to enjoy the stillness, the peace, the wide-open space and even the chill in the air. But the idea of what she was doing and where she was going eclipsed all of that.

Six months earlier, before Rosewood had come into her life, the scenario would not have been imaginable. Shaking her head, Miranda thought how life was like that—unexpected happenings and random events strung together that could all lead to an unavoidable intersection. Or maybe barely avoidable.

Miranda had driven by earlier in the day to get a visual in her head of where the trail was. Now, getting near, she flashed her cell to make sure. It revealed the cat symbol on a tree at about her height. Pausing to calm her nerves, she listened through the quiet for any new noises. But all was the same so she began a slow and careful creep into the woods.

The trail was narrow but filled with disturbing shadows

created by the "cold moon" against the sparse December foliage. Five minutes in, the path opened wider. Stopping before the opening in case anyone was there, Miranda could just make out what looked to be stacked logs set up for a campfire beside an ad hoc altar of some sort.

Furtively looking around for a vantage point, she finally settled on an area of dense shrubs to hide under. She worked her way in and under the low hanging branches which snagged her outerwear with a couple of pulls while getting into position.

Miranda settled in for the long haul. A quick assessment had Miranda register that her toes had already started to twinge and her nose felt like an ice cube. Otherwise, the rest of her body felt like it had some good mileage left. She was counting on the feet and hand warmers to stave off getting too numb.

Becoming perfectly still, her brain began to filter all the noises and fine tune what she was hearing. When the loud snaps and crackles of branches and leaves cut in abruptly, her heart began to pound loudly in her ears. Without making any noise of her own, she peered out through the branches to see a hulking figure in dark clothes attempting to move slowly and noiselessly. But he was just too big for that to happen.

Just like Miranda, he approached the center area and then held back. He also seemed to look around for a hiding place. She held her breath hoping he wouldn't zero in on her spot. She had already figured out it was Brian.

He found a place on the other side of the path while Miranda debated about whether to reveal herself to him or hold back until he played his hand. But she knew it was too risky to get out in the open so close now to the midnight hour. Or the witching hour.

Ten more minutes ticked by with agonizing slowness. When the noises began to fill up the woods from a distance, Miranda questioned whether it was really happening or her imagination. Sounds ramped up in intensity as they approached and her heartbeat thumped in her ears. The woods had become loud with encroaching people. Working up the nerve, she adjusted her view to face whatever the gathering was going to be.

One by one, they trooped forward from the path into the center open area. The moon, now highest and brightest in the sky, unveiled all of them.

First was Caro. The dark cape that enveloped her body could not disguise her round form and, in fact, accentuated it making her appear more rotund than she was. She held a largish book out in front of her as she walked forward. Most remarkable was that her hair now hung long, draping down both sides of her face. At the thought that it was off putting, Miranda inwardly checked herself. A woman of a certain age should be allowed to wear her hair as she deemed fit.

Lizzie filed in behind Caro with her head bowed and a cape loosely draped over her shoulders, almost falling off. It took Miranda a moment to place the next woman but then she pinned her down as the sister of Mr. Maynard. Tall and thin, she held a candle in each hand. Behind her, three more women walked down the path but Miranda didn't recognize any of them. All were be-caped and carrying miscellaneous items.

Then, to Miranda's surprise, a young man stepped forward in the line. Staring intently at his hazy visage, his identity finally became clear: Scott, the over-enthusiastic student in Fiona's teaching assistant class and the same guy who offered to help her around Rosewood. This was an interesting twist. Someone Fiona was using as a lackey?

Finally, pulling up from the rear was the last participant, Fiona. She made her approach in a white cape, marking her apart from all the dark be-caped others. She held a tall staff with a round sphere at the top out in front of her. It reminded Miranda of something she had seen in a Catholic mass ceremony that she had attended once.

The small group positioned themselves in a circle around the logs and make-shift altar where the candles had been placed carefully on either side. Caro opened up the book that she held and began to—for lack of a better word—chant. It sounded indecipherable to Miranda's ear.

It went on for a while—too long a while as Miranda's outer extremities went into the achy numb stage. But she ignored it, pumped up on adrenaline and strangely almost eager for what was next.

Without much warning, the proceedings shifted all of sudden with Fiona abruptly thrusting both arms up towards the moon and letting out a string of indistinguishable words. Following Fiona's mumbo jumbo, one of the women unknown to Miranda walked over to the altar, placing an open blue bottle on top of it. Miranda held back an utterance at the sight. So, the blue bottles tied into all this craziness which made it more than probable that this crew, some if not all, were definitely the source of Rosewood's problems.

Each person proceeded one at a time to approach the altar and place something into the bottle. Fiona stood off to the side with her staff-like thing raised slightly above her head as some sort of symbolic gesture to oversee the action. Miranda vacillated between wondering what was going to happen next and incredulity at what already *had* happened.

Fiona began to talk in the gibberish again, and Miranda wasn't able to follow any of it until she heard filtered in her name here and there. She sat back a little more on her increasingly frozen haunches with the realization it was a ceremony focused on her apparently.

Scott had begun to make a fire with the logs as Fiona kept on. Once the fire was fanned into flames, Fiona grabbed the blue bottle and capped it with a cork and then held it high over her head. Miranda realized she was probably witnessing complete cult-like fervor in action at this point. After more strings of gibberish with her name thrown in, including her last name, Chesney, Fiona threw the bottle hard onto the fire resulting in a dramatic pop of shattering glass upon impact. The popping noise reverberated in Miranda's ears long after it was finished.

An hour later, they were all gone. They had cleaned up by putting out the fire and unceremoniously dumping all their accoutrements in a cardboard box, even the fired-up bottle. As they left, carrying everything out with them, Miranda stayed still in the bushes, stiff as she could ever remember being. She waited fifteen minutes more after they left just in case.

Brian had not moved. Now, she had to decide whether to wait for him or come out first. Was he playing her? Could he be hiding to report back to Fiona on Miranda's whereabouts? Was he operating apart from Fiona and she didn't know he was there? Could Miranda trust him? She just didn't know which way was up anymore.

While she tried to sort through the possibilities, Brian pre-empted her by moving out of his hiding spot. She watched as he shook himself off like a dog, shaking off any twigs and leaves. Then he stood on the path with hands on hips, looking directly over at where she was.

"Miranda, I know you're there. Come out now. It's safe."

She felt chagrin wash over and then stopped herself. She wasn't doing anything bad. They were.

She yelled out from her bush cover. "How do I know you aren't in on this crazy town scene?"

He let out a huge audible sigh. "Come on. You know."

She began to untangle herself from the bushes and crawl out from underneath, each muscle, tendon and ligament screaming out in dismay at her physical movement. She couldn't stop the groans from coming out of her mouth. When she finally worked her way up to a hunched-over, standing position in front of him, she said, "How are you not sore?"

"Who said I'm not?"

"Well, you are masking it pretty good bouncing out of your lair like that."

They stared at each other and then it all rolled over Miranda like a breaking wave and she began to laugh hysterically. At first taken aback, Brian then gave in and began to laugh also.

Tears streaming down her face, Miranda finally stood up tall and began to collect herself. "Okay. This is complete, un-hinged insanity going on around here."

"Yeah...it is."

"What was that pole thingy she had?"

"It's called a crozier. Not an easy item to find, I bet. Look...

let's start walking. We need to warm up. I'll walk you back to Rosewood, okay?"

"How'd you get here? How'd you even know about this?"

"Let's just say there might be a spy in their ranks."

"Make that two because Lizzie told me about it."

"Come on. Let's walk."

The moon had become obscured by cloud cover but still allowed enough light to see the path back towards Big Island Road. As Miranda followed behind Brian, she felt safer than when she had walked into the woods. But at the same time, more unsure than ever about Rosewood and what she needed to do.

She asked in the direction of his retreating back, "Why did you come out here after you were told what was happening?"

He turned his head back to give her a quick look and then said as he faced forward again, "I was worried. I thought they might be planning something at Rosewood. With another blue bottle."

"Worried?"

"Yeah. Worried about you."

"You've had a funny way of showing it."

"You'd be surprised."

Once out on the road, they walked side by side. Looking over at him, puffs of air from her breathing matched his, evidence of the intense cold.

"Okay, here's what I don't understand. Aren't the blue bottles supposed to protect the person they are showing up for? Isn't that what the research came up with?" Miranda asked.

He shook his head and then said, "I don't know. I don't know what to think about that anymore."

"Brian, if you think this is dangerous...if you think Fiona is dangerous...shouldn't you do something about it? Alert the authorities? Enact the protocol? Something?"

"Yes...and no. Not yet. Not until she has played her hand."

"What exactly is her hand?"

"I'm still trying to figure that out. But you're going to have to trust that I'm on your side. I always have been. Even if it didn't seem that way."

"Look, I know you have feelings for Fiona but...."

He stopped and took hold of both of her shoulders. "Miranda...that is just not the case. Please, trust me."

She could make out the intensity of his eyes in the available light and began to lose herself in them. Then she shook herself free. "Whatever," she mumbled under her breath.

They went back to walking and he spoke up after a time. "I've been watching the house every night to make sure you're safe. That's how I knew you were in the woods tonight."

"What? No, you haven't," she said. "I would have seen you on the cameras."

"I stay out on the road."

"Why, Brian? This is all so incomprehensible."

"I know...but I just need a little more time. Please."

They stopped with Rosewood within sight. The lights left on radiated a warm, cozy glow outward. Looking that way, Brian changed tack. "You haven't decorated for the holidays yet. No Christmas lights?"

She stared at him with an incredulous look. "You've got to be kidding. Decorations in the middle of all...all..." She waved a hand in the vague direction of the gathering site.

He grimaced. "Yeah, okay. I get it."

They stood in silence. Debating the wisdom of the offer, Miranda spoke finally. "Do you want to come in?"

"Yes, very much. But I can't. There might be watchers."

Miranda closed her eyes. When she opened them, his face was right there and he bent forward to kiss her lips with more gentleness than she could have imagined.

"Trust me."

"Do I have a choice?"

"You always have a choice. I'll stay here until you get inside. I'll wait for a few minutes. If anything is wrong, come back out."

She shook her head, trying to convey all her doubt, confusion and dismay and then turned and walked away up the driveway to her front door.

Chapter Twenty-four

THE CELL RANG, WAKING her up. Blearily looking at the caller's name, she answered, "Hey, Beau."

"What's all this top-secret stuff, Miranda? I feel like I'm on
some kind of spy show."

Miranda debated with herself on how much detail to go
into, but weariness overtook all else. Keeping it simple, she said,
"I'll tell you all about it when we see each other...but thanks for
checking in. I'm fine, at least for now."

"Uh-oh. I don't like the sound of that."

"Yeah. I may have to make some changes."

"All right. Well, look...I had a thought about us looking for
that secret way into the house."

"What's that?"

"We forgot to check out the crawl space."

"Crawl space?"

"Yes, ma'am. You remember during the home inspection
that tight space underneath part of the kitchen and the pantry?"

Miranda smacked her forehead and said, "Yes. Now I do."

"Yeah, I blame myself for forgetting about it. I don't know
where my head was that day when we went to the cellar...not
firing on all cylinders, I guess. I mean, it's not all that big of a
space but next time, we'll get on it."

"Not your fault, Beau. Yes, good plan. We'll talk soon."

Ending the call, the tug for more slumber pulled at Miranda
but all the thoughts began to crowd in, winning the battle instead. Her mind replayed the mysterious gathering, play by
play. She ended up analyzing Brian's role once again, second

guessing whether she could trust him or not. Finally, she settled back on that tender kiss which had both tantalized and comforted at the same time. What was his game? There was no more word from him since then—at all. But that seemed to be a part of whatever this all was. Whatever it was he was working to figure out.

Now, on top of all of it, was apprehension about the crawl space and what might be lurking under there. She sat up with a jerk. Moving forward with a purpose was what she needed to do, propelling herself into a hot shower.

Once settled in the living room, she took some comfort in the beautiful space she had created at Rosewood while at the same time purposely ignoring the crawl space area. The comfort was mixed with a pang of doubt that crept in. There were still a lot of things to straighten out at Rosewood. And it was all on her to do so.

With a heavy sigh, Miranda reached down next to the sofa and hauled up the box that now held all her research efforts to date. Spreading it all out on the coffee table, she knew she could figure it out. There had to be an answer in it somewhere.

Squeezing her eyes tightly, she opened them back up with another big sigh. First, she would pin down the elusive ancestor who had settled in the area, the one who gave her the thread to the place. Her earlier digging revealed it to be not a direct ancestor, but rather a cousin line via a great aunt. It had to be bound up in that somehow, whatever it was.

Picking up the research trail where she had left it, she drilled down into miscellaneous family trees that other people had configured. Again, it was an exercise in sorting out the well-researched ones over those just thrown together without validation. After an hour of mental gymnastics maneuvering among a fair number of the trees, Miranda sat back with a huff of satisfaction, fairly certain she had found her gal. Her name was Prudence Chesney.

The kitten interrupted her musings and looked up at her, meowing. Taking a break and dangling a wire toy Polly's way, she absentmindedly watched the cat's antics, mostly focused on where to go next with Prudence.

Walking around the house, Miranda looked out the kitchen window with some trepidation, gun shy that she would see something, or someone. But all was still and beautiful with the frozen morning dew still hanging on the tree branches. She didn't want to be driven out of this place. Despite everything, it was still her little slice of hard-earned paradise.

Determined, she got back into the research and dug deeper into finding more about Prudence. Upon finding a startling reference with the word, "witch," Miranda gasped out loud. Prudence had made a name for herself back in her day, the 1600s—because she had been accused of witchcraft.

Several articles later, Miranda discovered that the state of Virginia, while no match for New England, apparently had a healthy fear of witches during its earliest colonial period. Witches were pursued to various degrees and Miranda's distant ancestor had been one of them.

Pushing down further and further into the records, Miranda hit paydirt in finding an obscure reference to an article in an old Virginia Historical Society journal from the early 1900s. Using her William and Mary account to open it, she began to read the article. Her heart began to flutter as she realized that it was her "Ah-Ha" moment, tracking down the almost unbelievable tale of Prudence Chesney.

The original trial record had been rolled into the journal article:

"Prudence Chesney, spinster, living on her father's estate, 'Chesney's Hold,' is hereby accused of the crime of witchcraft and stands in front of this court of Gloucester in the great state of Virginie. Spinster Chesney has waged nefarious intentions against her neighbors in the surrounding properties of 'Chesney's Hold' to include placing a pox on crops, provoking illness in babies and causing strife between another and her betrothed. Spinster Chesney has long been under suspicion and afeared by her neighbors with her left-handed dominance and the mark of Satan on her visage. Her fine is the payment of one hundred pounds of tobacco to this court and thirty-five whip lashings in accordance

with the number of her years on this earth."

Miranda had to keep re-reading each word to digest the meaning. Once satisfied, she moved onto the remainder of the article which analyzed the trial record details. She dropped her pencil upon reading a big reveal, eyes opening wide. In all probability, Spinster Prudence Chesney had lived somewhere on Polly's Creek but the house no longer stood.

Looking up from the article and blinking several times, the wheels in her brain moved around. So, this meant that Prudence's house had been somewhere around Rosewood, but where? Could it be a part of one of the existing houses, maybe hidden inside one of them? Beau had mentioned that add-ons happened as good fortune allowed. Could it be hidden in Rosewood? A weird, creeping sensation came over her at the thought.

Bracing herself to read more revelations, her eyes went back to her laptop. The writer claimed that the "mark of Satan" was possibly a port-wine birthmark stain. In early days, birthmarks like that were considered the Devil's handiwork. Women who had them were seldom able to find suitors for marriage contracts. Added to that, left-handedness was also thought to be an abnormality associated with the Devil.

It was pretty intense stuff: a relative, albeit distant, stamped a witch due to her physical characteristics. Making her way over to the kitchen, Miranda picked up an unopened bottle of local rye whiskey, a house warming present from a colleague. After pouring a stiff shot, not caring about the time of day or her empty stomach, she downed it.

Miranda stared down into the empty jam glass at the residue of amber liquor, pondering over these findings and their meaning. It dawned on her that this really did not answer any questions but, rather, set up a slew of new ones. Mainly, where did she and Prudence connect?

The whiskey sloshed around in her stomach, a reminder that she hadn't eaten. She threw some pasta and sauce together and gobbled it down. Hastily cleaning up, she got back down to it, in too deep to stop.

Several hours later, as the late afternoon sun cast a rosy hue of light into the room, she knew more. If Prudence and her family had not settled in the Tidewater region, it was highly likely that Miranda's line would have never made it over to America. In fact, as Miranda stared down at her hands, she considered the possibility that she wouldn't even be there in her current form anyways. Maybe another form? A bee? A cat? It was nonsensical, yet here she was entertaining the idea.

Typing up her notes, she reviewed it all again:

Prudence was an herbalist and a healer. People in the neighborhood called upon her in times of crisis. And it sounded like she came through using herbs and maybe just a healing touch.

She was also an early feminist, it seemed, as she ran a tavern on her father's estate. So, she was a business owner at a time when women were not allowed to own anything.

She sponsored family back in England to come over to America, paying for their passage and helping them once they were over. So, an early supporter of immigration rights too.

Lastly, it was quite possible Prudence was able to achieve all this for the exact reasons that she was sent to trial: she wasn't messed around with because of her birthmark and the superstitions of the time. So, an early superhero.

It struck Miranda that Prudence's tale was a scholarly paper in the making, maybe even a book written by someone. Maybe that someone was her? There were more questions: where had this lady's home and tavern been located? Somewhere on Polly's Creek, but where exactly? Mentally and physically, she needed to step out of it for a bit. Looking out the window, she saw enough daylight left for a quick walk.

It didn't register until her feet started taking her there that she headed back to the site of the gathering night, feeling the compelling need to eyeball it in the light of day. Big Island Road was vastly different in the daylight. Miranda relished that she still had the road to herself, peaceful and silent so, in some ways, the same.

Just like the previous night, the nerves in her digestive tract brought another layer to it. It felt almost as though she was going back to the scene of a crime. But what crime, if any, had been committed? It had been appalling and freakish but, when she broke it down, there had been no wrongdoing exacted. Really, it had been more childish games than anything else. In fact, Miranda didn't even know if it would merit reporting to the sheriff or not, especially given his cavalier tendencies about all of it. Would this new wrinkle even register in his book?

Getting to the break in the woods, she verified the trail by the cat symbol on the tree. It was strangely comforting now that she knew its meaning. Or what she had assumed the meaning to be, if her research was right. Entering the woods, she patted her jacket pocket making sure her cell was handy, uneasy no one knew her current whereabouts. But there was still plenty of light.

Within a few minutes, the path opened up into the clearing. Evidence of the previous evening's activities was minimal, the only remnant left being some ash on the ground near where the campfire had been. Rubbing it with her booted toe, she thought about what she expected to find here. More answers? More questions?

Poking around some more, Miranda examined every stitch of the ground just in case with her eyes tracing over the fallen leaves and pine needles beneath her. She drew to a stop at an unnaturally straight line stuck out under a large brown leaf. She nudged the leaf gently aside with her boot. A gasp escaped from her at what it exposed. A photograph. A photograph of herself.

Her nerves buzzed into overdrive as she fixated on the photo, staring down at it for some moments. It was from one of the photo albums that lined up in her bookcase. She had not had any reason to look through them of late. Someone had come in and taken it out, maybe others taken out as well, either while she was gone during the day or, in the cover of darkness while she slept unwittingly above in her bedroom. Her heart began to bang in her chest over both possibilities, both bad but one worse, in her mind, than the other.

Finally, she squatted down and picked it up between her gloved thumb and forefinger. Holding it up to the light, she saw that part of it had been burned at the edges. A black marker had been used to cross an x through her body, but her face was the worst. A careful effort had been made to burn just where her eyes were, so they were like holes. The rest of her face was marked up as though raked with knife slashes. A massacre of her face.

The photo was taken during her time in England. She had been standing on the edge of cliffs in Cornwall. Her boyfriend at the time, Mark had been his name, had captured an expression on her face that was somewhere between bemused and questioning. She had taken full advantage of her time there during her two-year stint at Oxford, traveling as much as possible, loving every nook and cranny of England. To be saccharine about it, she had felt a spiritual pull for the place which now made sense given what she was learning about her ancestry.

Her knees began to complain in her squatted stance so she stood up slowly with the photo still held between her fingers. Taking in a deep breath, she gazed around at the benign tranquility of the Bisoux woods, so at odds with the ravaged photo she held. She didn't know what it was she was holding or if it was evidence of a crime but the sheriff's office was her next stop. Miranda also knew: she would not be able to spend another night at Rosewood.

At the Motel 6 room later, she placed a call to Ottawa, Illinois. After finding the sabotaged photo of herself, she had thrown a bunch of things in the car and headed right back to the motel with Polly. Looking in the rearview mirror at Rosewood in the early dusk of the evening, an all-encompassing bereft feeling came over her at leaving her house for who knew how long.

On the phone, her mother gave a chirpy "hello," and

Miranda said, "Mom, I'm taking you up on that offer for the holidays if it still stands."

Her mother cleared her throat. "Knock me over with a feather. What changed your mind?"

"Just..." Miranda's brain spun around all that had changed her mind and decided to save it for a conversation at a later date. Instead, she answered, "It's been too long. But I have a cat now, so if that's an issue..."

Her mother harrumphed and then said, "Well, if a package deal is what it takes to get you out here, sure. But Burt is allergic so we'll just keep the kitty away in the mudroom. How about that?"

"That's fine." Miranda thought about how she could keep away from Burt somehow, too. They firmed up more details with Miranda giving a vague time frame for staying until after New Year's.

Then Miranda added, "By the way, did you have any luck finding that photo album?"

"It's sitting right here on my coffee table in front of me."

"Perfect." Despite the travesty at Rosewood, she felt the stirrings of excitement at getting her mitts on that photo album.

Part Two
Chapter Twenty-five

SITTING ON A STIFF, floral printed couch, Miranda waited for her mother to join her before opening up the bulky photo album with the ugly brown cover that lay on her lap. She reflected back on the events that had brought her to this place, a 1970s ranch tract home in a small town sixty miles west of Chicago in the cold and bitter Midwest.

A loose plan had come together once settled at the motel. She could finish grading coursework and exams on the road or wherever she ended up, which had led to the idea of visiting her mother for the holiday.

She had called Beau for the big ask of keeping an eye on the place, made easier by giving him the remote access code. Since he still had a key, he could also enter the house whenever necessary. While sparing him the particulars, it was left that she was spending time with her mother out in Illinois. He didn't need her full load of worries on his shoulders.

The next morning, she headed out early making one stop: the sheriff's office. As she walked into his office, barely taking in the fake greenery festooned around the doorframe, annoyance had flitted over Billy Sanford's face—the now familiar "not wanting to deal with her again" look of bland irritation that she had grown to expect out of him. "I'm heading out of town," Miranda said, without preamble.

"Alrighty. We'll still patrol the place. Keep it safe while you're gone."

She thought about spilling it out quickly, with no preemptive words. "So, there was a meeting in the woods. A gathering of about four women and one man. They had a ceremony involving a blue bottle that they filled up with God knows what. Then they threw it in a fire and left a calling card behind." But she didn't.

Instead, throwing the photo down on the desk, she said, "I found this in the woods. Looks like there had been a recent campfire there too."

His usual imperturbable expression cracked just a little as he looked down at the photo before clearing his throat. Reaching into a drawer, he pulled out latex gloves and snapped them on. Picking out the photo from the plastic baggie she had placed it in, he stared at it. Sanford looked back up at her, cleared his throat, and said, "Well...we'll get this dusted for prints. You need to give your prints on the way out."

"I had gloves on the whole time. And then I put it in that plastic baggie."

He nodded and said, "All right, then."

"You have my cell if you need it." She turned on her heel but then swiveled back. "By the way, did you talk to Mr. Woods yet?"

"Nah. Too busy around here. Never got a chance."

After dumping it into his lap, Miranda left without a backwards glance. Sanford didn't want to deal with any issues in his county, but this was on him now.

Leaving Sanford's office, the fifteen-hour drive into the flat, mindless territory of the middle of the country began and Miranda had let her mind go over and over the ramifications of all of it: staying, leaving...

Noises from the kitchen filtered in as Millie bustled about in her whirlwind fashion, making coffee. While waiting, Miranda gazed around the room. Knotty pine walls were filled with shelves that held all manner of collectibles. Thick and nubby wall-to-wall carpet spread across the floor in a sea of turquoise-green. The baseboard heat that ran along the room's edge pumped out so much hot air that sweat accumulated under her armpits. It was all so very different from the smooth, crisp and cool lines of Rosewood. But then, she wasn't at Rosewood anymore.

In short order, Millie walked in holding two steaming mugs. "Phew, it's cold out there today. This should take the chill off." Handing one of the mugs over, she plopped down on the couch a little too close to Miranda.

Millie Jones, a petite woman, had always maintained her figure and prided herself on her appearance. Even now that she was older, nothing had changed. Dyed black hair, the same color it had always been, was arranged into a precise hair helmet with nary a root showing. Heavy layers of mascara lent her a perpetual wide-eyed gaze.

The whole package hung on tightly to her younger years. That was who she was. The only hint otherwise was the crow's feet edging in around her eyes which mascara could not disguise fully. Nor could the wrinkles in the space above her upper lip stay hidden as she beamed a bright smile in Miranda's direction.

Leaning away just a little from her mother, Miranda took some grateful sips from the mug. She needed the jolt of caffeine after her late night. Due to the delayed start getting on the road, she had rolled into the slumbering burg in the wee hours. Now, seated on the uncomfortable sofa in the overheated room in Ottawa, Illinois, what had seemed like a good idea at the time now felt like it was not so much. The good news was that Burt had already left the house, so she had not seen him yet. Small mercies.

"So..." Millie reached over with her brightly painted fingernails decorated with Christmas trees to tug at the photo album, but Miranda held tight to it.

With some exasperation, Millie said, "Come on. Let's open it up and take a look-see."

A part of Miranda wanted to hold off from opening it as long as possible. Once opened, the opportunity to find out more would be gone. It was this in between phase with it jealously guarded on her lap that kept her hopeful. When she could put it off no longer under her mother's pointed stare, she opened up the cover.

Sepia toned photographs were positioned in a symmetrical fashion and fastened with black corner tabs. She immediately recognized her dad as a youngster among a group of other youngsters. "There he is. That's your dad with his siblings," Millie said, verifying Miranda's recognition.

Moving on to the next pages, the photo album appeared to be a collection of her father's family life. Her mother began to pepper commentary throughout every page. It was difficult to focus while Millie made her comments. "Oh, look how thin Martha was at that age!" and "His mother with her pearls. She was never without," and "They did have a grand old house down in Carbondale, didn't they?"

There was a progression as the kids grew up that included lots of Christmas scenes, some high school graduations and, finally, male family members leaving for military service appointments. Reaching the last page, they found an older looking photo with a different tint of an elderly couple that Miranda had never seen.

"Who are they?" she said aloud.

Her mother screwed up her face. "Maybe grandparents? Pull it out and see if anything is on the back."

Miranda carefully lifted the photo out of the corner tabs and held the paper-thin photo between her fingers. Turning it over, there was no identifying information on the back.

Placing it back, Miranda then closed the album softly, disappointment seeping through. A sigh escaped from her mouth. "Not what I had hoped for."

Her mother gave her a pat on the shoulder. "Oh well, you'll figure it out."

Setting the album on the coffee table, Miranda sat back and rubbed her forefinger over a pattern of flowers that made a long line from one end of the cushion to the other. Questions about her father were a touchy territory but Miranda was at the point of not caring about touchy. She needed to probe her mother's memory. "So, did Dad ever talk about his...people?"

"People?" Her mother looked at her with a perplexed expression.

"Like if he knew his grandparents and great grandparents...and where they all came from."

"You mean his roots?"

"Yes," Miranda said. "His roots."

Millie's mouth moved into a frown as she shook her head. Then she said, "His mother was such a snob. You probably don't remember that. She passed when you were just little."

"Why a snob?

"Oh, pompous ideas about where she was from and who her folks were. That kind of thing..."

"Really? Who did she think her people were?"

Her mother lit up a cigarette and stared down at its end. "I can't really remember. It never interested me to tell you the truth." The space between them filled with silence as cigarette smoke wafted Miranda's way.

"Tell me more about where you live. I'd love to go to Williamsburg. You know how I love colonial furniture." With the change of subject, it was clear Millie didn't want to talk about Miranda's father anymore.

Miranda's gaze wandered around the room, taking in her mother's unique style that barely flirted with "colonial" and said, "Uh, yeah. I guess I do."

"When the weather gets nice, how about I come down and stay with you?"

"What about Burt?"

"He won't be interested."

"Well, can you leave him like that?" Miranda had thought her mother and stepfather had been attached at the hip all these years, which was why it was so hard to be around.

"Sure. He goes on hunting trips with his buddies all the time." It seemed that there was more to that than Millie was willing to say. Instead, she added, "Plus, I'd love to see your new house. Just imagine a girl of mine buying her own place like that. I'm proud of you!"

"Yeah, about my house...I don't know if I will be able to... stay there.

"Oh, honey. Are you in over your head financially?"

"No, not that. I mean, it's tight but not that."

"Well, what is it then?"

Miranda hesitated, unsure of whether to confide in her mother. It would sound so off the wall because, well, it *was* off the wall. And she didn't want to worry her.

Pressing in on Miranda's hesitation, Millie added, "You know you can tell me anything, don't you?"

"Okay, this is kind of a strange story but here goes..." Sorting it out in her head as she told it, the tale rolled out from start to finish. Millie did not interrupt even once as Miranda worked her way through the whole thing. Finally, it ended with the burnt photograph and she finished it up saying, "I dumped it off the sheriff's office, not that I have any faith he'll do much. So...what do you make of all of it?"

Her mother swallowed the dregs in her coffee mug first. "It's obvious what this is, Miranda," she said.

"It is?"

"Sure. This is just a simple case of mean girl stuff. You know like that movie that was out years ago? With Lindsey Lohan? Mean girls are always a thing, no matter how old you get to be."

Miranda leaned back in her chair taking in what her mother had said. Millie's observation was fairly astute. Was it as simple as that?

"So, the mean girl is..."

Her mother gave her a duh look and then said, "Well, that Fiona of course. Geez, you've been too long in the ivory tower, I think. This is pretty basic, hon."

"What does one do in a mean girl situation?"

Her mother gave a big belly laugh. "You mean, this is your first rodeo with a mean girl? Sweetie, I'll tell you exactly what to do."

Millie began to spin out the story of a girl named Cindy Baker at Ottawa High and her posse of right-hand gals who took it upon themselves to dress and act in accordance with Cindy's lead. Millie herself had watched from the sidelines maintaining a diplomatic distance from all the drama.

As her mother continued to go into incredible recall of the machinations of these "mean girls," Miranda started to lose the thread and let her mind wander from the one-sided conversation. Finally, Millie wrapped it all up with a tidy metaphorical bow and said, "You see, Miranda. All you have to do is identify them for what they are and then just stay the heck out of their way."

Miranda tuned in to this supposed sage advice. "Well, I was smack dab in the middle of the way. That apparently was the problem."

Afterwards, Miranda mulled it around in her head, seeing if she could connect the dots to all that had gone on to date. Could it really be down to Fiona just being a mean girl, or was it something far more sinister?

Chapter Twenty-six

THE WALLS OF HER mother's house closed in on Miranda between the weird vacuum of time between Christmas and New Year's Day. One and a half days in, and they'd already started to grate on each other. As always, when Miranda spent any time with her mother, she was completely baffled that they were related. They were just so different and, now that Miranda was in her thirties, the differences were even harder to process, not easier.

One morning, she interrupted Millie in the kitchen leaning over Polly with a plastic spoon in hand feeding her something white and globular. Polly looked up, mewed plaintively at Miranda and then went right back to licking the spoon.

"Mom." Miranda heard the grating irritation in her voice as she spoke.

"Good morning! What's the story, morning glory?"

"What are you feeding her?"

"Oh, it's just a bit of coconut oil."

"What? Why?" Alarm at Millie doing this to Polly set in.

"I had some on my hands and she started licking it, so I thought maybe she needs it in her diet."

When Miranda let out an audible groan, Millie added, "She's fine, Miranda. Stop fretting. Remember that old saw about cats and nine lives?"

Miranda made a mental note to check into cats and coconut oil later. She tried to focus on the positives of her mother taking an interest in Polly, mostly confined to the mudroom due to Burt's allergies.

Her mother stood up, brushing off her hands. "So, how about we head to town later?"

"Okay, that sounds...yeah, okay." Since this was Millie's hometown not Miranda's, she didn't have any particular pull for it. But Millie liked for them to wander around so she could show off all the usual haunts of her childhood and teen years. Miranda had already seen it all before but humored Millie. It seemed important to her.

Driving into town in Millie's Bronco, bundled up good for the breath-taking cold, the scenery had not changed a whit from Miranda's last memory of it. Parking near the town square, they got out and began to walk past the imposing sandstone court-house squat in the middle as the centerpiece, overshadowing all around it. Too big for a small town in Miranda's estimation. A few other brave souls were out in the cold walking in and around the still viable concern that housed court doings as the county seat, prone to the usual amount of traffic for its business.

On their way to their destination, the LaSalle Diner, they passed by storefronts that included businesses like the Posey Flower Shoppe, the hardware store and, strangely, a running store. Millie kept up a scattered commentary pointing out changes—changes that Miranda would have never noticed. This was her mother's entire world, so the changes were huge in her eyes.

Broad Street, Ottawa's version of Main Street, was a mix of mostly dark colored buildings of brick or concrete block. Eventually, they were in front of the diner. The bells jangled when they walked in and customers looked over their way, some waving a hand at Millie.

The hostess, who appeared to be around the same vintage as Millie, yelled over, "Hey, girl. Just grab a table wherever you like."

Making their way to a corner booth, Millie said out of the side of her mouth, "Susie and I went to high school together. Can you believe it?" Miranda gave a nod, thinking she had no problem believing it at all, small towns being what they were, and Susie's obvious comfort level with calling Millie, "girl."

Once seated, Millie segued into a story about high school and mascots. Miranda stared out the plate glass window next to her, sparkling clear as though just cleaned, at the sleepy street scene beyond. The bright winter sun bounced off the windows across the street giving off a 1940s Edward Hopper painting feel. The place was a time capsule really of a different America. She contrasted it in her head to Rosewood and Bisoux, which seemed like a different country altogether.

Her mother's voice then broke into her thoughts: "...did you hear what I just said, Miranda?"

Pulled back into the conversation, Miranda said, "Yes. Mascots at the high school. Good times."

Her mother beamed. "The best. Which reminds me. We haven't gone over there yet so I can show you the renovations they did."

They finished up at the LaSalle after polishing off their trademark cheeseburger and fries. Strolling back, Miranda suggested they walk down to the river, two blocks away from the diner. Once there, they stared down into its churning waters, fresh from a recent temporary thaw of winter snow and ice.

Miranda finally turned to Millie. "Mom...I think it's time now. Can we head up there?" she asked.

Millie looked back to the river for a moment. "Sure. Sure, we can do that."

Back in the Bronco, Millie cranked up the heat and they headed north out of town across the river. Up the hill at the ridgeline was where the town cemetery was situated and where Miranda's father was buried. Only a minute's long drive from town, the out of the way locale left the small-town hustle and bustle behind.

It was an effort to get out of the Bronco with its nice, comforting heat and walk over to the gravestone. Slamming the car door, the cold seeped back into Miranda's bones within seconds. His grave was in the corner that had a direct view of the river far below.

Standing side by side, they both looked down at it in silence. The only exception to the quiet was the wind's whistle in a few straggler trees along the ridgeline. The chill sank into her very bones and Miranda shivered, not just from the cold.

His stone read:

Robert Walter Chesney
Husband and Father
1955-2005
Gone but not forgotten

It all came flooding back because...how could it not? Miranda was already well into her teens when her father died. At the point where kids work hard at freeing themselves from their parents. She had been doing that, too, but she never wanted to do it in this particular way, a forever parting.

Her dad hadn't been perfect, she knew that. But he had been pretty good. Solid, dependable, reliable, and accountable which she knew was more than many experienced in a father.

She so wished he was still there to confide in late at night when he reclined in his La-Z-Boy, smoking endless cigarettes and watching the late shows. That was their time, time that was just theirs apart from Millie. Really, it was when Miranda felt closest to him. He had been there for her but not in the typical ways other fathers were. His was more of a steady presence, background kind of style of fatherhood. She missed it even now well into her thirties. Actually, especially now.

In the afternoon, they sat at the kitchen table and drank yet more coffee. Miranda idly perused through the photo album yet again while her mother prattled on, as was her tendency. Burt made a brief appearance but took off again. She knew that he didn't like her company any more than she liked his.

Miranda stopped on one page taking a closer look at a photo that was slightly off set. She prodded it gently and, as she did so, the edges of another photo slid out and escaped. Her breath caught. "Mom, isn't that you?"

Millie stopped what she was saying. "What?"

"There's another photo we didn't see before. Look at this."

The two of them crowded over it, their heads almost touching. Miranda pointed to a very young version of her mother seated closely to a very young version of her father. They appeared to be at a family gathering in the formal living room in someone's house.

Her mother took the photo and brought it close to her face. "Oh my. I had forgotten about this."

Impatiently, Miranda said, "What's 'this'?"

Millie looked up from the photo, a faraway look in her eyes. "We visited this distant cousin of Rob's once. We were still technically honeymooners, really. You know, when you are so into each other in those early days that you aren't really paying attention to anything else around you...oh...maybe you don't know..."

Miranda folded her arms in annoyance. "I have had relationships before, Mom. You do realize that?"

"I didn't mean to say—"

Miranda cut her off and prodded her. "Anyway..."

"Oh, yes. I didn't pay a whole lot of attention but this cousin had a beautiful old house, grand really, in this little town on the banks of the Mississippi. The name of the town escapes me right now, but it'll come to me."

"Well, who was it? What happened to them?"

"No idea but you know, now that I see this photo..." Millie's finger hovered over the photo and then pinned it on one person. "Right here, this lady. This was the cousin."

Miranda took her in, a petite woman elegantly dressed with a chin-length bob hairdo. "What was her name? Do you remember?"

"That was easily thirty-five years ago...it might come to me. Give it a moment."

"I wonder if she's still there." Miranda looked on the back for any marks but, just like the others, there was no identifying information. "Well, if she was forty or so then..."

"That's a big if," Millie said.

"She could be in her seventies or eighties now. Maybe?"

Miranda's gaze beamed down on the photo, willing it to divulge its secrets. After a bit, it registered that her mother had stopped talking and Miranda looked over at her. She had her chin in one hand and was gazing out the window.

"Mom?"

Millie straightened up and said, "Her name was Emily Clark. And the town was Keokuk."

Miranda reached over and gave her mother a fist bump. "Good job, Mom."

"It just popped in my head. Emily. Keokuk. I think it's in Iowa but almost on the state line of Missouri." She had pronounced Missouri like Missour'a as was a tendency in the Midwest.

Distracted for a moment, Miranda asked, "Why do people say 'Missour'a' instead of 'Missouri'?"

Her mother shrugged and said, "Beats me. It's the way I always heard it. Anyway, I think the town is almost in three states...Iowa, Missouri and Illinois. Maybe its claim to fame."

"Huh." Miranda's mind went to poking around Keokuk, Iowa, and finding what had happened to this relative, Emily.

Later, Millie loomed behind Miranda as she was fiddling with her ancestry tree. "Is that the tree you were talking about? Why are you so hell-bent to sort through this stuff? What are you thinking you'll find out?"

Miranda looked up from the computer screen and stared at the window, feeling her mother's nervous energy behind her. "I don't know." Her gaze wandered towards a bird in a feeder. "I guess I am getting a little obsessed."

"I'd say so. Especially since I can't figure out how it's going to get you ahead at all."

"Get me ahead? Probably won't do that...." But privately, Miranda wondered if it was more about staying behind than moving ahead.

For New Year's Eve, her mother walked out of her bedroom

decked out in holiday colors. Her form fitting knit sweater tied into the season with a jingle bell motif. Little Christmas bulb earrings lit up as she swung her head. Burt, not to be outdone, strolled into the room with a leather vest over his usual flannel for the event.

They both looked expectantly at Miranda sitting on the couch. They eyed up her outfit, her customary jeans with a cowl neck sweater, at the same time. Miranda had the niggling sensation that they might be setting her up to meet a local boy.

"What?"

Her mother immediately sidestepped it by saying, "Nothing. All set?" She plastered a brilliant smile on her face.

If Miranda had ever been curious about what would be on offer for New Year's traditions in small town America, she was finding out in an Elk's Lodge in the middle of America which was quite likely the same as an Elk's Lodge anywhere in the country. The main room of the lodge with its low drop-tiled ceiling, dark paneled walls and beige floor tiles had been made festive with Happy New Year banners and tinsel strands strewn from one side to the other and weaved around the entire room.

As the evening set in, Millie lit from table to table, hands on shoulders giving a squeeze before moving to the next table. It seemed she knew everyone in the room. At first, she dragged Miranda along with her, but Miranda had stuck her heels in and now stood off to one side. Burt also made the rounds in a lesser way. He maintained his place at the bar, glad-handing his way down from one person to the next.

Miranda held back a chuckle at the thought that maybe Millie and Burt Jones were one of Ottawa's power couples. They did work the room separately, however. In fact, she was beginning to realize she did not see them side by side all night and she pocketed that away to think on later.

Miranda began to feel invisible as the evening progressed, as if a ghost taking it all in from the corners. The room faded out and her mind turned to Brian. She wondered where he was and what he was doing. Earlier in the week, she had thought about texting him something lame like happy holidays or happy new year. But she had put it aside. Whatever he was involved with was just not something she could get in the middle of. That much was clear even if the rest of it was a muddle.

A barrel-chested gentleman came up and stood too close, interrupting thoughts of Brian. "Hey, missy. You by your lonesome over here?"

As he loomed into her face, Miranda took a step over to the side and said, "Nope. I'm with someone. How about you?"

"Wait a minute. I know who you are! You're a dead ringer for her. Surprised I didn't see it right from the first."

"I am?"

"Sure. You're Millie's girl."

"You think I look like her?"

He gave a snort. "Like a carbon copy, I'd say."

Miranda's gaze went over to where her mother stood. A half foot shorter than her, different hair color and no similar facial features.

"Well, I am Millie's daughter but..."

"She's mighty proud of you. Talks about you all the time."

"She does?"

"Sure. I probably know more about you than you know about yourself." The man gave her a hard pat on the shoulder and headed off to his next pursuit. Miranda looked back over at her mother, bemused by both the thought that she might look like her and also that she talked about her a lot.

Miranda had not realized so much of the evening had passed and was startled when someone walked by and blew a loud noisemaker in her face saying, "The countdown is going to start soon!" When it got down to the last ten seconds, the whole room of people began to scream it out together. "Ten... nine... eight...!" and then, at the stroke of midnight, helium balloons were released and filled up the entire space with the room cheering, the merriment fueled and amplified by the many hours of drinking.

As Miranda took it all in, she realized that this diversion from her life had gone on long enough. This wasn't her place and these weren't her people—with the exception of her mother. Genetically-speaking, anyway. She needed to get back and figure out exactly her place and her people.

During breakfast on New Year's Day, Miranda announced she was leaving the next morning. Millie looked at her, her expression tinged with dismay. "You can't stay any longer?"

"Mom, it's after New Year's. I need to hit the road to get back to Virginia. Classes start up in a few days."

"I know...it's just been such fun having you here." She leaned back into her chair and eyed Miranda critically. "You're stopping by that cousin's house, aren't you?"

"Yeah. I am."

"What do you think you're going to find?"

"I don't know. I don't know at all. I'm just trying to pull it all together."

"Miranda, what if there's nothing to pull together?"

"What if there is?"

They stared each other down for a long moment. Millie then broke it off and said, "So what are you going to do about Rosewood?"

"Still haven't decided yet."

"Don't let those mean girls bully you out of there. You've put too much blood, sweat and tears in the place, you hear?"

"Yep. And remember it's your turn next. You'll come out to visit me?"

"You betcha."

Chapter Twenty-seven

MIRANDA CALCULATED A HALF day's drive to Keokuk heading in a southwesterly direction. A green light for clear weather meant no worries of snow in the forecast to contend with. She had already identified the house and, as best she could pin down, Emily Clark, her newly found cousin, still lived there. She had not been able to get a hold of her on the phone, so she would wing it once in Keokuk.

Waving goodbye to her mother in her rearview mirror, she felt a stab of something. Maybe it was nostalgia for when it had been the three of them: her mom, her dad, and her. She had locked that away, deep inside, though it would still peek out at times.

Or maybe it was a pang totally unrelated to her mother and father. Maybe it was worry over Millie's personal situation with Burt. She ruminated over whether Millie was happy with Burt. Did it matter? What did Miranda know about long-lived marriages and how people who stayed together for years and years felt?

It took about an hour into the drive before her mind could settle down and leave thoughts of the past and parents aside. The empty, open road gave her a feeling of release, a weight that lifted off her. Miranda started to get excited at the prospect of meeting an obscure relative whom she never knew about.

In her research, she pinned Emily Clark down in her ever-expanding Ancestry.com family tree. Emily was her dad's first cousin twice removed, making the connection between Miranda and her first cousin thrice removed. Or maybe it was a second cousin once removed. Whatever the semantics of their connection, Miranda fervently hoped that Emily was still living in the house.

Several hours later, the rural landscape swapped out from countryside to town in that all-of-a-sudden kind of way common in farming communities. It was a minimal and gradual buildup, just an immediate line separating town and country. The rural numbered road became Main Street and she followed it into the heart of Keokuk. As the town filled in, it seemed fairly lively with small shops not outsourced to big box strips somewhere else.

Using Google maps, Miranda found the right turn off Main Street towards the river. She entered a residential street populated by a variety of large Victorian era homes situated on largish-sized lots. Squinting to read the house numbers, she finally found 3000 Riverside Terrace and pulled alongside the curb.

The house and lot were squared in and protected by black wrought iron railings with a gate for opening. Constructed of red brick, the house loomed above and beyond the fencing. An unusual flat roofline was emphasized by ornate cornice detail at its eaves line. It was also accented by black shutters and a bold inset entrance of two doors with brass fixtures.

In the rearview mirror, Miranda fluffed up her mop of curly hair. It formed a wreath around her face, offsetting its somewhat sharp edges. One attribute that did help her was the genetic double layer of lashes that saved money on mascara. She didn't get those from Millie. In fact, she did not recognize any of her body parts as coming from Millie.

Would any of her be recognizable to the woman she was about to meet? The lashes? Pert nose? Angular cheekbones? Maybe something intangible? Staring into her chocolate brown eyes, she wondered if she might even see similar eyes staring back at her. She took in a deep breath. Truthfully, she was a bit nervous.

The sound of the car door shutting cut into the quiet of the neighborhood. Despite an empty driveway, the place did not have an air of abandonment. Encouraged, Miranda opened the elaborate gate lock and took the brick walkway to the imposing entrance. She pressed the bell once at the top of the stairs. A deep gong resonated in the interior, echoing throughout the entire house—not a promising sound. She bit her lower lip and waited.

After several minutes, Miranda headed back down the stairs and looked around to see if she could peek into a window. Just before she began to move towards one, a loud, grinding noise from the entrance caught her attention and she saw the door slowly move open.

A tiny, shriveled up figure stood, birdlike in appearance, at the threshold. Her eyes blinked rapidly as though not used to daylight. She stared down at Miranda with a questioning expression.

Miranda's voice came out scratchy. "Hello! Are you Emily Clark?"

"Young lady, I am not interested in anything you have for sale. Good day." With that, the little figure turned to go back inside.

"Wait..."

Emily slowly turned back as if rotating on a spit. Miranda fought to find the words she needed to make her understand how they were connected. Feeling tongue-tied, she finally managed to say, "I'm Miranda Chesney."

The other woman's brow furrowed. "Chesney?"

"Yes. We are related. My father's father was your second cousin...or maybe your second cousin removed. I get those confused."

"Well, why didn't you say so? Come on in." Emily Clark gestured to Miranda to come back up the stairs.

She followed Emily inside into a spacious foyer. A tall ceiling set a dramatic tone and made Emily even more diminutive. Miranda herself felt suddenly a lot shorter than she usually did. Eyes wide, Miranda looked around, taking in the dated, but clearly—at one time—spectacular space. Wide plank hardwood floors led to a generous staircase with a rich, mahogany newel post and banister.

"Let's have a seat in the parlor."

Miranda just about stopped her jaw from dropping once in the room to the right of the foyer. She recognized the room right away as the setting of the event her mother and father had attended so long ago. The same scale as the hallway, it included even more ornate detail with a showcase fireplace surrounded by intricate woodwork. But, most spectacular, the windows were the showstoppers and ran from floor to ceiling in an unusual fashion.

"I've never seen windows like that! All the way down to the floor."

"Oh, yes. Daddy told me once that his father ordered them special and it was quite a big deal. Italianate style, they're called."

Emily gestured for Miranda to take a seat opposite her. Two plush couches in a faded brocade fabric faced each other. "So, let's see. What would you care to drink?"

Miranda waved it off saying, "I'm fine really."

"Okay, well...Let me have a look at you."

As Emily peered over at Miranda, Miranda did the same on her side, taking in the snowy mane of hair pulled back loosely in a bun, the heavily wrinkled skin that maybe spoke of a cigarette habit either past and/or present, and the very few teeth remaining in her otherwise pleasant smile. In fact, it looked like only her bottom teeth remained, looking like little worn down and polished gray pebbles.

Emily was the first to break off their mutual staring contest. "I can't say we look like family, necessarily, but that's okay. What brings you to Keokuk?"

"Oh...where to start? Well, my mother—Millie—lives up in Illinois and I was spending time with her over the holidays."

"Your father?"

"He passed away a long time ago."

"Oh, that's right. Pardon me. I do remember hearing about that from Cousin Leonard some time back. When you get to be my age, time starts running together a bit."

Miranda nodded. Then she continued. "Anyway, I've been sorting out some family history and my mother remembered visiting you here years ago. In fact, we found this photograph." She reached into her bag and pulled out the image of her young parents in the very same room Miranda sat in now, a deja vu moment albeit with a degree of separation.

Emily brought it close to her face for several beats, her face crinkled even more in concentration. She looked back at up at Miranda. "I remember that day! Such a delightful gathering with the family."

"Yes, my mother said the same. Anyhow, I was hoping you might have some family stories to share?"

A light, tinkling sound came out from Emily—her laugh. "Oh, I did take a great interest at one point in the family lore. Maybe more than others in the family. But can I ask, what has gotten you interested? Why now?"

"It's kind of a crazy story."

"I've got time," Emily said with a smile.

Both women settled back into their respective couches and Miranda began to tell her saga about Rosewood and all the rest leading right up to the present moment. Emily listened attentively and held off from commenting, only giving the occasional nod or raise of the eyebrows along the telling.

Miranda finished the long and overblown story by saying, "I've been talking a long time. I hope I'm not boring you..." she hesitated suddenly realizing she didn't know how to address the woman in front of her and then added, "...Cousin Emily."

"Please just call me Emily. I don't stand too much on ceremony anymore. Doesn't seem to be worth it at my age."

"I know it's a lot to take in. What do you think? Did you ever hear about witches in the family?"

Emily looked thoughtful for a moment. "It does seem to ring a faint, distant bell. But I can't quite pin down what the bell is yet."

Miranda felt dismayed. Maybe Emily didn't have anything to offer to her search. But then Emily spoke again. "I do have a couple of banker boxes in my attic though."

"You do?"

"Yes. Filled with our family's history. I'm embarrassed to say I haven't looked at them in years. But those boxes aren't doing anyone any good up there by themselves."

Miranda felt a pilot light of excitement flicker on at the thought of getting into those banker boxes.

"So..." she began.

"Yes. So, I think we should bring them down and have a look-see, don't you? In fact, it's high time. Maybe we'll find what you're talking about."

Miranda tapped down acting too eager. "As long as you are sure it's okay."

"Now, my doctor has me on strict orders not to lift any-thing. Says it's to avoid a hernia or some such nonsense. But you look capable enough."

"Absolutely. I can carry them down."

Emily glanced at her wrist where Miranda noted an old-style watch sat. She hadn't seen a wrist watch like that in years: a thin gold band with a delicate oval that held the face. "It's get-ting late in the day so I'm thinking we should do this tomorrow. How long are you in town for?"

"I...um...really, I was just passing through. But, sure, I could stay into tomorrow. Is there a motel in town?"

"Oh, that's ridiculous. With this huge house, you might as well stay here. Good to put one of the rooms to use, I say."

Taken aback, Miranda didn't know how to respond. She knew that the elderly could tend to become gullible. She couldn't gauge whether it was okay to accept the invite. She demurred. "I couldn't ask that of you."

"Young lady, I may be old, but I *am* an excellent judge of character. If I am inviting you to stay in my house, be assured it is the right decision."

After a brief internal debate, Miranda accepted but real-ized she had a caveat to confess. "I do have my cat with me. I can keep her in her crate, of course."

"I love cats. Not a bother at all. Now, let's get you organized."

After lugging in a few bags and Polly in her cage, Miranda

followed Emily to the upper level, again marveling at the staircase as they climbed up. Emily took slow steps with one hand tight on the stair rail the entire length. Miranda was fine with that pace herself, still feeling a slight residual twinge in her ankle. Once at the first switchback landing, Emily stopped and Miranda heard a slight wheeze.

"Are you okay?"

"Oh..." she waved a hand. "It's just this angina that kicks in a little."

They continued up and arrived at the hallway that was just as wide and spacious as the one below. Emily paused. "I think I will put you in the blue room. How does that suit?"

"Whatever room works is fine. And thank you again."

Emily opened the door of the first room on the right and a rush of cold air came out with a bite. "It will warm up soon. I keep all the rooms shut off up here because the bill gets so outrageous, you understand."

Inside, the room was a time warp. The walls were indeed blue, a robin egg blue in Miranda's estimation. There were more Victorian era furnishings that filled up the space including a wash stand with a bar for a towel and nightstands that flanked a tall, ornate headboard with a marbled wood finish.

"So fancy," Miranda said, out loud.

"Yes, our forebearers were very fancy." Emily looked around the room with a wistful expression. "Well, I'll let you settle in. When you're ready, come back down and we'll have a bite to eat."

After Emily left, Miranda set up a station for Polly and sat on the bed, testing it out. It was a bit lumpy from age, but a feeling of comfort and connection washed over Miranda. Her father had stayed in this house, maybe even in the same room and, even though it was long ago, it brought him closer to her.

Casting her gaze over the entire space, her eye caught a little, round hole with a molded surround on the wall near the door to the room. She moved over to examine it, unable to identify it as anything she had ever seen before. Maybe it was something electrical. Peering into it only revealed complete darkness.

Later, over a dinner of canned tomato soup and ham sandwiches, the two women got to know each other, trading stories about their lives. Emily, Miranda discovered, had also been an educator. A teacher of elementary level students, she had taught at the Keokuk Elementary School for her entire career. But she threw a curve ball mentioning her missionary work in China for five years, earlier in her life before teaching.

"I guess you could say that was my grand adventure. It opened my eyes to the big, wide world. But then Daddy and Mother needed care, so...." The inevitable rest of that thought was left hanging. She continued. "That was when I got into the family history. It was such fun to share the discoveries with Daddy and Mother. The goal was to become a DAR. But I eventually lost interest, I guess."

"A DAR?"

"Yes. Daughter of the American Revolution. You have to prove a connection to an ancestor who served in the Revolutionary War. Which I did. A couple of times over actually."

Miranda mulled that over. She knew about the organization but didn't quite understand the draw. "Were there a lot of members in the DAR here in town?"

"At one time, yes. It was considered quite the coup in my day. Probably seems silly now."

"No, no. Not at all."

After helping with the dishes at the heavy, white porcelain sink, Miranda wiped her hands off a dish rag and said, "I think I'll take a quick walk. Take in the sights."

"Of course. It's a hop, skip and a jump to town and easy to figure out your way."

Miranda headed out and took in the attractions of yet another small Midwestern town thinking along the way about Emily's life here over the span of years. There was just enough light left to walk through the sleepy downtown and take in the storefronts. She imagined Emily strolling these streets, going about her day-to-day business, year after year.

The quaint downtown bordered the river but was different from Ottawa, her mother's hometown. Less gritty and a bit more refined. She assumed certain manufacturing and businesses accounted for nuanced differences in small towns like that perhaps based on whatever hydropower was available from whatever river flowed through.

Back at Emily's house, Miranda entered through the massive front doors. Inside, she heard television noises from the rear of the house. Venturing in that direction, she found Emily in a small sitting room off the kitchen. Looking up, Emily smiled and asked, "How was your walk?"

"Really nice. Your town is, well, delightful."

The other woman nodded. "You could say that."

"What are you watching?"

"One of these Dateline murder mysteries. I just gobble them up."

Miranda was taken aback by this interest of Emily's. "Really?"

"Oh yes, love them. This one here is about a guy who was murdered by his wife for cheating on her." She let out a delighted cackle and Miranda again was taken aback.

"She dismembered his body and carried out different parts of it in bowling bags. Really something. Eventually, one of his feet somehow was found at the edge of a river. The foot was still in its shoe. A Timberland boot, they said. Can you imagine?"

Miranda gulped at the graphic description coming out of the petite, elderly lady in front of her and the contrast of the words with her benign appearance. A gleam in Emily's eyes over the gory details of the crime made Miranda wonder what simmered under the surface.

After saying their good nights, Miranda made her way to her room, puzzling over Emily and her TV appetites. She wouldn't have guessed the woman to have an interest in that kind of thing. But then, she really didn't know her at all yet.

Falling into a deep sleep, Miranda was jarred in the night by noises entering into her dreams. Moaning, groans, and whispers. Coming to consciousness, she tried to figure out the direction they were coming from. Stumbling out of bed, she headed to the doorway and realized before opening the door that the sounds seemed to be emitting from the tube on the wall. She rued the fact she had not asked Emily what the tube was earlier. She fell back into a fitful slumber, punctuated by the noises, for the remainder of the night.

Chapter Twenty-eight

POLLY'S MEOWS LOUD IN her ear cut into her slumber and Miranda rolled over to look at her cell, immediately embarrassed at sleeping in past eight. The noises had kept her tossing and turning for most of the night. Getting up, a deep fatigue rolled over her as she looked around the room with bleary eyes.

Once she pulled herself together, she headed downstairs through a very quiet house, ready to apologize to Emily for sleeping in so late. Pondering on how to politely bring up the groaning and moaning from the night, she walked into the kitchen where someone stood at the sink. Someone with a wide backside and a mop of salt and pepper hair who was not Emily.

"Uh...hi," Miranda said, announcing her presence in a moderate tone so as not to startle.

In an almost delayed reaction, the person turned from the sink to face her. It was difficult to distinguish gender at first glance. It was a woman, Miranda decided. But a decidedly manly woman who stared, saying nothing, as Miranda absorbed a snarl on her thickened facial features.

Awkward silence filled the room as Miranda noticed an array of pill bottles behind the woman on the counter next to the sink. A tray with individual pills scattered on top of it also sat on the counter along with a mortar and pestle.

Miranda spoke up first. "I'm Miranda. Emily's cousin." Still nothing from the other woman. "And you are?"

Instead of answering, an accusatory glower came over the other woman's face as she said, "Emily had too much excitement yesterday."

"Oh, she seemed okay when we said goodnight…"

She cut Miranda off. "It was too much for her and now she's overtired."

"Who did you say you were again?"

"I didn't." Relenting a bit, she said, "Most folks call me Dee."

"Emily didn't mention anyone else living here."

"She gets confused. I'm her housekeeper. I had a day off yesterday. Otherwise, I would have been able to supervise what you two were up to."

"Well, Dee…I'll just go ahead and get started with what Emily and I agreed to. I'm getting some boxes down from the attic. Did she mention it to you?"

"I don't know that you need to go through all her stuff like that."

Miranda found herself in the strange position of having to ask this woman for permission. But did she really? Instead, she said, "It's family papers and I'm family, so…"

As they faced each other in a détente, Miranda sized Dee up. She was bigger and physically imposing. It could make for an interesting showdown. She cleared her throat and started again. "Look…why don't we just run it by Emily?"

Dee finally broke her gaze away from Miranda. "Only for a minute. You wore her out last night, like I said."

Dee turned on her heel and headed to the sitting room off the kitchen where Emily had lingered the previous evening. Once there, Dee opened a door on the far wall of the room, revealing Emily's bedroom. Which made sense given the challenges of a staircase at her age. Emily's tiny figure on the bed was almost swallowed up by a thick comforter and multiple pillows surrounding her head. With her eyes shut closed, she looked like a bas relief sculpture.

"You got company." Dee's voice came out harsh and edgy into the room.

Emily's eyes slowly blinked open a couple of times. "Whaatt?"

"Good morning, Emily. Uh…Dee and I were just discussing

the boxes I was going to get in the attic."

"Boxes?" She looked at Miranda with no recognition.

"Yes, remember we talked about them yesterday?"

Emily suddenly shifted in the bed, weakly trying to pull herself up. "Oh...I remember now. What did you want with the boxes?"

"Um...we talked about me looking at them for the family history...." Miranda's voice trailed off. She was taken aback by the change in the woman's attitude.

"That's fine...you can do that. But you better leave after that. I think that's best." She cast a skittish glance towards Dee.

"Oh, okay...well, should I take the boxes with me then? And bring them back when I have had a chance to go through them?"

"Yes...yes, do that. But then...but then...you have to bring them back." She blinked her eyes again in a confused manner.

"I will. And I'll call you about my progress with them in the meantime."

"Okay, that's fine then...Dee, do you have my breakfast ready yet?" Her voice was plaintive and she seemingly had dismissed Miranda altogether.

"It's coming...just hold your horses, missy!" Dee let out a raspy chuckle.

"Okay, well thanks for everything, Emily, and it was nice to meet you."

Emily nodded and gave a curt smile.

Back in the kitchen, Dee looked at her pointedly.

"Well, I'll go find those boxes in the attic and then...um... then I'll pack up."

"I'll come up with you."

"I don't think that's necessary. I can do it myself."

"No, I'll—" her sentence was interrupted by a text ding somewhere. Dee let out a groan and mumbled a "what now?" under her breath. After looking at her cell, she let out another groan and said, "My kid needs a jumpstart over Hamilton. When I get back, you're gone, right?"

"Sure, but what about Emily's breakfast? Do you want me to make—"

"No!" Dee let out abruptly. "No, she'll be fine until I get back. Just…just get the boxes and get out of her hair."

Miranda put her hands up. "Okay, okay."

Heading to the staircase, she halfway wondered if Dee was going to follow her up to the blue room and watch as she packed up. She cast a glance back down the staircase where Dee stood at the bottom with a glare on her face and hands on hips. It felt like she had just been fired in an office and Dee was the security guard making sure she didn't take pens, pencils and pads.

In the blue room, Miranda sat heavily on the lumpy bed letting out the breath she had been holding in. What fresh hell had she landed in? What authority did Dee have here, anyway? What the hell was wrong with Emily this morning? She had acted like Miranda was public enemy number one. One thing was for certain: Miranda was not leaving without those boxes.

Dee's voice yelled up from downstairs. "Hey, hey up there!" Miranda's body gave a jolt and, with a pounding heart, she went over to the top of the stairs and looked down. Dee, even more menacing from that vantage, said, "I'm heading out so wrap it up as quick as you can."

"Sure. Packing it all up now."

Miranda gave a fist pump into the air back in the bedroom at Dee leaving. She didn't know how far away Hamilton was but maybe this was a chance to see what was wrong with Emily. Dee made departure-like noises downstairs and finally a door slammed. Tip-toeing out to the end of the hall, Miranda peeked out the window.

Dee strode over to a beat-up truck parked in the driveway. The truck sputtered to life and backed out with its muffler making popping noises as it headed along Riverside Avenue away from the house.

Miranda paced back and forth; her mind scattered in all directions. Should she go to the attic and get the boxes first? Or should she try to talk to Emily and figure out if she was okay? Or maybe just pack it up and get the hell out of there and away from Dee? The lack of sleep made her off-kilter and indecisive, not her norm at all.

She shook herself. It was boxes first—they were up in the attic waiting for her. Heading up the attic staircase, it became narrower as it rose to its top. The level of dust indicated that no one had been up there in a long, long time.

Once at the door, Miranda pulled on the latch but it was stuck. Working it back and forth, panic rose until the latch finally gave way and the door burst free. Before entering, she stood still and listened. All was quiet.

The short, final flight up to the top consisted of rough-hewn, unfinished steps. Her cell illuminated a steep climb. She shuddered at the thought of falling, especially with her ankle, still weakened. But with the weird and looming threat of Dee, slowing down was just not an option. She hastened up but moved carefully.

At the top, she flashed the light over the space revealing a mass of nondescript lumps: furniture, clothing hanging off standing racks and boxes. Seeing a string for a bulb in the center of the space, she picked her way over to it and pulled. The added light was enough for her to size up the entirety.

The low ceiling met at a slight pitch in the center which made sense given that it was a flat roofline. The flooring consisted of wide and unfinished planks, seeming even wider than the floorboards on the lower level. It appeared organized in a fashion with all boxes pushed together in one area off to a side. Making her way over, she hoped against hope that the boxes were labeled or marked in some way.

Some of them were banker's boxes and she said, under her breath, "Bingo." Upon closer examination, three of them had been marked in cursive, "Family Papers". They had to be the ones Emily talked about. Picking up the closest, she gauged its weight. Not too heavy but it would take a couple of trips to move them to the Toyota.

On the second trip, her nerves caught up with her and, moving too fast, she fell on the way up the stairs, banging her calf. With no time to stop and examine, she kept moving until finishing up and sitting on the Toyota's trunk to get it closed. Looking up and down the street nervously, there was no sign of

Dee and the pick-up with its broken muffler—yet.

Hustling back into the house, she wiped her hands on her jeans before looking up to find Emily standing in the foyer. "Oh, Emily," she said, strangely embarrassed, like she had been caught out on something. "I was just..."

Emily cut her off. "Why are you still here?" she said, with a dazed look on her face.

Miranda was lost for words. Finding her voice, she said, "I'm moving as fast as I can. Almost done, just need to pack now."

Emily shook her head. "I'm very tired. You'll have to excuse me." She drifted out of the foyer without saying anything more. Miranda briefly closed her eyes before hurrying back to the blue room to collect her bag and Polly.

Back downstairs, all was quiet again as she puzzled over what to do about Emily. Then she began to hear similar sounds to what she had heard the previous evening, moaning and groaning. Near the door with Polly in the cat carrier in one hand and her bags in the other, her steps began to falter and come to a stop. She couldn't leave Emily like this. She just couldn't.

Placing all her things and the cat carrier down, Miranda moved towards the noises, back beyond the kitchen to Emily's bedroom again. Peering in through the open doorway, she saw Emily curled in a ball on the bed making the noises. Miranda's eye caught on the same strange hole that was in the blue room. So, this was how she had heard the sounds.

She leaned over and said softly, "Emily?"

The elderly woman's eyes opened slowly. "What?"

"I'm about to leave but your housekeeper isn't back yet. Do you need me to get you anything?"

Emily began to sit up and Miranda helped her to right herself.

"I'm so groggy today. I wonder if Dee gave me too much medicine."

Miranda cleared her throat. "Is there...is there anyone else I can call for you? Other than Dee?"

"No. Dee's good to me. She just gets a little overzealous

sometimes."

"So...you'll be okay alone with her?"

"Oh, yes. She loves me very much."

Miranda was astonished by the idea of Dee loving somebody very much. "Well...I'll be on my way then. Thank you for everything and about the boxes..."

Emily waved a hand and said, "Take your time with them. It's fine. But...before you go, could you get me a glass of orange juice? My throat is so parched."

"Of course. How about a cup of coffee also?"

"Oh, yes. That would be wonderful."

Miranda nodded and said, "I'll be right back."

She headed to the kitchen and made herself at home, casting aside any fears of Dee's wrath. She didn't know why she had cowed to the other woman, but it stopped now. She was going to make Emily as comfortable as she could before she hit the road.

Working her way around the kitchen, she again looked at all the pills on the counter and the white powder that lay in the pestle bowl. A barb of concern went through her. What exactly was going on here?

While coffee brewed, she rustled through the refrigerator finding sandwich fixings. She threw together a quick sandwich and then sat at the table, munching on the sandwich and puzzling out what she would say to Dee. "So, Dee, are you poisoning my relative?" came to mind.

Several minutes later, she heard the muffler noise outside in the driveway. Dee was back. She braced herself. Dee came through the back door and stopped cold when she saw Miranda sitting at the table.

"I thought I told you to be gone by the time I got back."

"You did. But I'm not. I didn't feel comfortable leaving Emily alone...she was groaning and such."

Dee made a growling-like noise in her throat and Miranda took a step back. "She's fine. Just tired out like I told you." She glared at Miranda. "I'm back so you can go now."

Dee began to move with her threatening bulk towards

Miranda, who had stood up.

"Dee. I talked to Emily. She mentioned some medicine. Could she have taken too much?"

Dee began to sputter. "How dare you come in here..."

"Look, I'm not accusing you of anything, but she's a small woman. Maybe her meds need adjusting."

"She's fine. And she'll be better once she can get some peace and quiet around here!"

"All right. I made her some coffee and she wanted juice. I'll just take that—"

"No, you won't. I got this."

"Fine. I'll just go in and say goodbye then."

With Dee right on her heels, Miranda hastened back one more time to Emily's bedroom. Emily had fallen back to sleep. Both women stood silently by her bedside and then Dee made a shooing motion to Miranda.

Back in the kitchen, Miranda knew she had to stand up to Dee. There was no way she could take off with a clear conscience if she didn't. She swiveled towards Dee, hands on hips, and said, "Is something going on with Emily's meds?"

"What? Why would you ask that?" She watched the other woman's face crumple into a hurt expression, a transformative expression, as if emphasizing her words. Her face almost took on a younger look.

Miranda waved a hand towards the pills on the counter. "Because of all those and because...because Emily seems completely overmedicated this morning."

"I love that woman to pieces. I would never, ever do anything to hurt her!" Her voice had changed along with her facial expression, conveying more hurt and dismay.

Miranda checked herself. Had she misread the whole situation? The two of them stared at each other, unyielding, until Miranda spoke. "Okay, okay. Maybe I got the wrong idea here. Just...take good care of her, will you?"

"Yeah. I'm...look, maybe I got too harsh with you. But, believe me, I would never hurt the elderly, just like I would never hurt a child. In fact, I was more worried about you hurting her.

But let's just call a spade a spade."

Miranda nodded, picking up the general intent even though confused by the odd and incorrect usage of that phrase. When Dee thrust out her hand for a handshake, Miranda shook the other woman's large hand, feeling as if something was resolved.

Driving away from Emily's house, she looked in the rearview, half expecting to see Dee watching her departure on the lawn. Instead, she just saw the house. She felt better about leaving and she made a vow to herself to return with the boxes on her next trip out to see Millie. It seemed like she had not understood Dee at all...kind of like how she had misread Lizzie and Lizzie's involvement with Rosewood.

Chapter Twenty-nine

THE SNOW STARTED SWIRLING an hour into the drive. Looking through her windshield wipers with dismay, Miranda chastised herself for forgetting to track the weather in her hasty departure from Keokuk. Because now, it looked like there was a situation.

As it began to come down in earnest, Miranda pulled onto the exit to Hannibal, Missouri, needing gas anyway. She shook some snow off her shoes inside the gas station entrance. The middle-aged clerk behind the counter looked out at her through his horn-rimmed glasses. "Roads getting bad I heard on the radio. How far you gotta go?"

"Virginia."

He gave a guffaw in response.

"Can you tell me if there are any good motels nearby?" Miranda asked.

"Sure. One block down is the Becky Thatcher."

"Becky...oh. Like in the book."

"Yeah, we got a lot of that going on here."

By the time she pulled into the parking lot of the Becky Thatcher Motel, the snow had thickened on the pavement to a couple of inches, a sea of white. The motel was a 1960s throwback style, a one level motor lodge. The vacancy light was on but missing the "y" at the end.

In the motel office, an acne ridden teen clerk manned the counter and gave her a room assignment without much fanfare. She piled in with her bags and Polly, then went back for the banker boxes, lugging them all in. Being snowed in might just be the perfect opportunity to pore through them.

Looking around the motel room, there was a barge-style boat design on the café curtains, shag carpet maybe as old as the establishment but she hoped not, and a chenille bedspread in a bright, cheery color. This was not the generic Motel 6 she had become accustomed to in Williamsburg.

First order of business was to find some food after being drained of energy from the combo of the Dee situation and the long drive. She popped back into the office, where the teen was back to scrolling through his device as if it was the most important work on the planet. "Hey...do you know if anyplace is open in this weather to get a bite to eat?"

He looked up at her with eyes dazed from screen activities. "Huh? Oh yeah," he pointed towards his right. "Around the corner."

"I can walk there?"

"Sure. It's like I said. Around the corner."

Back outside, the snow drove hard to one side. Miranda hoped the kid had his directional sense in order after all the scrolling. Stopping short after a few feet, she discovered the clerk had not been wrong. A restaurant really was at the corner which was actually attached to the Becky Thatcher. Pulling on the cold metal of the door handle, she busted her way in from the weather and stomped her feet.

"Getting bad out there?"

Miranda looked up to see the person who asked the question, a woman parked at a table near the front. She stared at Miranda over the half glasses perched on her face.

"Yep. Um...are you still open for a meal?"

"Sure thing. I don't have anywhere I need to be. Just watching the world go by here." She let out a gravelly smoker's laugh that turned into a cough.

"Oh, good. Thank you."

Clearing her throat, the woman said, "Take a seat, honey. Anywhere you want."

Miranda took a booth in the middle of the place, away from any drafts off the front plate glass windows. After taking off her coat, she sat down and got her bearings. A placemat in front of her was emblazoned in the center with, "The Huck Finn Diner," and surrounded by a United States word game.

The woman came over with a glass of water and a menu. "Here you go." After placing them down, she asked, "You just passing through?"

"Yes. Well, stranded now due to the weather."

"It'll happen. Catch you by surprise, huh?"

"Sure did."

"Take your time and call me over when you're ready."

Miranda perused the selections. They took the theme seriously with choices like Tom Turkey Sandwich, Huckleyberry pie, Duke's Rich Reuben, and Jim's Special, a classic diner cheeseburger with fries. She wondered if the entire town was like this. She felt she could use a stiff drink, but that wasn't on offer at the Huck Finn Diner.

After placing her order, Jim's special with a soda, and some more chit chat, Miranda stared again at the placemat and her thoughts turned to Mark Twain and ideas of westward expansion. She wondered if it had been down to certain personality types taking the leap to go west, a very American type. It had all started out east, where Rosewood was with the first people settling along the Atlantic coast. They were followed by those of the same ilk who kept moving westward until there was no further to go. She thought about tying this in somehow to her new classes of the semester, maybe even making it a theme of sorts.

The sudden jolt of the door opening crashed into her thoughts, startling both her and the proprietress. Even more startling was the man that walked in, shaking snow off a double-breasted, dark wool coat. With a direct view from her booth, Miranda was awestruck by the full effect. He lifted his head to reveal a long, straight nose and a thick mane of wavy, white hair that swirled off to one side from a side part. An unwieldy, yellowed, handlebar moustache covered his mouth. It was as though Mark Twain in the flesh had just been whipped up out of her reveries. Miranda gave herself a mental shake at the silliness of that thought.

"Hey, Mark. Getting bad out there?" The woman repeated the same question she had asked Miranda, strangely calling him the name his appearance conjured up.

"Coming down nicely," the man answered in a slightly twangy accent.

Giving Miranda a nod, he walked to the booth across from hers. She gave a slight smile in return. He positioned himself so that he was opposite from Miranda and gazed right at her. Shifting uncomfortably, she stared back down at the mat, half fascinated, half put off.

"How are you keeping this evening, young lady?"

She looked up. "Uh, fine."

"Haven't seen you in our humble town before, have I?"

"No...no. The snowstorm left me stranded."

"Ah, well. The weather can present difficulties at times in a prescient way."

Taken aback, Miranda was, at the same time, bemused by the formality of his speech and demeanor. On closer view, now that the double-breasted coat had been removed, his outfit included a beige cravat paired with a dark suit jacket. She knew that some took on personas of famous figures as a sort of hobby and, sometimes, even to an obsessive level. Perhaps this was the case with "Mark."

With a steaming coffee pot in hand, the proprietress began to pour him a cup. "Many thanks, Lorna," he said.

"Brewed fresh. I know how you like it."

"Indeed. I was chatting with our snowbound stranger here. Snow can make for strange bedfellows, I think."

Lorna let out a girlish giggle in contrast to her not girlish age. "I guess so, Mark." Again, Miranda wondered what he was talking about. Lorna headed back towards the kitchen taking the coffee pot with her.

"So where do you harken from, young lady?"

"Right outside of Williamsburg, Virginia."

He gave a sniff and wiped an imaginary something off his jacket. "There's a lot of history here too you know..." Miranda got the strange feeling he felt she was one upping him being from Williamsburg.

She changed the subject and asked, "So did you have an event that got canceled?"

"An event?"

"Yes. I mean, you look like him and are dressed like him. It's a reenactment thing, right?"

The man's pleasant demeanor took a sudden shift and his gaze became steely in front of Miranda's eyes. "Pardon me, young lady?"

"Oh, I'm assuming you play the role of Mark Twain somewhere in town?" She cushioned it with a question.

Lorna came barreling out from the kitchen with a plate of hamburger and fries as the question hung in the air. She plopped it unceremoniously in front of Miranda and gave her a slight shake of her head as though trying to communicate something. "Here you go, miss. Jim's special."

Miranda looked down at the plate in front of her and said, "You know, I think I'll take it to go." She could feel the man's eyes drilling into her.

"All right. Lemme grab a box."

As Lorna walked off, silence filled the space left behind. Miranda fiddled with her silverware and did not look up again.

She heard rather than saw the man suddenly get up from the booth which made squeaky noises as he did so. She looked over to see him pulling on his coat with abrupt movements before rushing out the door, back into the night.

"Oh, man," Miranda said, under her breath.

Lorna walked back into the room with a Styrofoam container in one hand and the coffeepot in the other. Looking around, she said, "Where'd he go?"

"He just left."

"Huh."

"I hope I didn't offend him. I asked if he was posing as Mark Twain. Like a reenactor or something."

"Yeah, I heard that and tried to give you the high sign. You shouldn't have gone there. He's real prickly about that."

"That?"

"Well, he thinks he really is Mark Twain. And we all just go along with it."

"Why?"

Lorna shrugged. "Doesn't seem to do anybody any harm, I guess. Look...just stay and eat your food while it's hot. He won't be back anytime soon."

Miranda let out a puff of air. "Okay, yeah, thanks. I'll eat here."

As she began to plow into the plate, Lorna came back with a bottle of wine and pulled up a chair to the table next to her booth. She poured herself a glass of wine. "Do you want one?"

Miranda nodded. "Thanks, yes." Rattled by the Mark Twain encounter, she welcomed the offer of alcohol.

As they drank wine, Lorna regaled Miranda with tales of Mark as well as other eccentrics that the town seemed to attract. Characters that came from other parts of the country to bask in the ambiance of Hannibal, it seemed.

"What about you, Lorna? Where did you come from?"

"I'm one of the few you'll meet around here that was born and raised." Then she added as a throwaway comment, "And I'm actually related to Mark Twain."

Miranda let out a soft "wow" and pushed her glass forward for a top off of more wine. Hannibal had become quite the diversion.

Miranda's head was spinning as she headed back out into the snow to her motel room. She ended up splitting the bottle of Chardonnay with Lorna. They hugged after she had paid the bill as if old comrades in arms. Lorna said, in parting, "See you at breakfast!"

Miranda kept one eye out as best she could to see through the swirling precipitation for any looming Mark Twain look-alike figures. All the stories that Lorna told made her want to explore all the nooks and crannies of the place the next day... but she had run out of time. Rosewood was calling her back.

Chapter Thirty

BACK IN THE MOTEL room, Polly scampered up onto the bed after being released from the cage, purring her gratitude. Miranda stroked her orange fur back and forth absentmindedly. The boxes twinkled at her in the corner where she had piled them up earlier. It was time.

Several hours later, she yawned so widely that tears sprung in her eyes. Her head was spinning with all the names, dates and places she had sifted through and, maybe, the Chardonnay as well. But she had not uncovered anything leading back to Rosewood. All of it so far had related to the Midwest segment of the family's sojourns as best she could find.

She checked herself and thought again maybe it was just an obsession with no point to it at all. Kind of like Mark's obsession with being in character. Maybe her mother was right and it wasn't serving any purpose to spend her time this way. Maybe, in fact, it was just a way to avoid the here and now which was really what she needed to focus on.

"Just one more box," she said aloud to Polly curled up next to her. It was the last one, anyway. Opening it up, she could see right away this one was different from the others. The paper looked older and even had a different smell. It smelled a little like...lavender. But that was impossible. She shook her head to clear her senses and began to pick items out one at a time.

Halfway down, elation filled her at the sight of a file marked "Virginia." Pulling it out, the very first item on top was a yellowed copy of a land deed. Her stomach leapt to her throat. Holding it under the murky light from the bedside table lamp,

Miranda read it line by line slowly, not wanting to miss anything, even the slightest detail.

Reaching the last paragraph, she set it down and thought about what she had read so carefully. It laid out the property in Bisoux—her property—in exacting detail. But, from what she could decipher, the property had originally included much more land. In fact, her ancestors seemed to have owned that entire peninsula—meaning the neighbors' parcels had been divvied out much later. She puffed up a bit at the thought that she, as a descendant, was not the outsider—they were.

Her phone made a bird tweet noise and interrupted her discoveries. Grabbing it off the table with impatience, she went still after looking down at it. It was a text from Brian that read, "When are you coming back?" Just a simple question. On the other hand, *not* so simple because it was loaded with possible meanings and interpretations.

Miranda paused, torn between continuing to the end of the document and the revelations in the box or Brian. Did she want to text him back?

He had not reached out even once over her absence and contacting her now seemed almost suspicious. But...a side of her couldn't let that emotional connection with him go quite yet. There was still a chance that maybe, just maybe, it could work out with him. It was against her better judgment, but she did want to text him back.

She typed back, "On the road home. Bad weather. Stranded in Hannibal, Missouri. There are worse fates." She added a smiley face emoji.

He came back with, "Can you talk?"

Whoa, she thought. Was she ready to talk again to Brian? She held off longer than the situation merited and finally answered back, "Sure."

The phone rang right away.

"Hi," she answered.

"Miranda."

The sound of him saying the three syllables of her name sent a spark through her system. She had pressed down her feelings for him for so long but now they came back hard.

"So...?" she said with a question in her tone.

"Yeah, so it's been a while."

The conversation was getting off to a stilted, uncomfortable start. After a brief silence, he blurted it out. "Fiona is in a mental hospital."

"What?"

"Things...things took a turn. They got worse after you left."

"Is Rosewood..."

"Rosewood is fine. Not involved at all. She...she spiraled out of control after that night. You know, the night of the...I guess we could call it a ceremony. The last time I saw you."

"What was all the secrecy about Brian?"

"She was obsessed with me, Miranda. And then it got really twisted with these ideas that you and she were battling it out for some kind of ancestral curse or something. She ended up posting all this crazy stuff on her Instagram stories nonstop over a couple of days."

"Wow." Miranda tried to take it all in and, also, tried to imagine Brian on the other end of the line. What his posture might be, what expression lingered on his face. There was so much that she literally couldn't see over the phone.

"Yeah. I mean things got so weird. I thought I was handling it okay, but it reached a point where I felt the only way to protect you was to keep away from you. Just until I sorted out what could be done about her. She is one of the most brilliant undergrads I have ever had...." His voice trailed away at that thought.

"I don't even know what to say. Where to even start?"

"I know...it's a lot."

"Brian, I have to ask again. Were you ever in that kind of relationship with her? A romantic relationship?"

He let out a big sigh. "I get it. I get why everyone thinks that. But no. Not even an 'emotional affair,' like the kind people talk about. She just...she just zeroed in on me. And I couldn't deflect her—as hard as I tried to. It's all been such a mess."

"I don't know what to say."

"Say you're coming back."

She felt flutters in her nether regions. "I am coming back. And I guess I'll be safe and sound now at Rosewood."

"Yes. All the weird stuff that happened was down to Fiona. It all came out when she was hauled away."

"God, that's a relief. What about the others though...Lizzie, her aunt, that other kid in the dig crew?"

"They are all embarrassed I think."

"What was the finale that led to her being taken away?"

He was silent on the other end.

"That's okay. You don't have to talk about it."

"No...no. It's not that I don't want to tell you. It's just that... I'll tell you the whole sad tale when you get back. How about that?"

"Sure. It's fine."

"It's just so good to hear your voice."

Miranda gulped. "Same."

"Listen."

"Hey."

They'd both spoke at the same time and then laughed.

Brian spoke again first. "It's late. I'll let you go...for now."

"I'll hold you to it. And I'll see you in a day or two."

Hitting the end button on the call, a slow smile spread over her face. Maybe, just maybe, things were getting fixed. Realizing she didn't have any bandwidth left to finish the box, she set all of it aside, wanting her mind to be fresh for the next go 'round. Thoughts of Brian flooded in as she settled down to let sleep take over.

Chapter Thirty-one

MIRANDA WOKE UP IN a cold sweat in the pitch-dark room. Instead of a peaceful slumber, her subconscious had another plan. Her dream had been a twisted encounter with Fiona and more than one Mark Twain look-alike as a collective against her in anger, trying to stab her with kitchen knives. What was the dream trying to tell her? Something about people caught up in their own realities? People too caught up in the past? She mulled over the similarities between Fiona and Mark from the diner. Her sojourn to escape was getting more and more bizarre and making the shenanigans at Rosewood feel tame—almost.

The wine left her with a headache and a metallic taste in her mouth. She tried to shake it off, all the thoughts and the physical challenges. Stumbling over to the window, she ripped the curtain back to discover no plow had been through yet. She would be staying put.

It was okay to stay in the little cocoon of the motel room with the cat, the boxes, and the family papers. It was fine, she told herself, tamping down the desire to get back and be with Brian.

After a hot shower, she got herself organized with the motel coffee maker and a bag of Doritos squirreled away from Millie's larder, opting to bypass the diner for breakfast. Once Polly was fed and her travel litter box cleaned, Miranda sat back down with the papers in the bottom of the last box.

It was the very last paper in the file folder. Of course, it would be. She skimmed it at first, not really processing what she read. Slowing down for a closer read, a flush started to rush up her face. She dropped it from her shaking hands like it was red-hot. Scrambling over to the bed and curling up with bent knees, Miranda stared at it across the room where it lay on the floor. It was a curse. A curse in the box.

Polly, curled herself in a rounded ball, looked over with slit drowsy eyes. Staring directly at Polly, she said, "This is ridiculous."

Picking it back up, she studied the paper again. After some time, she laid it aside and made the call. Brian answered right away on the first ring. "Are you back already?"

"What, no? Still snowed in. Listen...did Fiona talk about a curse when she was having the meltdown?"

"Yeess..." Brian dragged out his answer. "How did you know?"

"Because I found it."

"How...what...?'"

"Just listen."

She took a deep breath and then read from the paper in front of her:

"'I, Prudence, seventh daughter of the seventh son of the seventh tribe, will from this point forward cast a curse on the seven generations afore me. A curse on affaires of the heart. Unless a besotted man or woman of the Chesney family line places a curled hangnail, a clot of blood, water from the kidney, a cat's hairball, a lock of raven tress, a globule of spittal, under seven moon cycles but only at the exact point when the moon intersects with the celestial beings known as angelus minor they shall nevermore affect the chosen liaison of his or her heart. Only in this fashion may they be bound to the beloved of their choosing casting aside through witchcraft the others forsaken. Seventh generation will be cursed in affairs of the heart unless they or their blood ties do not harken from the region of the Anglo-Saxon lands bounded by the estuary of the River Thames, the North Sea and the lands of Essex, also known as the Kingdom of East Anglia. None others are contained in the web of the particulars of this incantation.'"

"My god...So, you mean she actually based this on something real?"

"I guess?"

"Where did you find this? Is it online?" he asked.

"No, I...It's a long story. It's in family papers I got a hold of. But this must be the basis of what this has all been about."

"So...she made it a love triangle about you, me and her?"

"I think so...I'm going to study it some more. But I think there was a method to her madness after all—"

Brian cut in saying, "Hey, I have another call coming in."

"Oh, okay. So, I'll see you..." Realizing the call had ended, she stared at the phone. His goodbye had seemed oddly abrupt. Had Brian gotten upset by her findings?

She sprung up and paced the narrow space between the motel room door and the bathroom, trying to get her brain cells fired up. None of it made much sense. Where it started, how it started, there were so many questions. Why was Fiona so focused on Brian? What was it about Brian? She checked herself, realizing that she was drawn to the guy, so why wouldn't others be too? But still, Fiona was a lot younger and could have her pick of any guy.

"Think, Miranda. Think. There is more to this," she said aloud. A sudden thought made her grab the laptop and dig through to find the article on Prudence's witch trial. She skimmed through until the description where Prudence had protested her innocence. Which was in direct contrast to the document that Miranda held in front of her. The curse spelled out a seemingly strong and rooted belief in witchcraft. So, for public consumption she had said otherwise; private being a different story?

Something nagged at Miranda and she kept reading back and forth between the laptop screen and the document several times, getting hung up on the ancient script of the curse. It made for hard work to decipher specific letters. Finally, what bothered her edged out like a hangnail. She worked through the curse's gobbley-gook about location, realizing that it was particular to families from East Anglia who had settled in the region. In fact, it was absolutely clear that persons outside that purview were not included.

Miranda sat back and lifted her arms up into a stretch. It made no sense that Fiona wrapped Brian into all of this, unless it was just part of the manifestation of her crazy. But, Miranda knew that Fiona was nothing if not precise and methodical. She and Fiona were alike in that way, she had to admit.

Fiona would have followed this to the letter. Which could mean that Brian...Suddenly, it snapped into place. The missing piece had to be Brian.

With that thought, Miranda scrambled around on her laptop until she had Ancestry.com up and running. She opened other windows to pin down as many pertinent details as she could plug in about Brian and his life. Digging deeper for any other tidbits she could find, she put pieces in from his bio on the college's website.

All of a sudden, it spit back in her face one finely delineated family tree. Brian had Tidewater roots. Just like Fiona. And just like her. Not just any Tidewater roots. In fact, his ancestors included the East Anglia connections from Bisoux. Miranda shook her head a couple times and then leaned in for a closer look.

After another hour, she had the connection. Brian and she were eighth cousins once removed sharing the same seven times back grandfather—along with ten thousand other people. But apparently that was enough to cause Fiona to go off the rails. It explained everything about Fiona's relentless obsession. It was down to the seventh generation since that was how the curse was set up. All three of them—Miranda, Fiona and Brian—fit right into the model cast all those years ago.

She sat back in the motel chair tenting her fingers. The bigger question came out of all of it: why had Brian never revealed this about himself, especially after all the Fiona stuff came to the forefront? Brian, like Fiona, was a local guy. Why was he keeping these connections to the place a lie by omission? It wasn't possible he didn't know this. With his background as an archeologist, there was no way.

Was it absentmindedness or something sinister afoot?

Brian's role was more, just so much more. It went beyond just trying to keep a lovestruck student at bay. The pressing issue that rose to the surface was: what were Brian's true motivations?

Miranda's earlier hopefulness deflated like a balloon. She felt a chill come over her. Rubbing her hands together to warm up, she wondered if she could trust Brian on any level, personal or professional. Was he playing her in some kind of weird game with Fiona and the others from Bisoux? Was it even safe to go back after all?

Her head was pounding when she stood up and away from her laptop. A late afternoon sun streamed into the room, bright off the snow. The post-snowstorm weather was a welcome sight, but it was too late to get back on the road.

Grabbing her phone and wallet, Miranda headed out the motel room. From the Becky Thatcher's hillside location, the town proper splayed out below. Beyond a small and quaint commercial district, the sun glinted off the majestic Mississippi River in the background, beckoning to her. As she descended the hill, her mind began to release everything else. She passed through the town, saving it for later. She needed to sit by the river first.

Miranda brushed snow and ice off one of the park benches located along the riverfront. She sat, letting the wet, cold chill seep through her jeans. Breathing in the crisp air, she gazed outwards into the swirling, turbulent waters with ice chunks floating on top.

Thinking about curses, she wasn't paying mind to much else until a shadow crossed over her view. Looking up, she covered her eyes against the sun and saw Mark Twain. In full costume. She sprung up from the wet seat.

"Good day, madam," he said, swirling his cape-like overcoat off to one side.

"Hello," Miranda said in a guarded tone.

"Wonderful sunshine we are having!"

She nodded.

"The tour is about to begin. Make haste."

"The tour?"

"Yes, at the museum." He pointed over to a stable type building that now had doors wide open. A sign hung above proclaimed it to be the Hannibal Museum.

Miranda pondered it. A museum was a public place so things would not be able to get too weird with Mark. Plus, she could use it to take her mind off other things.

Mark began to march away, and she found herself following along right behind him. Once they reached the entranceway, Mark swept an arm to one side with a flourish inviting her in. Walking behind him, she stepped onto brick flooring. Exhibit kiosks were positioned throughout the big open space and rooftop skylights provided some light.

Miranda blinked a few times to adjust to the dim inside lighting in contrast to the bright sun outdoors. As she moved to the first exhibit, Mark sidled up right next to her and began to pontificate.

She groaned inwardly, not really wanting a full-on theatrical performance worthy of a Broadway stage. She tried to focus on the nicely done panels of the exhibit in front of her and ignore him. But his booming voice seeped in and she started to realize that his speech was actually quite compelling. She turned her eyes away from the panels as she listened to Mark give details of "his" time in Hannibal, speaking in first person, of course.

When he finished his soliloquy, he made another dramatic flourish with his cape as he waltzed over to the next exhibit. Miranda followed right behind, now drawn in by him rather than repelled. Once at the second kiosk, Miranda interjected into Mark's patter and read aloud to herself the quote that the top of the exhibit was labeled with, '*Whenever you find yourself on the side of the majority, it is time to pause and reflect.*'

"That is one of Mark Twain's quotes, right?" she asked.

He gave a harumph and said, "Yes, it is something I said at some point. I have made many astute observations through the years."

"Oh, I get it now. Every exhibit starts with one of his quotes.

Very clever."

"Yes, I do have to take my fair share of credit for saying many lines of substance. Along with my writings as well."

Picking up right where he had stopped, he continued the talk about the steamboat era in Hannibal and how it had changed the economy of not only the town but the region as well. As they moved to the next kiosk, Miranda caught on to how each kiosk tied into the timeline of the town side by side with the timeline of Mark Twain's life.

Finally, reaching the last one, Mark began to speed up his talk after glancing over to a small group of school aged children just entering. Pointing to the photograph of Mark Twain sitting on his front veranda in Connecticut, he said, "So, he ended his days..."

Miranda interrupted him. "He?"

"I mean...me...I..."

She pointed to the quote above the kiosk. It said: *'Never tell the truth to people who are not worthy of it.'*

Gazing at him, she wondered if he would go back into a little tantrum like he did at the diner. But he did not. Instead, his face creased into a broad grin making his bushy yellowed moustache move widely from one side of his face to the other.

"You got me. I guess you are worthy of the truth."

"So, you know you aren't Mark Twain?"

He rolled his eyes. Then he put a hand by the side of his mustachioed mouth and whispered, "Don't tell the rest of them. Our little secret, okay?"

"Got it."

They parted with Mark going over to greet the schoolchildren using that same theatrical voice and Miranda going to the booth where a clerk now sat to pay her fee. After settling up, the clerk handed over something.

"What's this?"

"Just a little token of our appreciation."

She looked down at a keychain with a pudding award on it—the award that Twain had won.

She held it up to the clerk and said, "Thank you."

Heading back up Hannibal's main drag with more of a spring to her step than when she had started her jaunt, the last bits of sunshine petered out. In her motel room, she thought about truth. She was worthy of the truth and she would ferret it out, one way or the other.

Part Three
Chapter Thirty-two

AS MIRANDA NEARED THE outskirts of Williamsburg, both the heavy weight of fatigue and a need for a hot shower overcame her. The fourteen-plus hour drive had taken its toll, and she felt a wash of relief that it was almost over. Popping into a grocery store on the outskirts of town, she made quick work of buying a few essentials to get her through before a bigger shopping trip. She was due on campus the next day, bright and early.

Finishing the last half hour leg of her trek, she found herself back on Big Island Road with its bowered overhang of shadowy trees and its emptiness, just as she had left it. Her stomach began to knot up, getting ready to face whatever was ahead. Returning to Rosewood, she had to claim it for what it was—hers.

She had talked to Beau on the road a couple of times and had gotten his reassurances that all was as it should be at Rosewood. She recalled the last conversation with him. He had heard some rumors of "the girl from the college" as he put it. But details on his end had been scarce.

She also heard from the sheriff. At a rest stop break, she discovered that Sanford had left a message on her phone at some point between Kentucky and West Virginia. Calling back, he had been strangely available to take her call in a distinctly marked contrast to the other times when Miranda had never been able to get him on the line.

His usual laconic tone had been somewhat altered when he said, "Mizz Chesney, Sheriff Sanford here. Needed to fill you in on a few things." He had gone on to relay what Miranda already knew from Brian. Fiona had been caught out in a psychotic state, talking nonsensical stuff about curses and her rightful place among other things, by a deputy patrolling Rosewood. Once taken to medical care, it had all come out that she had been the perpetrator of all the hijinks (Sanford's word) that had gone on at Rosewood over the past months. He finished by saying, "I think you can rest easy now, Mizz Chesney. This was all just the goings-on of a delusional mind. But the case is closed now, safe to say."

After finishing the conversation, Miranda had sat for a bit to digest the conversation while staring at the brick utilitarian rest stop building in front of her. The sheriff's version of the tale still did not give the full story, much less the details that Brian had alluded to. The details that she may never actually hear from Brian about what lay behind it all. It felt like the other shoe hadn't dropped. Not yet.

Turning her music off, she kept the car silent for the last mile before pulling into Rosewood when the only noise was the sound of crunching tires on the driveway shells. Thanks to Beau, an outside light by the front door was on as well as the stovetop light in the kitchen. Even so, nerves kicked in as she made her way to unlock the front door.

Taking a deep breath, Miranda opened it up, pausing on the threshold. The smell of Rosewood hit her full on with its familiarity, that distinctive scent that had drawn in her so many months back. Despite all the struggles, she had missed it. Walking through the space, she flipped all the lights on, carefully looking around as she did so. All was exactly as it had been when she left two weeks prior. A two-week time warp.

The next morning, the scramble of readying herself for the first day back on campus superseded everything else. Her mind scattered in various directions; office hours, two lectures for new students, a staff meeting, the works. It was always this way at the start of a new semester.

After saying goodbye to Polly, she left Rosewood by eight a.m. into the stillness of the winter morning. Stopping for just a second to look around and still half on alert for finding things amiss, it appeared that all was as it should be and in its place. Feeling the knots of worry in her shoulders begin to loosen a little, she even found herself singing along to the radio as she drove off.

Maybe it would all be okay. Even the Brian thing. Maybe it was all okay. She hadn't contacted him at all since that last call in the motel. He had texted her several times but she just... couldn't. She wasn't ready yet. She just didn't know what to say. And he had seemed to drop off after not hearing back from her. Was that weird, too? Or was it just the crush the semester's start taking off? They were both caught up in the thick of it, as far as the academia bullrush went.

Back on campus, the day went by in a blur. By noon, Miranda was running late for the meeting that the department head had called. Dashing across campus, she entered the area called the Sunken Garden, the college's version of a quad, and headed to the other end where the John Lathrop sat. Her mind on the meeting ahead, she almost bumped into Brian before processing he was right in front of her path.

"Miranda!" he said, grabbing her by the shoulders.

"Oh, Brian," she sputtered out. She shrugged just enough for him to let go as she gazed at him. His face seemed open, not marked by deception of any sort. But Miranda had the fleeting thought that lack of guile might be deception in and of itself.

His eyes took her in with an intensity that she couldn't figure out. "Why didn't you call? Or answer my texts?"

"Long drive, late night. Look, I'm late for Abernathy's meeting," she said as she began to walk away, looking back as she talked. "I'll...I'll text you...later."

He stared at her with an inscrutable expression. She felt her stomach sink as she walked off, not knowing what to do about Brian.

Later, standing in the lecture hall for her last class of the day, a weariness set in as she felt the need for the day to be wrapped up. She stared out at the panorama of faces in front of her, a bigger class than usual. There was a buzz around campus that students thought her class was an easy "A" to fulfill a Gen Ed requirement. She didn't think she gave out easy "A"s, but somehow that was the word on the street.

Letting her mind relax before starting up the lecture, Miranda's own flinch took her by surprise, realizing her focus was on one face in particular: Scott. Fiona's henchman or her right-hand man or her overzealous student. His gaze beamed on her, laser-like, from behind the reflective glass of his wire-rimmed specs.

Feeling a chill run down her spine, Miranda looked down, rifling through the roster in front of her. What was his last name? She couldn't remember. Her stomach plummeted at the idea of that stare all semester long. She pulled herself together realizing it was a minute past start time.

"Hello..." she began and then smoothly picked up the thread of her practiced spiel for the start of any semester. It was a spiel that included what the class would cover, the fundamentals of logic, and a few tidbits about her background.

She avoided looking at Scott to keep her train of thought in check, purposely staring out beyond him which was not easy since he had positioned himself front and center. In the back of her mind, she was already planning out the frank chat she needed to have Dean Abernathy about Scott's presence in her class.

An hour later, the lecture wrapped up with the week's as-signment: "...so the first two chapters of Wittgenstein's Logic Primer, to be read by our next class. Got it?" A few nods here and there in response indicated that the message was received.

Miranda gathered up the books and papers that she had spread out during the lecture as she had consulted them. Then she smelled Scott's presence before looking up to see him. He wore the all-pervasive cologne that seemed to be a favorite of the majority of college guys: Ralph Lauren Polo Black. A scent that spoke one word in her opinion—juvenile.

"Hello, Scott. I don't see your name on the roster," she said tersely.

"That's because I'm not on it."

"Why are you in here then?"

"Don't press charges against Fiona," he began in an impassioned tone. "She was only doing what she felt was right and you, of all people, should understand that."

Miranda raised her eyebrows. "Of all people?"

"A professor of logic, I mean. She doesn't deserve the law on her. She's suffered enough as it is…"

Miranda was flabbergasted but quickly found her voice. "Suffered? Are you kidding me? Do you have any idea what I've been through at Rosewood? You shouldn't even be allowed on campus after the stunts you participated in with her!"

"You just don't understand her. You don't appreciate her like I do. And others too. She's a very special person."

"Wait a minute, did she send you here? Is that what this is about?"

His face shifted to one side and she knew right away she was right. He was still playing the role of Fiona's lackey.

"You know, Scott, I just realized you haven't even apologized for your role in all this."

"My role?" he said, having the gall for incredulousness seep into the statement.

"Yes, your role. You know, special or not, under the eyes of law, you can't break and enter into peoples' property. Also, it might be a gray area but 'gathering ceremonies' might also be frowned upon in a court of law. So, back off."

"But what about the charges? Are you making any?"

"I am done with this conversation."

He stared at her with complete malevolence in his gaze. "You are such a witch. Fiona is so right about you." He turned on his heel and stomped out to the door.

Watching his departure, she shook her head at Scott's brazen gall. The sheriff was leaving it up to her whether she wanted to press charges against Fiona or not—or any of the others, for that matter. But it was crystal clear that the pull that Fiona had over others was, in a word, potent. It may well be necessary after all to follow through on those charges.

Chapter Thirty-three

THE LONG DRIVE, THE first day of classes, the Scott issue and the Brian dilemma all caught up with Miranda by the next morning, leaving her exhausted and groggy upon waking. After tossing and turning for most of the night, she had resolved that she had to talk to some of the others involved before she confronted Brian. With no classes for the day, she got ready by fortifying herself with a strong cup of coffee then headed straight to Fiona's aunt's house.

Pulling up in the Toyota, Caro's place looked exactly as it had at her previous visit. Miranda strode over to the front door, not giving herself the chance to hesitate at all. After knocking several times, the door finally opened. Caro stared back at her with dull eyes, her gray hair hanging down long. Miranda's pulse quickened to see the hair like that, not in its usual updo, rather in the style from the gathering night.

"Yes?" Caro finally said.

"Um...hi. I think we need to clear the air, Caro."

The other woman gave a big sigh opening the door wider. Miranda walked in and took in the interior, astounded by the sight. The place was filled to the brim without one barren spot. It was obvious that Caro was a hoarder.

"It's crowded up here in the front. Come on back."

As they squeezed their way through the tight hallway cramped by stacks of boxes and magazines, Miranda was overwhelmed by all the stuff that obscured figuring out the basic floorplan of the house. But she could still see enough that it appeared to be just like Rosewood with the kitchen in the rear.

In the kitchen, a very small area had remained carved out enough from all the hoarding for a table. Two chairs were pressed close together, with just enough table surface cleared for dining. Caro pointed to the chairs and Miranda seated herself.

"You want coffee?" Caro asked in that same dull voice.

"Sure. Thank you."

As Caro fumbled around the kitchen for coffee, Miranda took in the packed-out room, riddled with so much inventory. Her mind could barely process any of it. After a few minutes, Carol brought two coffee mugs to the table where they both had to sit way too close to each other.

Miranda murmured her thanks as she stared down into the cup, half-silted up with coffee grounds and the other half, murky liquid. As Caro watched her, Miranda lifted the mug to her mouth and took a delicate sip to show her appreciation. Inwardly grimacing, she set the mug back down and started up the conversation.

"How's your kitty doing?"

Caro's eyes gazed towards the wall. "Miss Janie left again."

Miranda was momentarily jarred by the mention of Miss Janie, but then remembered the cat was named after the previous owner of Rosewood. In a way, "Miss Janie left again" could have had meaning on several levels.

"Oh, I'm sorry. I'll keep a look out for her." Miranda wondered if the loss of the cat was contributing to Caro's demeanor in part, or if it was all Fiona. Or maybe the loss of the human Miss Janie. Or maybe a combination.

She started up again. "Like I said, Caro, I'd like to clear the air. We're neighbors and I'd like to be...well, neighborly?"

Caro stared off at a spot to the left of Miranda. Then she spoke. "That's fine. I don't have a problem with you."

"Um...well, I know you were a part of that ceremony with the blue bottle back before the holiday..."

The other woman grimaced. "Oh, that was just letting Fiona have her fun. I do what I can to keep her happy. I try to, anyway..." Her voice drifted off.

"Yeah, so, I don't really understand yet what that was all about. Why she felt the need to...to, well, to curse me like that."

Caro sniffled, not saying anything. Rather, she fiddled with her long, gray hair. Miranda gazed at her, again triggered by the hairstyle with its associations to the gathering. Setting her nerves aside, she reminded herself it wasn't the hair as much as the history behind Caro's appearance.

Almost as though Caro had read Miranda's mind, she said, "You like my hair down like this?'

"Uh...sure. Sure. It's, um, nice."

"I know it makes some feel anxious. Letting my hair down long. On a woman my age...like I'm trying to be a witch, right?"

"Are you?"

"Am I what?"

"A witch? Or trying to be a witch? Is that what the ceremony was really about?"

Caro shook her head. "Nah." She paused, still fiddling with the hair. "You have to understand.," Caro said. "Fiona has always been a sensitive child...she always had intense emotions."

First, Scott had gone on about Fiona being "special," and now Caro was trying to cover it up by calling her "sensitive." It was too much. Miranda stopped any more of it by putting up a hand and said, "She's not a child."

"Well, I think of her as a child. We didn't see any harm in humoring her with it because...."

"Because why?"

Caro gathered up the long strands and pulled it back with a hair clip.

"Because she's my family, that's why."

"Okay, but, apparently, it took her to a very dark place."

The woman shrugged and Miranda found her more disturbing somehow with her hair up rather than down. Distracted, Miranda wondered if it was a sexist thing on her part about the hair.

"So...I'm sorry she's in the hospital now. I hope she gets the help she needs. How is she?"

Again, Caro shrugged. "She won't let me in to see her, they

said." Her chin wobbled and she became more emotional, sniffling again. "Don't know where I went wrong. All I ever tried to do was help."

"What got her into the whole archeology thing, and working for Brian Beckett?"

Caro breathed in deep and got lost in thought again before answering. "It was at the high school."

"The high school?"

She nodded. "He went over there and put on some kind of dog and pony show. Hawking his wares about his archeology gig."

Caro went silent again for a pause. Then she added, "Fiona came home that day and I'll never forget it. She was spell-bound."

Caro seemed to check herself, realizing her word choice was ironic and looked at Miranda with some chagrin.

"I mean...I just mean, she was real taken with him. And then she busted her butt to make the grades and get into the college. And she did it."

"Sounds like you're not a fan of Brian."

"He's the one that caused all this hubbub. With his fancy ideas about the dig and leading Fiona on like he did."

"He led her on? How?"

"I don't know exactly, but...you know, he's like the hometown boy in my stories."

"Stories?"

"My soaps that I watch."

"How so?"

"Well, in the stories, the hometown boy who done good comes back to lord it over everybody else."

"Really? Wait...did Brian grow up around here?"

Caro shot Miranda an incredulous look. "You don't know?"

"Know what?"

"He lived during his teens at Rosewood. With Miss Janie. She took him in when his daddy died."

Miranda felt as though the air had been sucked right out of her. When she found her voice again, she said, "He never said... why wouldn't he have said anything..."

Caro shrugged and then looked at her shrewdly. "Shouldn't you be asking him that?"

"Yes. Yes, I should."

The two women sat quietly and Miranda distractedly raised the mug to her lips, forgetting what was in it. She placed it down quickly instead as she realized something. "So...did Fiona know Brian as a child?"

"Sure. Everyone knows everyone around here."

"Yeah. I know that." A claustrophobic feeling suddenly overcame Miranda and caught up with her. She wiggled out of the tight space and stood up abruptly.

"I need to go. Thanks...for the coffee and, again, I want to put all this behind us," she said half-heartedly. She lost her train of thought as her gaze cast over the disorder of the place again. But then she remembered one more thing. "Do you know where I can find Lizzie Gooding this time of day?"

"Well, she's probably at her daddy's house I'd suspect. Where else would she be?"

With that, Caro reached behind her head undoing the clip that held her hair back. As her hair flowed down to either side of her face, Miranda looked at her one last time, again rattled by the effect. She picked her way out of the hovel-like interior and softly closed the door behind her.

Once outdoors, she gulped in fresh air. Digesting the scene with Caro, she felt prickles of worry, disturbed by the visit. The most disturbing was most certainly Caro's revelation about Brian.

Chapter Thirty-four

DRIVING DOWN TO THE Gooding's house, Miranda's mind went round and round, not able to justify Brian's secrecy on any level. He had never once mentioned or alluded to the fact that he had actually lived at Rosewood. It seemed devious. It seemed wrong. It seemed the ultimate in deception.

Turning onto the Gooding's rutted drive, she absentmindedly took in how different it looked from her other trip down it with all foliage now pared down from the winter. Just like the rest of the area, there was a barren bleakness that pervaded. Getting closer to the house, it appeared to be maybe a little grayer, maybe a little more deteriorated. She startled at the sight of a figure sitting on the front porch despite the cold temperature of the day.

It was Lizzie and, once closer, Miranda could see that the horrible, big dog was actually sitting on Lizzie's lap, as if it was a small dog, almost shrouding her entirely. Since it *wasn't* a small dog, it made for an incongruous sight.

Miranda rolled her window down and said, "Lizzie. Can we talk?"

Lizzie gave a slow nod but made no move to get up and come over to the car.

"Um...can you put the dog in the house?"

"You scared of Cletus?" Lizzie asked with a tone of disbelief. "He wouldn't hurt you none."

"Well...could you just put him in the house? Please?"

Lizzie with some effort lifted herself up with Cletus in

her arms. The dog struggled to get down and then Lizzie said, "Git," nudging him with a sneakered foot inside the house. The Doberman looked back at Miranda with a baleful glance but did as told.

Miranda stepped out of her car slowly, worried Cletus might come crashing out of the door. Standing at the bottom of the porch steps, she looked up at Lizzie. "I wanted to thank you."

"What for?"

"For telling me about the gathering. Because...I think I've figured out a lot since then."

Lizzie gave one of her characteristic shrugs and started trilling.

Miranda decided on the direct tack. "I'm sorry to hear about Fiona. I know you and she are close."

Lizzie stopped trilling and got silent.

"I'm sure they can help her get better," Miranda said.

Lizzie spoke up. "Maybe. Or maybe not." Miranda did not know what to make of that response so she bypassed it with another question.

"Do you remember the guy that was at Princeton store that day? He was with me and he tried to talk to you?"

"Hhmm."

Miranda took that as a yes and continued. "Lizzie, did you know Brian when he lived at Miss Janie's?"

She nodded up and down in an exaggerated fashion.

"Why didn't you...um, okay. So, what do you remember about him?"

Lizzie's face took on a mulish expression and she folded her arms across her chest either from the cold or from the memories. "He thought he could make Miss Janie like him better than me. But he was wrong."

"Ah. So, did you get to know him when he lived at Rosewood?"

She didn't answer.

"Was he nice to you?"

Lizzie shrugged and started trilling louder, not looking directly at Miranda.

Finding out more about Brian's machinations from Lizzie would be a dead end probably. Miranda scrambled to come up with what else she needed to ask the enigma in front of her that was Lizzie. If only she could tap into what Lizzie knew. It might help her figure the entire mess out.

"Okay...so, I've been wondering how people could have gotten into Rosewood after I changed the locks. I mean, the crawl space might be one way but do you know? Are there any secret ways into Rosewood?"

The trilling started up louder again.

Miranda tried again. "Did Miss Janie ever show you another way in, maybe?"

Lizzie stopped trilling abruptly and said, "There's a tunnel."

Miranda stood very still. "A tunnel? Where...why?"

Lizzie finally spoke again in a low voice. "Cuts under the kitchen. Used to, anyways. Before you got all these folks riding herd over the place." Miranda heard some bitterness in Lizzie's voice.

"There's a way through the crawl space then?" Miranda's question hung unanswered as she gazed at the woman trilling in front of her. She was unsettled at the idea of a tunnel possibly underneath what she considered her private sanctuary. People might have been in that tunnel when she had not been there and, also, when she had been there, sleeping. Maybe it had only been Fiona, or maybe not. Was it all done now that Fiona was safely ensconced elsewhere?

Miranda would figure out if there was a tunnel and make it secure. Heck, maybe she could turn it into one of those fancy wine caves that were all the rage. She had read something about the perfect temperature being the ultimate in wine storage. Her mind meandered in that direction but she shook herself as the trilling from Lizzie intensified.

Looking at the woman in front of her—the peroxide-bleached out hair, dark roots showing through, the ragged, painted fingernails and the heavily made-up face—Miranda realized she was no longer disturbed by Lizzie. Instead, she felt a warmth towards this remarkably odd woman who had clearly, in her way, done Miranda a good turn.

After saying goodbye and driving away, Miranda's mind wandered back to her earliest research efforts into the Gwynn family when three sisters or three daughters had cropped up. It had stuck in her mind as something, but she didn't know what that something was at the time.

Now, it occurred to her that she too had become a part of a loose triangulation of sisters. Clumsily stepping in as a sort of replacement by proxy into a trio of females that included Miss Janie, Lizzie and Fiona, she had taken Miss Janie's place at Rosewood, blissfully unaware that she'd been playing a role she didn't understand. But she did understand there was power in that symbolism of three connected females. She just didn't know what to make of it, exactly.

Chapter Thirty-five

MIRANDA SHRUGGED OFF HER morning with Caro and Lizzie as best she could and drove out to meet Beau for coffee at Joe's Restaurant in the afternoon. She'd missed him and was eager for a chatty reunion.

When Miranda approached the table, Beau half stood up, his face wrinkling more into his smile. "Look who's back! Good to see you, young lady."

Miranda leaned in towards him for a hug. They had not been on hugging terms before but she felt the need to do so. After having been through so much by this point, she needed the hug too.

After Miranda got a coffee, Beau said, "So, fill me in. What all have you been digging up now?"

"You go first while I get some of this coffee down."

"We already covered the college gal having the meltdown, right?"

"Not all the details but the gist of it. And the sheriff called me and said he was satisfied that all the 'hijinks' had been down to her."

Beau nodded and said, "Yep. Me too. 'Cause Rosewood was quiet as could be every time I checked on it. I think your problems have been solved, missy."

"Except, well, there is one thing that sticks out now..." Miranda went into the tale of Brian and how he had lied by omission for unknown reasons.

Beau's brow was furrowed as he listened. After she finished, he said, "How about that? He never mentioned a thing that time I showed it to him and the college gal. Huh."

"Yeah, so, now...What do I do?"

"Ask him straight up, right?"

Miranda said, "Maybe. Or maybe just leave it. And say nothing."

"Could do that. He's all finished with his digging so...yeah, you could do that."

They both paused and took sips of coffee. Around them, the rest of the diner filled in with comforting noises: the sizzling of the griddle, the idle chatter of the old timers sitting at the countertop and the waitress' shoes squeaking on the floor as they walked back and forth.

Miranda broke the pause. "I almost forgot. Before I left, you told me about the crawl space. Did you ever take a look at it?"

Beau smacked himself on the forehead. "Oh, geez. I plumb forgot about that. With all the other things going on and the cameras to look at and everything."

Miranda immediately felt guilty. "I'm sorry to have put so much on you."

"Not at'll. Not at'll. Things settled down after that gal was hauled off..." He left the rest unsaid that surveillance duties at Rosewood had not been as time consuming after Fiona's downfall.

"So, I don't know how fanciful it might be, but Lizzie Gooding told me this morning that Miss Janie had told her there was a tunnel."

"A tunnel?"

"Yeah... Said it connected somehow into the kitchen. Or she said it used to. She didn't know if it was still there. I was thinking about the crawl space. Do you think that's where it could be?"

Beau sat back in the booth. "Hhmm. That's a real mind bender. I don't see how something like that would have not been figured out already. Either by us, or the home inspector you had."

"I mean, I've looked at it from the exterior as best I could. I don't see anything at all."

"It could be a red herring on Lizzie's part. Just something to throw out in conversation, you know? She's an odd duck like that."

"That she is."

"I don't think I would give it much thought right now. It might involve too much tearing up of the place to pin anything down. And you've had enough of that."

Miranda nodded. "Yeah, I'm so over any more workmen in the house. Forever."

"I hear you."

After they parted, Miranda felt bolstered. Beau reassured her everything was back on track. She had made peace as best she could with Caro and Lizzie. In time, maybe the rest of the community would follow suit with how they acted towards her. Hopefully, she could settle back in at Rosewood without worrying about more nonsense going on. There was just Brian as the last nagging thorn.

After driving back from the diner, Miranda stepped out of the car and headed right to the rear facade of Rosewood. The afternoon light had shifted enough to get a good hard look at the crawl space area. She ran a hand over the freshly painted white lattice work that covered it up. Examining closer in a squatting position, she could not see any area where a piece had been taken apart or was out of whack. Tugging at the corner, nothing gave. There was just no way someone could have been using this as an access point that she could see. In fact, she would place a fair wager on that fact. She dusted her hands off and stood back up.

Taking her investigation indoors, Miranda examined all around the kitchen area where the crawl space was underneath. Getting down on all fours, she took a hard look at the floorboards to see if any of them met funny. There was nothing. She ran a hand over the wood that had been polyurethaned to a gleaming finish, reminded of how the details of Rosewood had drawn her in and how much she loved it. Standing back up, she felt comfort in the space around her for the first time in a long while.

As she settled into her evening, Miranda fell into the routine of making dinner and later watched Polly enjoy her new cat cave. But the matter of Brian lingered, like an itch that she couldn't avoid scratching.

Finally, she plopped down on the sofa and stared at her cell as if it might have all the answers. The last real contact with Brian was the first day back in the Sunken Garden rushing to class. She had basically been ghosting him since then. Miranda still hadn't formulated exactly what to say.

But he had just sent a text several hours earlier. She looked at it again: "Miranda can we talk". Oddly, there was no question mark at the end of that line. Or any punctuation, for that matter. Like it wasn't a question or, he gotten interrupted. She wasn't going to do this by text or phone. It was going to be face to face. She would carve out time first thing the next day to go to his office. In the meantime, she would figure out what needed to be said.

Chapter Thirty-six

THE DRIVE INTO TOWN early the next morning made Miranda's stomach go all aflutter at the thought of confronting Brian. She had already gone over it in her head a hundred times since waking up. She considered it to be an indictments list, mainly comprised of lies by omission. She reviewed it again as she drove, glazing over the passing scenery and the bright day outside the windshield. Instead, her thoughts churned through all that he had not said and not done. The indictments list.

It started with Brian not revealing his viewing of Rosewood with Fiona when it had been up for sale. Beau had told her that. Then Brian never indicated being from the area, or that his family roots went way back in the Tidewater region. In fact, he even hinted being from other places; places more sophisticated, more liberal-minded. Miranda's mind snagged on that point. Was that just how she wanted to see him? Had she projected that onto him? The so-called "woke" academic persona?

This ultimately led to the whole Fiona debacle. He only let out bits and pieces until the night of the gathering when he claimed to be protecting Miranda. Had it *really* been protection when the reality felt like ghosting? Finally, the top hit on the list: not ever saying he had lived at Rosewood for a period of time with Miss Janie.

As her nervousness heightened, she wondered if he would answer for any of it. Would he just have a glib response for each red flag? Would she be suckered and charmed out of questioning the validity of anything he said? All she could do was try.

Miranda pulled into the parking area closest to Brian's office building and could see a thin veneer of frost twinkling on the pavement. The morning was colder than normal, but weather in the Mid-Atlantic was seldom predictable. She hurried towards the building, pulling her polar fleece jacket closer, thinking about her ancestors putting up with the region's mercurial weather patterns. All they had been through made her current trials seem so much less odious.

As it was very early, activity on campus was minimal. She hoped to catch Brian before his student office hours. But she also hoped there would be a few people wandering around, maybe at least the department secretary. On the off chance that...Miranda stopped in her tracks. Did she worry that Brian was dangerous? Someone she had slept with in her very own bed. The thought sent more of a chill through her that had nothing to do with the cold. It didn't bear focusing on. It was too uncomfortable.

Her footfall made a dull sound as she walked down the empty hall. Too empty. There was no one else around—at all. She went back in her head to the very first time she had met him in his office. His larger-than-life presence sitting at his desk in the middle of a mountain of scattered papers and books and eating a pastry.

Getting closer, his office door was slightly cracked. She stopped a few feet away to catch her breath and calm herself. Moving forward, she pushed gently on the door to open it. It didn't register at first, the sight in front of her eyes. She was expecting the larger-than-life presence and the mess and the books and the papers. What she saw instead was something totally opposite.

The room had been stripped of all contents other than the desk, chair and bookcase which were completely empty, save for some dust bunnies. Her eyes roamed around the space trying to understand what had happened. Brian and all parts of him in his office had seemingly vanished.

Suddenly, there was a voice saying, "Can I help you?"

She swiveled to see Myra behind her, the department secretary. The one she had hoped to be already in her office at this early hour.

"Oh, Professor Chesney. I didn't recognize you from behind," Myra said in her refined Tidewater Virginia accent.

Despite the early hour, Myra was attired crisply in pantyhose, a navy skirt and a violet cardigan, daintily clipped with a cameo brooch. Her silver hair was styled in a tasteful, page girl bob. It was like she had stepped out of a photography book from another time and place.

"What...what happened? Where is Brian...I mean, Professor Beckett?"

Myra shook her head with a grim expression. "It's a bad situation."

"Is he okay?"

"I doubt it. He was escorted out by the campus police last night...late. I had to stay until it was resolved."

"What? Why?"

Myra looked over her shoulder and then bent closer to Miranda with a confidential air. "I don't know all of it, but, apparently...." She paused again, looking to see if anyone else was within hearing distance but the hall was completely silent and bereft of all others, especially Brian. "He was bilking funds from the department. Covering it up somehow with his archeological digs. Especially that one at Rosewood. Oh, wait...isn't that your house?" With that, she peered at Miranda with some suspicion.

Miranda closed her eyes for a second to close out the other woman's expression, to close out all of it. Opening her eyes, she said, "Yes, it's my house. But I had no idea, of course."

"Well, anyhow, I need to lock this room up, Dean Abernathy said. He just called me. It was a late night for all of us as you can imagine. A lot of damage control now." She edged Miranda out as she pulled the door closed.

Miranda shook her head with disbelief. "I just can't believe this. I was coming here this morning to catch him before his office hours with his students. His students...What's going to happen?"

"Like I said, damage control now. But don't you worry,

we've dealt with worse."

"Do you know by any chance where he went?"

"No idea. I would hope for his sake he's lining up a good lawyer about now."

"Can you...can I...can you give me his address?" The thought that she had never been to his apartment or even thought to ask about it seemed strange to her now.

"I really shouldn't," Myra answered.

"Please...I wouldn't ask unless it was important." She finagled the truth and added, "He had results of the dig for me about my house. If I don't track him down, they may be lost forever."

The woman stared at her as if deciding before nodding. "Okay, come with me to my desk."

Leaving the building with the post-it note that Myra had written out for her with Brian's address, Miranda wandered in a daze back to her car. Sitting in the cold car, her mind puzzled out what to do next. Go directly there and confront him? Hold back and wait for the college to do what they needed to do? But what if he took off?

All the answers she wanted, she would never get. But did she need to get them? What was the point now? After all, he was clearly a liar and, apparently, a thief too. A flare of anger shot through her. The point was to make him answer for all of it. To her face. That was the point. She started up the car and headed over to the apartment complex where he lived.

Even though she had never been invited to his apartment (disturbing in itself and something that should've been a tip off, she now thought with chagrin), she knew the complex well. With high rent costs in the historic area of town, many professors chose to live in this particular complex constructed in the 1970s in a bland style. Devoid of any charm, it was the antithesis of the historic allure of Williamsburg. Mundane but practical, Miranda had always thought, when visiting other faculty members there.

She pulled in with the post-it note in hand. Checking the number, she drove deeper into the complex. As she got nearer to his apartment, she sighted him outside, carrying items towards a dumpster. Upon the sight of him in his customary flannel shirt and jeans, that flare of anger burned more than ever. No flare of passion anymore. Just the anger left. She busted out of the car and made her way over. He looked up in surprise.

She came to an abrupt halt at a closer view of him, his hair standing on end, his clothes in disarray as though they had been slept in, and his eyes darting left to right. His gaze shifted to the left and stayed put, not looking straight at her.

"Miranda," he said with a hoarse voice.

"What is this, Brian? What is all of this?"

He stared at her as if evaluating what she knew. She beat him to the punch. "I know all of it. Well, maybe not all of it. Apparently, your stack of secrets is pretty high. But I know you got kicked off campus last night."

He looked down at the box of miscellaneous items and trash he was holding. "Yeah...but they're wrong about me. I just need a chance to explain..."

"In the meantime, explain to me this..." Miranda spun off her indictments list to him. When she finished, there was nothing but silence.

He turned his back on her and walked over to the dumpster, tossing in what he was holding. Then he passed right by her, saying nothing.

"Are you kidding me? You aren't going to say *anything?*" She followed him as he strode back to the apartment complex. She kept badgering him until he finally reeled around at her with fire in his eyes. Miranda stepped back.

"I don't know, okay? I don't know why I didn't tell you any of it. I didn't want to...want to..."

"What? Want to what?"

"Make you think less of me, I guess."

"But you did so much worse, Brian. So much worse."

"Yeah, I get that. I know."

"What are you doing right now? Moving boxes...what is that about?"

He rubbed his hand over his face. "I don't know. I don't

know yet."

She felt sorry for him all of sudden, which caught her off guard. But she couldn't be pulled into all of his mistakes. Standing there in their weird, frozen diorama in the apartment complex parking lot next to the dumpster, it struck her that she shouldn't be there, confronting the man in front of her.

Feeling the slight chill in the air around them, goosebumps prickled up on her skin, bringing her back to her senses. She was done. Done with all the mixed messages and attempts at divining the meaning of his words. Done with the two of them being awkward and stilted actors in their roles. What remained was the need to step out of the weird, frozen diorama.

Finally, Brian looked at her directly with his golden-brown eyes that hid so many secrets. Too many secrets for her to ever take on. Miranda turned and walked away.

Chapter Thirty-seven

LANDING BACK ON CAMPUS, Miranda burrowed into her office, a space far smaller than Brian's. She slumped over her desk, miserable with all that had happened and still not understanding much of it. Brian had come so far in his career and now, it had been blown to bits.

Maybe he was one of those people that could not tell the truth. Compulsive liars, she'd heard them called. Maybe all their interchanges had been like that and she just hadn't let herself realize it. She'd been blinded by lust, or something like it.

A note then slipped under her closed door with a whisper of paper against tile, and she roused herself to go pick it up, fighting a heavy weight of lethargy as she did so. Dean Abernathy wanted to see her in an hour, the note said.

"Ugh," she groaned, knowing immediately it must be about Brian. She could only hope she wasn't somehow implicated in his problems. That suspicious look on Myra's face flashed through her mind. College politics being what they were, she needed to stay in Abernathy's good graces. She didn't imagine he was too happy with all of the swirling drama around of late.

An hour later, Miranda found herself sitting on the other side of Dean Abernathy's enormous desk making her feel like a child in contrast. After he greeted her at the door, they had seated themselves: Abernathy in his plush looking leather swivel chair and Miranda in the hard backed visitor chair. She fleetingly wondered why he didn't care about his visitors' comfort.

An uncomfortable silence filled the space as Abernathy sat back, tenting his fingers. Waiting for him to speak, Miranda processed the man behind those tented fingers. His gray hair lay flat over to one side. Heavy frames on his glasses only went so far to cover an acne scarred face from his youth a lifetime earlier. The eyes under the glass were beady and sharp.

He cleared his throat as if to emphasize the gravity of the conversation. "Well, Professor Chesney, as you can imagine, we have a PR situation here for the college."

She nodded in what she hoped was a grave nod.

"Those higher up the chain want to make sure all this is handled appropriately. Again, I am sure you can understand."

Miranda was getting the sneaking suspicion some blame had been cast her way. She spoke up. "So, I want to say up front I knew nothing of any of this."

Abernathy nodded in a conciliatory manner. "We know that, we know that. Your house, though, was the tipping point unfortunately."

"How? How was Rosewood the tipping point?" Miranda asked.

"Well, because of an anomaly in the Rosewood expense reports, we uncovered that monies had been siphoned off to a phony account. Not just for Rosewood but other digs Beckett had set up as well. Prior to Rosewood, that is. But Rosewood puts you right in the middle of the frame, doesn't it?"

Again, she felt that underlay of blame. "Yes, but again, the contract I signed with Brian—I mean Professor Beckett—and the college was all above board. There was no way I could have known—"

Abernathy put up a hand and interrupted. "Of course, of course. All legitimate on our ends. Beckett, however, was another story." A shadow fell over his face and he said, almost to himself, "I kick myself that I didn't pick anything up in that initial interview. Anyway..."

"Any idea why he was up to all this? What he needed the money for?"

The dean shrugged. "Who knows? Why does anybody steal

money?"

"I mean, could it be a drug habit? Or an addiction of another sort? Gambling maybe?"

He leaned forward towards her and spoke in a lower tone. "I probably shouldn't be divulging this but...we have been contacted by a federal investigator."

Miranda sucked in some air as she let out a "Whaat...?"

"They suspect him of buying and selling artifacts on the black market. And, if that's the case...Needless to say, he's in a lot of trouble."

"I can promise you I knew nothing—nothing—at all about what was going on with the dig. Or black-market doings. Or misappropriated funds. All I did was offer my house up as a dig site—which the college signed off on." Miranda looked down at her lap and the two of them sat in silence for a bit with the heaviness of Brian's actions.

The dean cleared his throat again. "So, you had a personal relationship with Beckett?"

Miranda jerked reflexively. "No...no. I mean, well, yes... but..."

He looked over the heavy rims of his glasses. "What is the answer, Professor Chesney? It should be as simple as yes or no."

It wasn't that simple. That was the problem and she didn't know how to convey that to the dean. Also, she didn't know that it was any of his business who she slept with. Feeling pinpricks of irritation, she knew she was walking a fine political line but the college bore more responsibility for Brian's machinations than her at the end of the day.

She avoided answering directly and, instead, blurted out, "The bigger issue might have been his teaching assistant, Fiona Lassiter."

The dean raised his eyebrows. "How do you mean?"

"Well, you know about her breakdown, of course..." When he nodded, she continued, "She apparently had an obsession with him. I asked him about it pointblank before we...before I... anyway, he denied that he was doing anything inappropriate. Now, I don't have any idea whatsoever if that's the truth or not."

"I see...I see...well, I will do what I can on my end to make sure the people upstairs know that your role in this seems... fairly innocent. Hopefully, that will insure this doesn't need to go any further."

"Further?"

"A disciplinary action. That kind of thing."

Miranda pressed her lips together so she wouldn't let out a string of curse words. How dare Abernathy act like she was the one in the wrong here? She stood abruptly and dusted her pants off. "Right, then. I'll go back to work."

"Yes," he said as he stood up too behind his desk. "And... uh...we will keep you apprised of any developments."

She gave him a terse nod and then stormed out of the room. The absolute nerve of him. Miranda then stomped back to her cubby of an office and threw her things in her bag. She was skipping school. Not that she had any classes to teach, but still...she was skipping school.

In the half hour drive back to Rosewood, her head swam with all the emotions: frustration, anger, fear, despair. What a mess, what a muddle. She needed to vent it all out somehow. And she had just the idea of how to do it. There was still enough daylight left.

Back at Rosewood, Miranda headed to the carriage barn where her bike sat in one of the padlocked hay sheds. Pulling it out, she rubbed off cobwebs and dust with a rag. It wasn't an ideal time of the year to ride but she needed it.

Once on the bike, she hit the road hard, taking a route she had done a few times before. On the empty roadways, typical of any season in Bisoux, she began to pound out all the anxiety and stress. The ride started to work its magic about the same time that her muscles began to tighten and complain.

Miranda pulled into her half-way point, a public boat landing with a nearby dock. It stood deserted, with the sole exception of a beat-up pickup truck parked in the lot. Panting for breath, she faced the reality that the winter months had taken away her level of fitness, along with other things.

Disentangling herself from the bike, she began to walk

along the dock, stretching out the kinks as she went. Miranda shielded her eyes against the glare to view the clear expanse of water that shone as far as her eyes could see. Her breathing slowed down as she took it all in. It was all bigger than her, all of it. It was the reminder she needed.

After a time, Miranda turned her back away from the bay and headed back to her bike. Glancing over towards the pickup, she gave a start at the sight of a figure in the driver's seat. The figure had not been there when she had passed by the first time. That was weird. Had he been lying down and had now popped up?

Here she was, alone in the middle of nowhere with only the Chesapeake Bay for protection. She had nothing in the way of weapon on her person. Keeping one hand on her cell phone in her pocket, she rushed over quickly to her bike. Just as she stepped off the dock, the truck door creaked open in a high whiny noise and the person climbed out of the pickup.

Miranda continued to stride to her bike as he stepped towards her. Passing by him within several feet, she caught a glimpse of a dirt smudged t-shirt only partially covered by his flannel jacket and quickly processed the words that declared him to be 100% American emblazoned over a flag. His baseball cap hung halfway over his eyes but she knew those eyes were tracking her. He could easily be cast in a bad made for TV movie about a clueless woman biking out in the countryside and getting abducted.

Her heart pounding hard in her ears, he spoke up as she picked up her bike. "Where you off to in such a hurry?"

"No hurry. Just getting on my bike."

His eyes squinted at her underneath the ball cap labeled, No Fat Chicks Allowed. "Wait a minute. I know you. You're the one everybody says is that witch that moved to Bisoux."

Her day couldn't get any more ludicrous and she decided to just own it. "Yeah. I'm the witch."

He gave her a dumbfounded look. "You call yourself that, too?"

"I'm being sarcastic." In case he didn't know that word, she added, "I know that's what the gossips are saying, but have no fear. I'm not a witch."

It was a laughable scene, Miranda trying to convince a 250-plus pound brute of a guy that she wasn't a witch.

He let out an unexpected peal of laughter. "This place... people got too much time on their hands. They need to shut their traps."

"I'll agree with you on that point."

"I'm Ronnie, by the way. Lizzie Gooding's cousin. You know Lizzie, right?"

"Yes...she's a...um...she's a good neighbor."

His face lit up in a smile. "She's a sweetheart, ain't she? Folks don't understand her..." His voice softened. Sweetheart wasn't the description that came to mind, but Miranda nodded.

"She told me some about you. She was real worried for you...for a time."

"Really?" Miranda placed a foot down to stabilize her bike, now curious with the turn the conversation had taken.

He spit a wad of chewing tobacco to the opposite side of Miranda before he spoke again. "Said she had to untangle some knots and help you out. Sometimes, she talks in riddles like that. But you can be sure she was taking care of business."

"Taking care of business?"

"Everything settled down at your place, right?"

"Well...yeah. I guess you could say that. Except that everybody around here still thinks I'm a witch."

They both laughed and, in that moment, in the sunshine with the crisp air and the light reflecting off the bay in front of her, Miranda felt more connection to the place than she ever had.

"You ride all the way out here from your house?"

"Yep. It wasn't that bad. No headwinds. Just cold. I needed the exercise. How about you?"

"Huh...oh, I'm just staring at the bay. Wanting to get back out there. Chomping at the bit more like. Waiting for better days, I guess."

Wanting and waiting for better days...Miranda thought he

had summed it up nicely. She said aloud, "Good to meet you, Ronnie. I'm Miranda, by the way, and tell anyone you can that I'm not a witch."

"You got it, Miranda." He tipped his ball cap towards her and stood there as she pedaled away from the dock.

As she biked down the narrow road, she thought how she had misjudged him on first sight. Just as people had been misjudging her. A mile or two into the ride back, she could hear the battle-weary engine of Ronnie's truck get closer behind her. As he passed, he gave her a honk and a wave. She knew it would take time, more time, but she would eventually find her place in Bisoux and not be known as the outsider witch... someday.

Chapter Thirty-eight

THE WEEK THAT FOLLOWED was a whirl-wind of department meetings, phone calls and regular duties. Wherever Miranda was on campus, talk spread like wildfire about Brian's transgressions. She felt underwater keeping up with all of it: the theft of the monies, the federal investigation, the black-market stuff and then more trickling out about his past. Apparently, he had played similar con games prior to this one. Despite the same behavior at his last university post, he had somehow managed to get the position at William and Mary.

The very same day Miranda had seen him at his apartment complex, a dumpster fire had been ignited followed by the discovery that Brian was gone. No one knew where, but theories abounded. His vehicle hadn't been traced but it could have easily been exchanged for something else with his cash, another supposition floating around campus. With the monies he had stolen, he could live for a while out of the country. Maybe Mexico or South America. It was sometimes too much to take in—Brian was a devious criminal and she had been so painfully ignorant of that fact.

News of Brian's doings spread out of the community and flooded into the national spotlight. It vied for competition in luridness with the cheating scandal, Operation Varsity Blues. Who was to say which was more egregious in nature?

Miranda sat in her office a couple weeks into the whole affair, still mulling all of it round and round when a call from Dean Abernathy came in.

"Professor Chesney. Hope you are well today."

Miranda murmured something non-committal and the dean continued. "I took the liberty of arranging an interview for you. A fellow named..." As he paused, she could hear papers shuffled. "Ah...here it is. Drew Connor."

"Um...interview?"

"Yes, we have decided to cooperate with a news source that has guaranteed that the college will be portrayed in the most appropriate, and favorable I might add, light."

"Okkaay..." Miranda dragged out the word trying to figure out how to ask why she was involved in this. "Why am I going to be interviewed?"

Abernathy cleared his throat in that now all too familiar way. "This gives you an opportunity to settle the score, so to speak. To make it perfectly clear that all was—as you said yourself—above board at Rosewood. It's really the least you can do."

Miranda inhaled before saying, "All right, I understand. And...thank you, Dean. I'll make sure to set everything straight." She knew that this was Abernathy's way of giving her a leg up. As much as she didn't think she had anything to be blamed about, she also knew she had to give him his due. It was how the game was played.

"Certainly, Professor. Soon all of this will be in the past."

Miranda arranged to meet the reporter off campus at a coffee shop. As she sat waiting for him, she recalled her most recent phone call from Abernathy telling her no formal disciplinary action would be taken against her and, as he said, she was essentially being let off the hook.

She had kept her mouth shut but was furious—let off the hook? She had her fill of the college's scheming and after this one last task, the interview, she would be free of it.

A figure was suddenly in front of her. "Professor Chesney?"

He introduced himself as Drew Connor and she took him in as they exchanged pleasantries. A tall man with thinning dark hair, he was attired in an oxford button down shirt with khakis, the de facto uniform around campus. She wondered if he had graduated from the college, which would explain that. Most marched forth into the world from the collegiate experience at William and Mary keeping that preppy persona close by.

Once seated with his coffee, he looked at Miranda with intense dark eyes. "So, can you tell me some about Brian Beckett? He was undertaking an archeological dig at your house?"

The question took Miranda back to those early days when she had first met Brian. The excitement of the dig along with getting Rosewood to move-in readiness had been followed by the thrill of the blue bottle find. But then the dominoes had fallen and all else that had come afterwards. It now felt like a lifetime away.

To the man in front of her, she said, "I had just purchased my house. It's a house called Rosewood."

He opened up a notebook and looked back up at her. As Miranda explained about Rosewood's architecture and how it was important to the history of the Tidewater region, he jotted a note down here and there but mainly looked at her with those intense dark eyes.

She finally wrapped it up saying, "So the dig was a good idea because it could reveal cultural information—that was my understanding anyway."

He nodded. "And did it?"

"What?"

"Reveal..." he looked down at his notes and then said, "cultural information."

"Well...things got sidetracked because of the blue bottle."

"What was that?"

"It was a pretty amazing find. I actually was the one to find it." She remembered the feeling of her gloved fingers brushing against the glass for the first time. The rush of that and then the digging around it to uncover until it was exposed fully.

She realized Drew had repeated his question. "What was it?"

She refocused on their conversation and explained all the research that had occurred to ascertain that it was a witch bottle.

"Whoa…" He sat back in his seat. "So…witchcraft and witches at your house?"

"Yes, but it apparently was a way to ward off evil spirits—I think. I don't know that I ever got the full understanding of it."

"Okay…" He tapped his pencil against the notepad then said, "So, did that distract Beckett or did it lead to him doing what he did?"

She thought: what had happened really? And what was the college politics here that she was supposed to stay on the side of? She realized with some chagrin that Abernathy did not remotely prep her for this, except for saying that this guy was supposed to paint the college in the best light.

Instead of answering his question, she asked him one. "Did you go to school here?"

He raised his eyebrows but answered right away. "Yep, I did. Class of '08."

"Huh."

"Huh, why?"

She smiled at him and said, "Just curious. You dress the part."

As he smiled back, she made the decision that there was no need to go into detail about her persecution under Brian's right hand gal or girlfriend or whatever she was to him, or that more fake blue bottles had been planted everywhere or that there was a gathering ceremony of supposed present day witches in her neighborhood. She figured Abernathy would think the same.

All the man in front of her needed to know was what Brian was capable of. "I had assumed that Brian…Beckett…put all the remaining funds into the research about the blue bottle after that. And that was the end of it. I had no idea about anything else." She was struck by the thought too that she did not know if the stipulations of the dig had been met.

Drew was silent for a pause and then spoke. "This is where I am struggling to pin down Beckett's motivations. I mean, if the dig stopped, didn't the funds stop? I looked over the terms of the agreement with the college and it reads that the funds are cut off if work ceases. Couldn't he have just kept the dig going and kept the money flowing? Unless...."

They looked at each other and both said it at the same time: "He didn't need the funds?"

Miranda said the rest, "Because...he had found something else to leverage. Something from Rosewood." She slapped her hand on the table. "That bastard."

He let out a sigh. "This takes it to a whole other level. The black market for buying and selling artifacts and antiquities. Of course, that is why the Feds are investigating and what I need to pursue next."

He closed his notebook and they looked at each other again.

"So...what he found—and took—was my property." She had spoken it out loud more for herself to hear than the man in front of her, who nodded his acknowledgement. "Let me know what you find? Please?"

"Sure thing." He rifled through his pocket and pulled out a crumpled business card. "Here is my number. So, call me if anything comes up." Their fingers brushed against each other as he handed the card over. He gave her a crooked smile.

Miranda watched him leaving the shop as she tapped his card on the tabletop. In another time and place, she might give a guy like Drew Connor a call. But, not now...now, she just needed to close this chapter with Brian Beckett and get some distance.

Later, she dialed Abernathy's number and was put through. Once he was on the line, she said, "I met with Drew Connor."

"Who?"

Irritated, she said, "The reporter you wanted me to talk to."

"Oh, yes...yes. Sorry. We have so many spinning plates with this Beckett thing it's hard to keep track."

"I can imagine...So, the thing is I was reminded during our conversation that the terms of the contract I signed were not fully met."

"How do you mean?"

"Landscaping was supposed to happen at the end of the dig. I just have big holes in my yard right now."

There was silence on the other end. She continued, "And, of course, Brian dropped the ball on any follow through. But spring is sprung. It was in the contract. And it's the least you can do." She took great satisfaction in throwing his own words right back at him.

He inhaled sharply and then, after some silence, said, "I'll put in a work order for the college landscape crew to get out there."

"Thanks, Dean. I'll keep a look out for them."

She grinned and thought to herself, "Well played, Miranda, well played."

Several days later, she watched out her window as a crew worked in her yard with a backhoe, filling in all the channels and holes. All that hard work being filled in took just an hour or so. They followed it up with laying down grass seeds finished with strewing hay on top of the entire area.

Once they left, she walked outdoors and stood with her hands on her hips, taking in their handiwork. It would soon not stand out as any different from the rest of the yard. It would be like none of it never happened. But as she gazed at all of it, she had to ask herself what Brian might have found underneath... and taken.

Miranda shrugged that thought off and concentrated on the fact that Rosewood was becoming the sanctuary she had always envisioned it to be—finally.

Chapter Thirty-nine

MIRANDA WALKED OUT OF John Lathrop into the waning light of the day. She had stayed late again. The meeting with a particular student had gone on too long, but it had been gratifying to help him with his graduate school application. Showing a lot of promise, he just needed that leg up in the cut throat world of academia.

With the semester drawing to a close, a number of students had been asking for her advice in mapping out post graduate plans. She was happy to do it, remembering how that time had been for her—as though she had been set free into the wilderness with a rudimentary compass to direct her path.

It was later than she realized when she pulled up to Rosewood and saw the kitchen light flickering. She didn't remember leaving one on, but it had become second nature to do so as part of her morning routine. Now, she was glad for it due to some residual nervousness at coming back to Rosewood at nightfall. Once out of the car, she breathed in the burst of spring in the air and felt that, despite everything, she was definitely getting her groove back.

After unlocking the front door and walking in, Miranda threw her keys on the hall table and dumped her bag on the floor beside it. Her vision was drawn to the flickering light from the kitchen. Why was it flickering? She had just replaced that bulb. Moving in that direction, she turned on the other lights along the way. "Kitty, kitty," she bellowed out, letting Polly know she was home to serve her.

At the threshold of the kitchen, Miranda's legs stuttered

to a stop as her mind registered the scene in front of her eyes. The light that was flickering was a pillar candle on the floor. The pantry door was wide open and Polly was milling about. In the middle of the kitchen floor, near the pillar candle, sat Fiona. Or, an alternate version of Fiona, almost unrecognizable with disheveled hair, limp and unwashed, obscuring her face. She wore a ripped-up t-shirt and dirt-encrusted sweatpants.

As if that wasn't enough to take in, Miranda moved her gaze to the foot Fiona held up in the air with one hand. Blood dripped down from it onto the floor where a small pool had accumulated beneath. Miranda blinked to try to clear the vision as Fiona finished the process of ripping one of her toenails right out of its nailbed.

Once finished with her task, Fiona looked over at Miranda and her mouth broke open into a wide smile with blood dripping off her teeth. Complete horror washed through Miranda as Polly meowed and daintily picked up a paw, shaking off a slight spray of blood. As the cat stepped away, leaving stained paw prints in her wake, the two women stared at each other for a beat.

Moving at lightning speed, Fiona scrambled upright. Frozen for a second too long, Miranda bolted, racing towards the front door for her cell buried in her bag. Sensing Fiona right on her heels, Miranda lunged for the bag near the front door. Just as she grabbed for it, the bag was kicked out from under her hand, droplets of blood flying into the air with it.

Fiona moved her back against the front door. "Where ya going, Mir---an---da?" she said in a high falsetto tone, drawing out each syllable of Miranda's name.

"Fiona, what do you want?"

"Jes' a little chat..." Her speech came out slurred.

Miranda started to back up and her hip hit hard on a chair behind her. Fiona pressed forward towards her and Miranda glanced down at the bloody pulp of a mess on Fiona's feet where the toenails had been. "My God, Fiona. Why are you doing that to your feet?"

"Seemed like a good idea..."

"How did you get in here?" Miranda kept edging backwards as she talked.

Fiona took a feint forward and Miranda jerked. Fiona laughed maniacally. "You don't know *anything* about this house. Anything." Raw anger tinged the slur this time.

Miranda kept her eyes locked onto the woman while moving back, hoping she could keep Fiona talking until she could make it to the back door. "Well, tell me about it. Tell me about the crawl space. That's got to be the way you got in, right?"

Fiona was now stepping gingerly on her feet but kept pressing towards Miranda.

"Those feet look painful...maybe you should sit down. We could talk sitting down."

"'Maybe you should 'sit down.'" Fiona parroted the words back at Miranda in a mocking imitation. "Maybe I don't want to sit down, bitch."

"Okay, well, let's chat...like you want to. You first." As Miranda said the words, she kept moving in inches towards the back.

"Why didn't you leave things be? Why'd you have to ruin everything?"

Behind her, Miranda's hand grazed an occasional table between the kitchen and dining space, remembering it held a heavy paperweight. Her fingers grabbed the edges of it and surreptitiously held it behind her. Meanwhile, she got more words out of her mouth. "Ruined everything? I didn't plan on doing that. I didn't know you felt..."

Fiona cut her off and screeched out, "You should have! You've got eyes and ears! You should have seen how we were together. We had everything and you ruined it... you ruined it!"

"What, Fiona? What did I ruin?"

Her face crumbled in front of Miranda. "He took it all. It's all gone from the hidey hole. He said we were in it together. We were going to use the money to go to Belize together."

While listening with one ear, Miranda had managed to creep further away as Fiona talked. When Fiona looked back up, a murderous expression came over her face and Miranda did not wait any longer. She crashed through the kitchen, reaching out within inches for the door handle.

But Fiona jumped on top of her, slamming her with full body weight. The paper weight flew out from Miranda's hand as her head pounded on the hard tile floor, stars exploding in her vision. Tumbling to the floor together, Fiona began to pummel her. Miranda jumped into survival mode, dodging and fighting back with punching, scratching and moves she didn't even realize she knew.

Fiona's stale, fetid breath filled the air and nausea overcame Miranda but she held it down. Instead, she thrust her knee into Fiona's gut, lifting the woman off her with an audible "oof." It gave her enough purchase to scramble up again and try for the door. Fiona reached out with an ungodly strength and pulled one of Miranda's legs out from under her. Miranda was down again onto the blood pool on the floor. She pulled herself through, slipping as she did so but focused on heading back towards the front to get the phone. Fiona hung on tight to her leg and started up with the maniacal laughter again.

With muscles screaming and head pounding, Miranda moved in a partial crawl, partial lurch into the other room with Fiona being dragged behind her. As she almost reached her bag that had been kicked into the corner, the front door flung open.

Through slitted eyes, she could see Beau and Sanford among others. The cavalry had arrived, and Miranda let the effort of dragging herself and Fiona go. A dark cloud came over her vision and a part of her knew she was passing out. She let it happen.

Chapter Forty

AN UNMISTAKABLE ANTISEPTIC ODOR, heavy and clinging, filled her nasal cavity. It was rapidly followed by the jarring white noise of beeping monitors and other machines filling her ears. Coming to the surface and blinking eyes open, Miranda took in her surroundings in chunks and it all came together in a one word thought blurb: hospital. She hated hospitals.

She took a slow inventory. Her throbbing head was the most insistent. She tentatively moved fingers and then toes. Arms and then legs. She felt some relief that all parts seemed in working order even though she was achy all over.

It all came back in a rush: the horror at Rosewood with Fiona's deranged actions. Movie clips of trying to escape slammed her thoughts with the last vision being the Herculean effort to move to the front, Fiona hanging onto her leg the whole way. Feeling a shudder deep in her soul, Miranda knew nightmares of that scene would probably be etched as leftovers into her memory for life.

She heard a rap on the room's door and a man in a white coat walked in. Saying hello, he picked up the chart at the end of the bed. Repeating his hello again, he added her name to the end of it.

Moving to the bedside, he gave her an impersonal smile. "Well, Miranda, you gave us a scare last night with all that blood on you."

"Blood?"

"Yes. Took us a while to figure out it was mostly your attacker's blood."

She grimaced.

He continued. "Quite a street fight you were in..."

"It wasn't...forget it. What is wrong with me? I mainly feel a bad headache."

"That's the worst of it. You took a hard knock at some point and got a concussion. Some bumps and bruises all over but nothing broken. You got lucky on that score."

"Lucky..." She let the word sit on her tongue. It didn't feel lucky. It felt horrific and catastrophic. But now she also felt relief flowing through her at hearing "the worst of it."

"So...when can I check out?"

"Just waiting on your discharge papers. The nurse will be in." He lifted up the papers on the chart again and added, "And you have a ride so we can release you."

"I have a ride?"

"Some folks who have been waiting in the visitor room. Shall I send them in?"

"Please." Miranda wondered who it could be as she released her head back onto the pillow, exhausted from the effort of conversation with the doctor.

The door opened again and she looked over to see the worried face of Beau with a woman behind him.

The woman started speaking right away. "Lordy, have you had a time. We were just talking about it..." She continued on as Miranda looked between the two of them, assuming that the woman in the huge flowered patterned shirt draped over her large and generous bosom was the wife, the one she had never had a chance to meet. In the corners of her mind, she dredged up how Beau had described her one time as just a "little itty-bitty thing."

Beau said nothing, patiently waiting for his wife to wind down. She finished with, "You had this guy in a dither I can tell you, gal. My Beau didn't know what to do with himself. So, we headed over to your house and got it all cleaned up for you, okay?"

With that, the woman peered in closer to Miranda with a

moonish fleshy face, her eyes bright and kind. Beau peered in as well with worried lines stretched to capacity as he nodded in agreement.

The silence went on for a beat too long and finally the synapses of Miranda's mind started to fire up enough for her to respond. "How did you know, Beau? How did you know I needed help?"

The wife jumped in again to speak and answered for him. "He never disconnected that program that was on. Not that he was spying on you...Lord knows, I wouldn't let that go on. I happened to walk by and see some weird goings-on and I..."

Finally, Beau piped in. "I couldn't figure it out at first. Couldn't make head nor tails of it. Two girls cat fighting like that is a scene to behold. It was set up to trigger on if something out of the perimeter had occurred, remember? So, she must have broken in—and we can look back on the tape and find that out, by the way—and then it went on. Lucky for us, Elaine just happened to be walking by like she said. And we are damned glad she did."

Miranda bobbed her head in agreement but grimaced at the pain. She stopped the movement and, instead, said, "So glad. Yes. I don't know how to thank you really."

A nurse bustled in before they could say anymore and began to talk to all them or no one in particular. "We got discharge papers for you, Miss Chesney."

As she proceeded to rattle off the rules and regulations for Miranda's issues, an impressive concussion along with some sizeable contusions, Miranda gave up processing and just let the words drift over her. The nurse wrapped up her discourse saying, "You get all that?"

"Is it all down on that paper?" Miranda pointed at the paper she was holding.

"More or less."

After Miranda signed the paper, the others all left so that she could change. Elaine had brought her an outfit of her own, leggings and a flowered shift like that one she was wearing. She winced as she pulled the hospital gown off and then outright grimaced as she pulled the outfit up against bruised and battered places on her body. Gingerly touching a blooming bruise on her leg, she had to remind herself that it would all heal. She would heal.

She walked out of the room, swimming in the outfit she had donned. Beau and Elaine hovered nearby and Elaine chirped out, "There she is! Don't you make my clothes look pretty."

Miranda gave a weak smile, still learning to take in stride the powerhouse that was Beau's wife.

"Alrighty then," Beau said, "Let's get you going." They made a strange trio as they took a slow shuffle down the hall, a tall and lanky Beau and a wide hipped Elaine on either side of a battered Miranda.

Once outdoors, Miranda blinked at the bright light and took in a deep breath. She felt funny...like she was coming back from another country. Beau and Elaine packed her into the backseat of Beau's Crown Vic as though she were spun glass wrapped in cotton wool.

Miranda made a weak attempt at a joke: "So, you Realtors really have to go above and beyond at times."

"Happy to do it. Weren't we, Beau?" Elaine said.

As they drove east away from the hospital and back to Bisoux, Elaine maintained a steady stream of chatter. Miranda let herself slouch against the comfy, cushioned back seat and watch the shadows cast by the sun over the upholstery.

There were so many scattered thoughts in her mind, but there was one that was trying to bubble forth amongst all of them. She recalled that in the midst of the whole macabre episode with Fiona she had said something...something...something. It was right at the edge of her thoughts, and she was struggling to reel it in...what was it?

Slowly, slowly it wormed its way out and into the front of her mind. She blurted it out, interrupting Elaine's stream.

"Fiona said something..."

"What? What did she say?" Beau asked as Elaine cast a glance back her way.

"She said there was a treasure. That she and Brian had

found things in the dig and squirreled them away. She said they put them in a 'hidey hole.' And was furious he had taken them and left without her."

"Huh..." Beau said, and it hung in the air as they were all silent for a pause.

Then Elaine started talking again. "Where the dickens do you think the hidey hole could be? Although, I guess it doesn't matter much now, if he took it all and it's gone. Does it?"

"I don't know," Miranda said. "Maybe it does?"

Beau cleared his throat. "Well, wouldn't do any harm to bring it up with Sanford."

As they pulled into Rosewood's curved drive, Miranda saw a figure standing off to the side. "Lizzie is here," she said.

"She was real worried about you when we were cleaning the place up earlier. Fretting something fierce," said Beau.

Elaine chimed in and added, "She was practically wringing her hands and what-not. In a real state over you."

As Miranda gazed out the car window at Lizzie, it suddenly clicked. Lizzie would know. She would know where the hidey hole was and she might even know what had been in it.

Beau pulled as close to the front walk to the door as possible. "Just hang on, Miranda, and we'll help you out.

Miranda, feeling silly, demurred. "I can get out..."

No sooner did she utter the words when the car door opened and Lizzie's face loomed in front of her. "I got her. I got her."

With a strong grip on her arm, Lizzie hoisted her up and out. Miranda stood and looked at the woman in front of her. "Thank you, Lizzie."

Beau and Elaine circled around her as well and they all hovered as she climbed up to the front door. Behind her, Lizzie began to start up with her trilling. Miranda stopped, once at the threshold, and fear overcame her.

"You doing okay, missy? You got this." Miranda could hear Elaine's voice in her ear and it provided the reassurance she needed to step into Rosewood. Pushing the scene of horror to the edges of her mind, she nodded as she crossed the threshold.

She cautiously moved her gaze to view the space in front of her. It sparkled and shined, cleaner than it had been in a long while. "Aww...thanks so much you guys. You cleaned up after... Well, anyway, it looks great."

She turned and faced the three behind her. It felt strange to have so many people inside Rosewood with her. It felt strange to be in Rosewood with others.

"So..." Beau spoke up first. "Let's get you situated."

Elaine took one of her arms and led her to the couch. "Prop your feet up here and settle in."

Miranda began to protest but Beau interrupted. "Doctor's orders. Come on now."

She gave in and let the three of them take over. Elaine and Lizzie went into the kitchen to "fix her a little something to eat" and Beau sat on the chair opposite from her on the couch. In a lowered voice, he said, "I don't know how you feel about this, but Lizzie wants to stay and tend to you."

"She does?"

Beau nodded then added, "Apparently, she had an LPN license at some point."

"Huh." Miranda let that idea sit.

"Anyways, I wanted to give you the heads up..." his voice drifted off as the two women entered with a plate of food.

"Now, I made some of my county-famous chicken salad and there's some fresh fruit on the side. It's a far sight better than the hospital food, I am sure."

"Oh, thank you so much, Elaine."

The other woman beamed in response.

Beau cleared his throat and then stood up. "I think we better head out so you can rest up some."

Lizzie broke in with a loud voice. "I got her. I got her. I'm tending to her now."

They nodded, Miranda included. After saying goodbye to Beau and Elaine, her eyes began to droop and then she was being moved like a baby doll into a more comfortable position on the couch. She fell quickly back into a deep slumber.

Chapter Forty-one

WHEN MIRANDA WOKE, THE daylight had all but faded into a few shadows on the hardwood floor within her view. Opening her eyes fully, she saw Lizzie seated across from her, reading a People magazine that she must have brought with her.

"Hi," she said in a croaky voice.

Lizzie looked up from the magazine. "How you feelin' now?"

Slowly, Miranda raised herself into a semi sprawl and thought about it. "Better. I think."

Lizzie nodded.

"I hate keeping you. I'll be fine if you want to head out."

"No'm. I said I'm tending to you and I am. Used to do the same for Miss Janie."

Miranda was surprised to hear that bit of information. "I didn't know that. Was she sick...at the end?"

"Yep. I got that license to take care of her and that's what I did."

"That was good of you."

Lizzie gave a shrug in response.

"So...Fiona...I guess she escaped...or something?"

"She ran out of that place they had her in. Hitched a ride, I heard."

They were both silent and Miranda mulled over the particulars of Fiona's escape. Then she spoke. "She told me some wild stuff during...well, while she was here."

"How's that?"

She repeated to Lizzie what she had told Beau and Elaine in the car about the hidey hole. Lizzie began trill as Miranda talked but she pressed on. "Do you know where a hidey hole would be?"

"Yeah. I do."

"Okay. Because I think maybe the sheriff needs to see it."

Lizzie exhaled loudly. "Probably nothing in it now. If he took everything."

"Yes, but it could help with the investigation to find him."

Lizzie did not answer. After a while, Miranda asked, "Can you show the sheriff?"

"Okay."

Knowing that Lizzie might change her mind, Miranda rallied and pulled herself up. "I need my phone. It's in my bag..."

"Sit back down. I'll get it."

When Lizzie handed the bag over, Miranda cringed as she saw the dried blood splatter on it. Fiona's blood. She reached in, careful not to touch the blood, and pulled out her cell phone. It had just enough battery left to make the call.

After she made the call with Sanford saying he would be right over, Miranda began to sense Lizzie's mounting agitation. She began to pace from the front door all the way to the rear door in a rhythmic fashion back and forth in her scuffed-up, dirty white Ked sneakers.

After a number of rounds, Miranda spoke up. "Uh...Lizzie, do you think you could put a can of soup on for me? There's a chicken noodle in the pantry I think."

The other woman stopped in her tracks and stared at Miranda for a beat. Then she nodded. Miranda breathed out a sigh of relief as Lizzie got busy in the kitchen, rustling through the pantry and banging some pots around. The agitation was now being carried out in the kitchen which was preferable to the pacing.

No sooner did Lizzie bellow out "It's ready" than there was a knock at the door.

"Hold off on it, Lizzie. The sheriff is here. Can you get the door?"

Lizzie pounded with a loud footfall to the door as Miranda worked herself up to standing. Once up, she evaluated and told herself she could do it. She could move to wherever Lizzie was going to take them.

Sanford stood in an awkward stance at the open doorway and took his cap off. "How you doing, missy?"

Miranda was taken aback at his different tone and demeanor. Maybe they had turned the corner from him not believing her and taking the threats seriously. The validation left her with a hollow feeling rather than a triumphant one. A part of her wished he had been right all along. But he had not been, and proof of that was him standing in front of her.

"I'm doing okay. So, Lizzie has some place to show us like I told you on the phone." She turned towards Lizzie. "Are we going outside, Lizzie?"

Lizzie nodded and turned on her heel as she headed to the back door. Miranda followed in a slow path behind her with the Sheriff following. "This place cleaned up good," she heard him murmur under his breath.

Lizzie opened the door and soon they all gathered behind the house. The silence started to become awkward with Lizzie staring at the back of the house and Miranda and the sheriff staring at Lizzie.

The sheriff cleared his throat and said to Miranda, "You checked out the place thorough-like, right?"

Just as Miranda opened her mouth to respond, Lizzie moved forward towards the lattice of the crawl space. Miranda fell silent instead and watched, curious about what she had missed. Lizzie walked around to the corner where it jutted out. When she pressed hard with both hands, the corner sprung open with a suddenness that made Miranda take a step back. Both sides released a foot or so. Lizzie pulled one piece outwards so that a space was created to slip through. "Lizzie..." Miranda spoke out as Lizzie vanished into the space.

Sanford made quick work of going in behind her, pulling a Maglite off his holster as he did so. Miranda struggled her way through behind them, an earthy smell of the dirt floor rising up and making her nose twitch immediately. The other two were crouched in the space as Miranda cast a cautious look around to determine if there were spiders or worse to see in the limited lighting. Another odor took over as predominant: what she had first smelled that first day inside of Rosewood, that hint of lavender that had seemed like a promise of some sort.

They all three fell silent. Lizzie finally moved crab-like several feet away towards the other side of the corner where they had entered. She began to scuff the dirt with her sneakered toe until the sheriff's light exposed a hatch clasp.

"Okay, okay. Step aside, Lizzie. I'll take it from here," the sheriff said.

Miranda felt her inner jangle of nerves start up again, the nerves that had been so close to the surface for months now. Lizzie moved back over closer to Miranda and her hand fluttered above Miranda's hand as if she wanted to hold hands. But she didn't touch her.

The sheriff paused with a grasp of the hasp between his forefinger and thumb. "Anything else you want to say before I pull it open?" He directed his words to Lizzie. She shrugged. "I'll take that as a 'no.'"

Miranda's breath caught in her throat as he lifted it up. He flashed the light down and they all moved closer to look. It was a perfect square about two feet by two feet in dimension that appeared to be lined in old timbered wood. "Geez, how old is this?" Miranda said.

"Miss Janie always said the wood came from the ship that brought her people here. Ballast, she called it."

The sheriff glanced over with arched eyebrows, his face distorted in the dim light, and it looked like punctuation. "So... pretty old," he said.

He crossed the light over every square inch of the area. It was clear for all of them to see it was empty of any contents. "What was in here when Miss Janie was alive?" he asked Lizzie.

"Papers..."

"Papers?" Miranda said sharply. "What happened to her papers?"

"Dunno...maybe Fiona got them."

Miranda reeled at this news, her mind scrambling to add that to what she already knew. She was also getting woozy and didn't know if it was the ongoing effects of the concussion or the dank environment of the crawl space.

The sheriff continued to pass the flashlight over the space and said off the cuff, "There always was talk of there being treasure somewheres around this place, but I had it down to being a canard."

"What's that?" Lizzie asked.

Miranda's mind jerked away from the papers and she answered Lizzie's question. "A canard is an impossible story. Like a false rumor. So, the sheriff means there was not really treasure here. Just talk of it."

She felt immediate ire towards the sheriff at dismissing her all those times if he had heard there might be treasure out here. That, in and of itself, should have made him pay more attention to the blue bottle incidents.

"Then a canard is a lie?" Lizzie asked.

"Sort of."

"But that's not a lie."

The sheriff moved to light to Lizzie's face. "How do you mean?"

"There was treasure here. Those fancy cups and..." She clammed up as if she had said too much.

"Huh. Well, I guess we won't know for sure what Mr. Beckett got his hands on unless the authorities track him down."

He moved his light again around the space for a final sweep and came to a sudden stop. He cast it back and forth over a small spot. "What is it?" Miranda asked.

He reached down into the space and pulled out something small. When it was in his hand, they looked at it. It was a scrap of paper. Numbers and a couple of words. Miranda stared at it for some time before she spoke. "That's my cell number. And my name. In my writing."

He looked at her pointedly.

"I'm pretty sure it's a scrap of paper that I wrote my name

and number on for Brian when I first met him."

"Huh...wonder why he left it here."

"Could it have dropped out of his pocket at some point?"

"That's possible or..." He gave her a funny look. "Was he trying to tell you something?"

"Like what? A final thumbing at me?"

The sheriff shook his head. "Hard to say, I guess. I'll let the G men have it to see if it gives them anything to go on."

"I guess I'll never know what he got and stole unless Fiona 'fesses up."

"Yeah. And given her state of mind, who knows if we can get a straight story out of her."

Miranda wrestled in her mind with Brian stealing from her. Did she need revenge? No, she did not. Besides, if he didn't get caught, he would be a fugitive for the rest of his days, always looking over his shoulder, needing to be one step ahead. Maybe he had always been doing that. Her choice was to let it all go. Her first choice was Rosewood and it was still her choice.

To Lizzie, the sheriff asked, "Anything else down here you need to show us? What about that tunnel somebody said was down here somewhere?" He seemed oddly attuned to Lizzie's ways and was now waiting her out and letting her take the lead when she was ready to do so.

Some time went by before Lizzie moved, still in a crouch, to where the exterior stone foundation wall of the house was. At the far corner, there was space that connected to the interior wall of the pantry. They watched as she moved her fingers lightly along the stone. Just like on the front façade on the house, it was the old fieldstone that had been dug up two hundred years earlier by the original builders. Miranda had a passing thought of admiration for those people and the hard job they had done.

On the other side of the stone was the basement. Miranda knew that the seam between the basement and the crawl space ran through both the kitchen and the pantry cutting in at about a third of the way from where that space began.

As the sheriff shone the light on it, they waited for Lizzie's next move. They were rewarded when she arched her neck and placed both hands onto the wide plank floorboards directly above. With the light zooming in, they could barely make out the hitch attached to a narrow wire that she pulled on hard. With that action, the floorboard closest to the seam connecting crawl space and basement moved to the side. Miranda gasped as light from the above pantry filled up the space where they crouched in. The sheriff mumbled, "If this don't beat all."

The floorboard pushed easily into an area next to the pantry wall. Miranda envisioned what was there: the shelving unit. Lizzie then placed her hands out on either side above, providing a grip for herself on either side and deftly hoisted herself up into the pantry with a grunt. She peered back down into the space at Miranda and Sanford with an inquiring expression. "Lizzie, stay up there. We'll be right up," the sheriff said.

Miranda and Sanford both made their way out of the crawl space corner where they had entered. Once out, Miranda took a shaky breath. They looked at one another. "So that's how Fiona got in," Miranda said.

"Yep. She must have known about it," he said with a somewhat abashed expression. "Let's go have a look see inside."

Back inside, Lizzie stood by the pantry door, arms hanging at her sides. The sheriff went into the pantry and Miranda pressed in behind him. He got down on his knees and looked at how the floorboard fit underneath the shelf. "That's an old timey gear mechanism if I've ever seen one."

Miranda looked closely at it, berating herself for not seeing the slightly higher edge of the floorboard before this. On the other hand, it was an ingenious mechanism. The wire underneath allowed it to be pulled out and then flipped underneath the shelving unit. It locked into place until someone unlocked it. There was a hidden pocket for the board to be pushed underneath the shelf.

When she stood up, she looked at Lizzie. "So, this is how Fiona got in. Why didn't you ever say anything, Lizzie?" The other woman gave a shrug and looked off into the room.

Miranda staggered over to the table and plunked herself down on a chair, all the activity and exertion catching up with her. She was overcome by the strange mechanisms that had lain right underneath her all this time. One thought rose up above all the others and she said it aloud. "What about the tunnel? Is there still a tunnel?"

Lizzie walked over to the sink, running the water. Miranda looked to Sanford who just shook his head. Sighing, Miranda said, "I guess that's it then."

Sanford rolled up his sleeves and walked over next to Lizzie, "Here, I'll scrub, you rinse."

Lizzie threw him a doleful glance but began to settle into the routine with him. Miranda didn't know what to make of the strange pair as Lizzie began trilling and Sanford took up humming. Turning off the tap when he finished the last dish, Sanford said, "What do you think happened to the tunnel, Lizzie?"

As she kept drying the dish she held, a look of confusion crossed over her face. Almost as if just to herself, she said, "Miss Janie said there was one. She was going to show it to me. She always promised she would. Just never got around to it..." Her voice trailed off.

Sanford and Miranda exchanged a glance. Then Sanford spoke up. "I didn't see nothing like that down there. Did you, Miranda?"

Miranda shook her head. "Maybe it got walled off at some point?"

Lizzie said in a mournful tone, "I always wanted to go in it. But we never did."

As far as Miranda was concerned, the tunnel would wait for another day. There had been enough unveiling for a while. The rest of Rosewood's secrets could sit tight for a bit.

Sanford patted Lizzie on her shoulder. "It's okay, missy. You got to know about a lot of other things, didn't you? You done good, Lizzie Gooding. You done good."

Later, with Miranda's head still swimming with questions, she and Lizzie sat at the kitchen table. Lizzie had made a fresh pot of coffee; stronger than even how Miranda usually drank it.

But it revived her and she needed it. Their silence together was now companionable rather than disturbing. Miranda realized she had come a long way in understanding the woman across from her.

But she still had questions. She made a one last attempt. "Lizzie, do you know what Fiona did with those papers?"

"Some things you know, some things you don't know..."

"So, you do know?"

Lizzie shook her head. "I don't know. What do you need them for?"

Miranda sat back and thought about it. What did she need them for? She had pieced it all together on her own. Short of a step-by-step instruction pamphlet of how to make a witch bottle, what could possibly be in those papers that she didn't already know. But...but...it was the niggling aspect of 'what if?' What if there was something else in those papers?

She answered Lizzie. "I don't need them anymore. I guess I know enough."

Lizzie nodded and said, "Yeah, you do."

Epilogue

MIRANDA WALKED ALONG THE brick lined paths of Colonial Williamsburg with her mother by her side. Millie had made the trek out to the east from Illinois to catch the best time to be in Williamsburg. In an almost overnight event, tulips had popped up all over town. Just as Beau had promised, they were a feast for the eyes.

The historic buildings gleaming in the sunshine were now also adorned with the spring flowers bursting on their grounds. The most magnificent sight of all was the centerpiece, the Governor's Mansion, which almost seemed burnished in the light. As they strolled, Millie's expression was consistent: wide-eyed bemusement and open-jawed wonder at the place, along with non-stop oohs and aahs.

The costumed employees of Colonial Williamsburg flitted in and out amongst the burgeoning numbers of tourists brought out by the excellent weather. The numbers almost seemed to swell before their eyes even in the short time it took them to walk from one end to the other of the historic district through the center green.

As they ambled along together, Miranda felt contentment that had been a long time in coming. Starting anew with her mother and their relationship meant cutting her more slack than she had in her younger years and finding appreciation in what used to be a cause for annoyance.

"Ooooh...look at that little house and garden. And it's open!" Millie pointed to a small house museum that indeed had an accompanying garden on its side.

"Okay, okay. We can go in, Mom." Letting herself be corralled, Miranda flashed her college ID for a bit of a discount and paid for two tickets from a woman garbed in a super tight white bodice that cinched in at the waist where several layers of billowing skirts hung below said waist. Miranda's suspect was that she was a college student or recently graduated college student.

"Please wait outside by the garden!" the guide said to the small group bumping into each other in the cramped ticket area.

Once everyone had checked in, the costumed woman began to give her spiel with remarkable poise. It was the Williamsburg touch, in Miranda's observation. They seemed to press these types out from a mold and they all kept to script notably well, seemingly buying in to all things Colonial Williamsburg.

Taking turns, all were granted a peek into the two downstairs rooms of the simple hall-parlor style dwelling house. Miranda began to tune out most of it. Millie, by contrast, watched with rapt attention, lips parted.

The group eventually crowded inside the white picket fence line of the garden which showed that it was off to a promising start for the spring growing season. Squeezing themselves off to one side, the view was twig teepees set up for plants to grow into, rows tilled out with perfect straight lines and sprouts already evident in the soil.

As their hostess began to lecture about the spring vegetables soon to be making an appearance, Miranda edged even further to the fence line placing one hand on a nearby post. Her fingers touched indentations on one side. Moving her fingers back and forth, she stopped suddenly suspecting what they were. Craning her neck for a view, the crude cat symbol boldly stood out.

Interrupting the guide's chatter, she blurted out, "What is this? On the post?"

Millie murmured, "Miranda!"

A slight frown came over the guide's face but she answered. "That's the mark of Goody Lancaster's profession. The woman who originally owned this house. Anyway, the plants here..."

"What was her profession?" Some of the group now frowned at Miranda.

This time the answer from the tour guide was curt. "A herbalist. So, back to the plants..."

Again, Miranda interjected. "So, she needed a mark for her herbalism practice?"

"Well...sometimes there was a fine line between herbalism and witchcraft in those days so...." The guide let the idea trail off.

"Wait...I researched that this symbol means kind-hearted woman. I never came across it meaning witchcraft."

The guide let out a sigh. "Yes, that meaning became attached to the symbol later. But our advanced research has shown it was witchcraft in the earliest years of the colony. Now, if you don't mind...."

She took up again with the information about the plants as Miranda's mind spun around what this meant. The blurred lines between herbalism, witchcraft and kind-hearted women. What did it all mean?

The tour guide winded down by saying, "And that concludes the tour. I have some sprigs of rosemary here if anybody wants a sample. It grows all year here in our Tidewater climate."

As they stood in line to get their sprigs of rosemary, Millie nudged Miranda. "What was all that about?"

"Just tying up some loose ends."

As they walked away from the house with its cat symbol post, she asked herself if she minded having the symbol at Rosewood. Truth be told, Miranda found that she actually didn't mind at all.

They meandered their way towards their final destination, the Duke of Gloucester Coffee Shoppe at the corner of Francis and Boundary Streets, near where the town and the college intersected at a central hub.

Walking into the busy eatery, Miranda searched around the place until her eyes lit upon them. "This way, Mom," she said, leading the way to a back corner where Beau, Elaine and Lizzie sat. Beau and Elaine were in companionable conversation and Lizzie was looking all around.

"Hi guys. I'd like you to meet my mom. Millie Jones."

Beau stood up and hellos were exchanged all around. They all sat down in the booth and Miranda squeezed herself in the spot next to Lizzie, giving her shoulder a squeeze. Once seated, her mother started right in and said, "I have heard so much about all of you. Thank you for taking such good care of my baby."

They all looked at Miranda with differing expressions, but with underlying affection. As they began to converse in an easy fashion, Miranda looked around the table at the other four, feeling a sense of being home at last.

Author's Note

A small article in the Washington Post in January 2020 along with a photograph of a jade blue "witch bottle" found near a Civil War fortification in Williamsburg, Virginia, was all the inspiration kindling needed to write this tale. The ensuing summer of 2020, the first pandemic lockdown summer, I scrambled for a focus, just like everybody else. So, I latched back onto the tantalizing tidbit snipped and saved months earlier.

A deeper dive to discover more about witch bottles revealed limited studies available. Even so, I did find plenty of rich and fascinating details. Typically filled with items that ranged from fish hooks to urine, their primary purpose was to lure and trap witches and/or malevolent spirits. They were especially employed during times of hardship and strife which explains why one was buried at the Civil War site. Research also pointed to the bottles as a tradition brought over from the East Anglia region of Britain.

The area where this particular bottle was located, Tidewater Virginia with its tie-ins to Colonial American history and its own unique idiosyncrasies and folklore, provided a perfect setting for my fictional use of the witch bottle. Cue some Southern gothic vibes along with these historical underpinnings and I began to piece a story together, a story that became my lockdown work.

The weirdness of 2020 no doubt colored the authorship of this tale and ramped up the volume on gothic and quirky overtones. But it also must be noted that all of my fiction writing harkens back to an early reading diet of Nancy Drew mysteries, later expanded and layered on top with gothic suspense and thriller reads. This novel is, without question, a product of those deep reading roots.

I am forever grateful to all who have supported this project including my wonderful beta readers, my fantastic technical support (Desmond Lavin), and Artemesia Publishing, who took a chance and picked this project up, then polished it to perfection. Also, a special nod of appreciation to you, dear reader, if you made it this far.

About the Author

Mary Kendall is first a reader of all books across the genres and, second, a writer of fiction. She brings her background in history-related fields to her writing along with some Celtic story-telling genes. Fueled by black coffee and a possible sprinkling of fairy dust, she tends to find inspiration in odd places and sometimes while kneading bread dough. She has two previously published novels and three short stories published in dark fiction anthologies for charity.